TABLE OF CONTENTS

STOLEN GIFT EXCHANGE
Bettie Boswell

Chapter One

Honey and the senior aqua aerobics class watched their substitute instructor climb out of the pool and head toward the locker room. A young boy and girl followed her from the room, chattering about their coming Christmas trip to the Florida amusement parks. Lorie and Lincoln's laughter echoed off the tiled walls as they talked about seeing their Grandma Lorna on their journeys.

"Bon Voyage, Miss Melody." Honey's commanding voice rippled over the water and bounced off the tiled walls of the indoor pool.

Melody turned with a weak smile. "Thank you, Honey. The twins have been looking forward to this trip for over a year. Their parents planned to take them last year, but..."

"Then you should all enjoy your brother's final gift." Honey blew a kiss to the little patchwork family. They'd been stitched together for over a year since Melody's brother and sister-in-law passed in a tragic automobile accident.

At one time, Melody led a children's choir at the church where Honey played bass in the praise band. These days, the former music teacher spent her time being a mom to the twins, teaching private piano lessons, and taking on odd jobs to survive. The college student who normally taught their aqua aerobics had left early for Christmas break due to the latest virus, opening the door for Melody to teach them some water dance moves during the last two weeks.

Honey looked over her shoulder as her other senior swim class friends moved closer and shared their well-wishes for the little family's travels to a warmer place than Ohio.

Loretta swayed, stepping sideways across the pool. "Be sure and say hi to the mouse for me." The semi-retired art professor's swim dress swished after her, creating a swath of Hawaiian colors in her wake. She had found the suit on last summer's trip to the islands and admitted to buying several suits of the same design. Chlorine did a number on the best of swimwear. A smart woman knew enough to purchase backups when she found a good outfit.

1

"Make sure you wear plenty of sunscreen to protect your skin." Annabelle's face expressed her caring nature as she marched next to the other ladies across the pool. The woman always had a campaign going to make life better for all. Her push for the vote to save teacher positions had been a failure, but at least the positive woman tried to support the issue through her broadcasts. She mostly stayed home, doing her weekly podcasts and taking care of her housebound husband. Annabelle had joined the swim class after discovering a dementia day care at the local senior center. For the last month, the three ladies enjoyed chatting together as they stretched and jogged away their aches and pains in the water.

Melody and the twins thanked everyone and made their way from the room. Several swimmers headed to the deep end of the pool to enjoy some free-swim time. Honey and her friends continued to move about in the shallow end.

"I hope they make their flight on time. We would have sent them off sooner if we'd known they needed to leave." Loretta twisted and twirled as she traversed through the water.

Tillie huffed as she floated toward the exit stairs provided for the less agile to remove themselves from the pool. "She shouldn't have taken the job if she planned on shorting us fifteen minutes of exercise."

The trio of friends gawked as the woman climbed up the ladder and marched away. Tillie's dark one-piece suit dripped, leaving a trail of beaded moisture behind her, as she flip-flopped her way from the room.

"That Melody is a responsible gal. I doubt she would have mentioned leaving early if the kids hadn't told us about heading to Florida to meet their grandma and see the sights." Annabelle walked backward in the water.

Honey jogged backward through the water, facing the other two as they moved in sync through the pool. "She's stronger than most people realize. Last Sunday at church, Melody asked for prayers to find a place to live. Apparently, her apartment building manager received too many complaints about her piano students coming and going, not to mention the wrong notes some of them played. He wasn't happy about the twins making noise either."

"Poor Melody. What's she going to do? If this happened during my summer travels, she could house sit the little bungalow I rent."

"I'd invite her into my home, but my sweetheart isn't doing well at night. I just don't know if the children would understand when he gets upset in the middle of the night." Annabelle flung flat hands down against the wavy surface, making splatters fly.

Honey wiped sprinkles from her brow. "No worries, for now. Ginny and Scott have a couple of empty bedrooms. They're going to put Melody's piano in their formal living room. She can still give her piano lessons, until an affordable place becomes available with management having a welcoming attitude toward her music and kids. There's a group of church people helping move their belongings when Melody and the twins get back."

Honey knew the Hallmarks' family of baby Treasure Hope and adopted daughter, Melissa, would one day grow to include more natural and adopted children. In the meantime, it looked like Scott and Ginny would be taking in Melody's little family.

Loretta pointed to the clock. "Swim time is over for me. I have an errand to run this morning."

Honey led her friends toward the same steps Tillie used earlier. "I need to go to a worship committee meeting at church." She knew Annabelle planned to meet her husband for a lunch date at the senior center.

According to Annabelle, on most days, the poor man thought he was meeting his girlfriend for the first time. Honey's thoughts turned to her long-gone sweetheart. If disease hadn't taken her husband away, next month would have been their fiftieth anniversary. She climbed out of the pool with a sigh. Time to get her day started, after retrieving soap from her locker for a quick shower to get rid of itchy pool chemicals.

Drips hit the floor tiles as the cluster of women shuffled to the ladies' showers, leaving puddles for the ever-present custodian to swipe away. Honey and Annabelle headed toward their customary lockers near the showers.

Loretta waved. "I'll see you ladies later. I used one of the bigger lockers in the back today so I could stow my delivery." She headed toward the rear of the facility, leaving a drippy trail in her wake.

Honey reached for her shower supplies. She jumped when a piercing cry split the air.

"What in the world is going on? Someone has dumped all my belongings out of my locker."

Honey hurried toward the back of the room and approached Loretta pawing through a pile of towels and clothing.

Loretta sank to her knees and wailed."Oh no. She's gone. I don't want to die!" Her screams rang through the dressing room chatter. Silence encompassed the room populated with senior women.

Honey slid to a stop on wet flooring. Pulling her towel tighter around her dripping floral one-piece, she gaped at the panicked woman kneeling in front of an open locker. Loretta tended to be over-dramatic at times. Maybe she should have been a drama instructor instead of teaching art at the local college. Perhaps this was one of her over-reacted moments. The panting breath and hand over the woman's heart gave Honey pause.

She reached for her friend's forearm. "What's wrong, Loretta?"

"I've been robbed. Someone took her. Now I'm in big trouble." Her terror turned to an angry flip-flop stomp as she turned and started rifling through scattered belongings.

"Which *her* are you talking about, dear?" Annabelle moved closer and organized some of the scattered items into a pile.

Loretta heaved a deep sigh. "I planned to deliver a commissioned portrait to Edmund Bradley after our aquatic exercise this morning. The painting was a likeness of his long-lost wife. I used the bigger locker in order to fit it inside. I thought his painting would fare better here than in the cold car. He's such a sweet fellow." A dreamy smile crossed the woman's wrinkled cheeks.

"The man is too young for you." Tillie snorted as she shouldered a huge beach bag and exited down a curved hallway.

A frown crossed Loretta's face. "I thought the portrait would be safe in my padlocked locker. Now her likeness is gone forever."

Honey bent over and picked up an open padlock. "Are you sure you closed the lock? Either someone knew your combination or it wasn't clicked shut."

"I thought I closed it." She took the padlock, staring at it with widening eyes. "It looks like the last number is correct. Maybe I forgot to give it a twirl and click, but someone shouldn't have taken the painting." Loretta moaned as she leaned forward with her hands covering her eyes.

"You're a good artist. I'm sure you can make another painting." Annabelle's comment brought tears to Loretta's eyes.

"No, I accidentally ruined his wife's only remaining photograph by knocking over a jar of turpentine. They were only married a short time before the woman's rich father caught up with them and annulled their marriage. The photo was the only keepsake he owned from his time with the woman. Her image was blurry. However, he liked how I captured her spirit when he saw the almost finished painting."

"I'm so sorry. Maybe you can redo it from memory." Honey lifted a moneyless wallet from the floor. "It looks like the culprit took more than your portrait. At least they didn't take your license or credit card."

Loretta wailed again. "My wallet still had Edmund's payment clipped together inside. Or did I put the money in the gift bag with the painting? I'm so confused. Right now, I can't remember where I put the clip." She brushed a hand across her cheeks. "I do know this. I can't even return the fee or buy any Christmas presents until my next pay day." Her face paled. Sweat broke out on her cheeks. "Oh, dear. I think I've thrown my blood sugar out of whack. There should be a bag of candy somewhere around here, unless they took the sweets too."

Honey rummaged through what Annabelle hadn't picked up and shook her head. "No candy."

"I keep some chocolate-covered peanuts in my purse for Gerald. Will that help?" Annabelle left for a moment and then returned with her husband's supply of goodies.

Loretta calmed down after a few handfuls of chocolate-coated protein. Once they'd cleaned up and changed into their street clothes, the ladies made their way to the front desk and registered a complaint. The bored looking worker admitted to being made aware of several thefts in the last month, but since the shower rooms had no security cameras there wasn't much he could do, other than suggesting Loretta make sure she checked her padlock each time.

He pushed a form across the counter. "Here's a form you can fill out and take to the campus police.

The middle-aged attendant's attitude could only be described as condescending to the women, unlike the usually cheerful students who manned the station during the semester.

The women turned away. "What a wasted conversation." Loretta sniffed. "I don't know what I'm going to tell Edmund when I see him at our meeting today."

Honey held out her phone, knowing Loretta usually left her device locked in her car during class. "Give him a call and ask if you can have an extension. Tell Edmund you need to redo the painting. Surely he will understand."

"I just hope I can remember her face well enough to keep that promise." Loretta started to accept the phone but lowered her hand. "I can't seem to recall his phone number right now. I'll take care of making contact when I get to my car. I think I'd rather meet with him in person to break the bad news. Would one of you be willing to go with me if he can meet this afternoon?"

Honey checked her watch. "I'm running late for a meeting at church. If you can wait until around three this afternoon, I could go with you."

Annabelle apologized. Dementia daycare ended at one. Her responsibility to her husband, Gerald, would require her attention for the rest of the afternoon and evening.

Honey settled into her classic red car and waved to the other women as she started her engine and headed to the worship committee meeting. Her father's long ago graduation gift still purred along, thanks to capable mechanics who kept the Mustang raring to go.

A few flakes of snow dusted her windshield. It was beginning to look a lot like Christmas. Too bad someone ruined Loretta's hopes for the holidays.

Chapter Two

A few hours later, Honey led the church committee in a closing prayer, mentioning peace for Loretta's well-being. She hadn't shared details with the group other than letting them know a friend experienced an upsetting event and needed a calm spirit for the next few days. The other members of the group scurried out quickly after the meeting ended, leaving Honey and Preacher Jonah behind to toss empty pizza boxes in the garbage and lock the building.

"Thanks for coming today, Honey. I appreciate you getting all the songs arranged for next month. I'm looking forward to hearing the praise band's new song during the Christmas Eve worship. I've got an idea about how to tie my sermon to the song." The minister's smile held extra warmth, giving Honey pause.

Jonah Farmer could have retired years ago. Instead, he chose to continue serving the church, demonstrating his deep love for the Lord. His widowed status was a frequent topic of discussion among the older church ladies. No one held his interest, unless... Honey wondered if her cheeks were blushing. He fidgeted with his tie, drawing her eyes to his fluffy white beard. Both cleared their throats and headed out of the church.

"Please pray for me this afternoon, Jonah. I'm going to meet with my friend and try to find a resolution for the situation. There's another party involved, and we hope they're open to a change in plans." Honey's voice sounded weak in her ears.

"If I can help, let me know." Jonah's hand rested on her arm. Feelings she hadn't experienced in years pressed on her heart.

She stepped back and made her way to the Mustang. Imagination played tricks on people. There'd never been any attraction to the man before today. Leaning a hand on top of her car, she firmed her voice. "Your prayers will help for now. Thank you."

"I will keep you in my petitions, Honey."

Her name almost sounded like an endearment as he opened Honey's car door and ushered her inside. Her imagination needed reining in. Her heart galloped as she put the Mustang in gear and hit the road for Edmund Bradley's estate. She couldn't imagine how Loretta wrangled a visit to the secluded home.

~~~~~

Jonah watched the little red car speed up as it headed toward the road leading out of town. The little woman was a whirlwind. He marveled at Honey's energy. She kept the praise band energized every Sunday with her rhythmic bass. If he couldn't think of a sermon topic, she always had an idea to share or song lyrics to stir up a new concept in his mind. Now she was off to save the day for a friend. He wondered what the church would do without the little dynamo.

He loosened his tie, which suddenly felt a little tight. The woman seemed irreplaceable, just like his departed wife. He still missed Darlene. She was another woman with a name befitting her personality. His darling, Darlene, lived a full life, embracing all the highs and lows of their ministry in a southern church. Together, they'd raised two children. Their son traveled the world when not teaching at the college level. Their daughter, Darla, and her husband blessed them with three busy grandchildren. Darlene had loved those babies and often found time to travel to Forest Glen from their ministry in another state.

When Darlene left this world for her reward almost ten years ago, Jonah accepted an interim ministry in Forest Glen to be near his daughter's family. Grandchildren and The Rock Church became his new full-time calling. Thoughts of an early retirement dropped from his goals as the church expanded in the following years. In addition to having Honey as worship leader, the staff now included an assistant minister and youth director.

He climbed into his used car and rubbed an aching knee. When Honey mentioned her friend from aquatic exercise needing prayer, reminders of the doctor's orders to find a way to exercise his stiffening knee came to mind. Maybe he should spend some time with Honey and her friends in aquatic exercises to see if his joints might loosen up a little. It might be interesting to see his worship leader in a different light.

He put the car in gear and squashed his wandering thoughts. The ladies' society at church would have a heyday if he expressed an interest in having a close friendship with anyone, unless they had a say. No way would he put Honey through that kind of inquisition. She was too valuable as a friend.

An alarm sounded on his phone. He needed to go get in line to pick up his youngest granddaughter from the middle school. A snowflake danced across his windshield. The Ohio weather was changing. Maybe his grandchildren would get their wish this year for a white Christmas.

~~~~~

Fluffy snowflakes landed on the arms of Honey's black coat as she climbed out of the Mustang. She hoped the meeting with Edmund didn't last too long. The rate of falling snow had increased as she'd wound her way down his curved drive. Older Mustangs weren't built for snow. She could always count on one of the praise band members to take her to church or the doctor when the roads became covered. She prayed for a quick meeting with the rich man and hoped the snow wouldn't stick until she made it home.

A dense forest surrounded the gated path she'd traveled to Edmund's home and the opening where she now stood. There were several protected arboretums in the area, in honor of Forest Glen's history. It looked like Edmund had his own personal forest glen.

Early in Ohio's history, previously untouched trees in the area were harvested for tall masts used on Great Lakes sailing ships. Once people moved to the area, homesteaders used the forests for log cabins and eventually lumber-built homes in the new town named Forest Glen. During the last century, parks and preserves sprang up to protect and replant the forests.

A rattling sound took Honey's thoughts away from history and the forest. Loretta often talked about getting a new car. So far, she still held on to her old sedan. Honey could understand the attachment. Her friend parked next to Honey's Mustang and exited her vehicle.

They stood side by side observing the rustic cabin in front of them.

"I thought his home would be larger." Loretta sniffed.

"Me too. I don't know anyone who visited here before, so I had no idea. The place is cute though." Honey admired the log structure sitting in the clearing. Small undecorated fir trees on either end of the cabin made Honey want to cover them in Christmas bows and lights.

"I'd like to make a painting of the cabin sometime, if I'm allowed after my confession." Loretta lifted her cell phone and snapped a quick photo. "It looks like a Christmas cabin in the snow."

Honey nodded in agreement. "Edmund has gifted the town with many Christmas gifts. I suppose he decided to share his wealth instead of spending it on himself."

"Hopefully his goodwill will extend to me when I let him know the bad news." Loretta led the way to the cabin's small porch and pressed her finger to the doorbell. Chimes could be heard from inside, along with footsteps.

Edmund answered the door wearing casual pants and a brown sweater over a plaid shirt. Honey and Loretta exchanged a quick glance. Honey couldn't read her friend's mind, but figured they both expected an employee to usher them in, even though the home was small.

"Welcome, ladies. Let me take your coats. We can meet in the den off to your left." After hanging their outerwear in a nearby closet, he glanced at Loretta with raised eyebrows. "I don't see the painting. Is it in your car?" His unanswered question hung in the air as he ushered them into the den. The two women sank into a leather covered couch and faced Edmund. He perched on the edge of a matching easy chair.

Loretta heaved a big sigh and pressed a hand to her chest. "That's what we're here about. Honey is here to support me as I share a tragic event from this morning." She looked down and shook her head. "Someone stole your painting while we were at water aerobics this morning."

Edmund frowned. "Did you report the incident to the police?"

"Not yet. We talked to the person at the front desk who gave us a form to fill out. He wasn't very helpful when I admitted that I might not have locked my locker." Loretta looked up with pleading eyes. Leather squeaked as she squirmed in her seat.

He stood and paced back and forth across the room. Edmund's hands brushed a bare Christmas tree before stopping in front of a natural rock fireplace. He crossed his arms and shook his head. His gaze focused on Loretta.

"First, you will report the robbery to the police. Next, you will begin working on a replacement portrait, in case the painting isn't found. I haven't celebrated Christmas in many years. All I wanted for this one was her portrait to hang above my mantelpiece. I even bought a few ornaments for the occasion." He pointed to an unopened box sitting under the Christmas tree. His demands faded to slumped shoulders.

Honey elbowed her friend. "Answer the man. Tell him everything."

He looked up with a frown. "There's more?"

"Well, I accidentally spilled some brush cleaner onto your wife's photo the other day. Her likeness faded into a mess of gray."

Edmund's mouth straightened into a flat line. His face paled then reddened. His fists clinched at his sides.

Honey held up a hand. "Loretta is a wonderful artist with a great memory. I'm sure with a little extra time she can recreate your wife's portrait. Are you coming to Ginny's late Christmas New Year's party?"

He nodded.

"Loretta, can you have his painting by then?" Honey glanced between a cowering Loretta and stern-faced Edmund.

"I will do my best." Loretta sounded winded. She began to nod, slowly at first, and then her hands waved through the air with her usual dramatic flair. "I can do this. I am so sorry for what happened."

Honey smiled at both of them. "Would you like to tell us about your wife, Edmund? It might help Loretta capture some of her personality when she recreates the painting."

Edmund returned to his chair and leaned back into the brown leather. His eyes closed. "She was a beautiful woman, inside and out. I fell in love with her on the day we met." A smile crossed his face.

"I graduated from high school and found a summer job working on the grounds and kitchen crew for a church camp. My military service didn't start until the fall. I was glad to have seasonal work that included a bed and plenty of good food.

"My Lorine came there as a youth leader for one of the weeks. She made friends with everyone, including the lowly hired crew. Her eyes sparkled as I dished out food for meals. During the morning class she taught in the chapel, I managed to be nearby, sweeping and picking up litter. Her love for all of God's children stood out like a beacon to my hungry soul. She waved at me as I wacked weeds around the campus. When she asked my name, my heart nearly exploded."

"You fell hard." Honey's mind drifted back to her departed husband, and their own whirlwind romance. When Preacher Jonah's face entered her thoughts, she forced his visage from her mind. "What happened next, Edmund?"

"During that week we grew very close. When my chores for the day were finished, we sat together for evening chapel times and campfire devotions. I helped her camp team with their Bible drama and talent night events. The week flew by. I learned she lived near the camp. She came by often throughout the summer. We fell in love.

"I proposed and she accepted. I didn't have much, but the military would provide a steady income and base-housing we could afford. When summer camp ended, my minister, who attended the last week of camp with his family, performed a small wedding ceremony for us at the camp chapel. The manager allowed us to stay in one of the camp's cottages for a honeymoon. We had the empty campus to ourselves. We didn't realize how short our time together would last."

"What happened to end your marriage?" Honey asked.

Chapter Three

Edmund sighed. "Whenever I asked Lorine about her family, she always said they weren't around. I should have asked more questions, but I was in love. All too soon, I learned her parents were alive. They pretty much ignored her until she did something that embarrassed them, like marrying a penniless nobody.

"They were a prominent family who valued money more than faith. They let their daughter play at religion, figuring it would help her meet the right people. Her parents used the mega-church they attended to make social connections with the elite and famous, not for developing a personal relationship with God. They didn't understand Lorine's devotion to Jesus and to those who loved her for herself. When they discovered our marriage, they literally hauled her out of our honeymoon cottage and threatened legal action against me if I didn't agree to an annulment."

Loretta gasped. "Did they have the right to make you end your marriage?"

"Unfortunately, because of her age, they did. Lorine talked about attending college the year before we met. My assumption of her being a year older than me proved false when her parents arrived and mentioned she'd skipped a grade and graduated from high school early. My wife was younger than I thought and her parents were threatening me with robbing the cradle, to put it mildly. I tried to fight for her, but I had no money. Resisting the desire to go AWOL, I headed off to boot camp a few days later. Survival forced my penniless hand as my heart broke from losing her."

"But you aren't poor anymore. Have you tried searching for her on the internet or with a detective?" Honey started thinking about ways she might do an internet search on her own.

"I've tried having her investigated many times. Lorine Kenworthy doesn't seem to exist. Her parents denied even having a daughter when I contacted them after boot camp." Edmund rubbed his forehead.

"I completed my military service without spending much of my salary. That savings provided the cash I needed to start my first company. I dreamed of finding Lorine and proving my business abilities to her family. After many attempts through the years, I'd given up. Then I came across this picture in an old box when I cleaned out a storage unit. I decided to at least have a small painting of my Lorine for my memories."

"And that is why Loretta is going to do her best to recreate your wife's likeness by Ginny and Scott's party on New Year's Eve. Right?" Honey elbowed her friend.

"Definitely. What you just shared helps me understand the woman better." Loretta scooted forward on the couch and groaned as she stood. "Thank you for your time. I need to get started with the new portrait."

"Don't forget to contact the police about the first portrait. I liked what I saw when you were almost done." Sadness etched Edmund's lined face.

"I'll make sure we let the officials know." Honey shook Edmund's hand, noting a slight tremor. The man must have truly loved his wife. She'd enjoyed many more years of marriage than Edmund, but could relate to his loss.

The two women headed for their cars and stopped to look back as Edmund waved from his porch. Loretta's face looked gloomy when she turned to nod in Honey's direction.

Honey used her gloved hand to dust a light covering of snow from her windshield, glad to notice flurries no longer filled the air. "Don't be sad about the painting. I know you can redo your work."

"It's more than just the painting. Even though I'm a few years older than the man, I hoped Edmund might notice me. From what I saw and heard, he will always be in love with his lost wife."

Honey reached over to swipe snow from Loretta's sedan. "You are an amazing artist who hasn't needed anyone before now. Having a husband would tie you down from all your adventures. Put thoughts about him away and put your best effort into this painting."

"You're right. I don't need a man." She paused. "But if you can talk Preacher Jonah into going with us to the police station, I wouldn't mind his support since he sometimes volunteers there."

"I can ask. He might be busy. I don't want to intrude on his time."

Loretta's downturned mouth lifted into a smile. "I have a feeling he would be willing to do anything you need him to do."

Honey shook her head. "I have no idea where you got that idea."

Loretta just smirked and plopped into her car. "Let me know when he's available."

~~~~~

Jonah followed Honey and Loretta into the police station. Honey had asked him to come along for moral support. He'd agreed to help the two women parishioners at her urging. The energetic woman suggested his being part of the volunteer Chaplain Association might influence the officers. Her reasoning might work if the personnel on duty recognized him.

Loretta led the charge with the others following. His arm brushed against Honey's. A shock traveled up his arm. He dismissed the charge as static electricity and hurried ahead to stand next to Loretta as she rapped on the glass partition separating the waiting room from the interior offices. He felt Honey's presence as she stood behind Loretta.

The female officer on duty slid the window open. "What can I do to help you, ma'am?"

"I'm here to report a robbery." Loretta's fists moved to her hips and waited with one foot toe-tapping as the officer clicked a few keys on her computer.

"I've got the form open. Now, where did this alleged crime occur?" The policewoman showed no emotion as she waited for Loretta to provide the details.

Loretta scowled at the woman. "There's nothing alleged about it. Someone stole some cash and a portrait I painted while I participated in water aerobics at the college."

The officer's fingers paused. "Did you report this to the campus police?"

"Not yet. We have a form to fill out but haven't had time to do so. Is that going to be a problem?" Loretta's voice grew louder. Jonah placed a hand on her shoulder. At the same time, Honey wrapped an arm around her friend's waist and moved to stand next to the angry woman. Trembling traveled through his hand, letting him know both women were steamed.

Jonah leaned closer to the window and plastered on a pleasant smile. "Hi, Officer Jones. Could you take Loretta's information and possibly share it with the college?"

She shrugged. "We don't normally proceed that way, but it may be hard to find someone at the college office right now. My daughter and I went over to discuss a parking situation yesterday. The only person in the office was a retired secretary subbing in for the regular staff."

She glanced at Loretta. "Go ahead and give me a description of the missing items. I'll share the information with the campus police and that's all I can promise at this point. Someone will get back to you from the college. I imagine you won't hear anything until after the holidays."

Jonah listened as Loretta described the painting and a money clip holding several hundred dollars. He thanked Officer Jones, before linking his arms with both Honey and her friend.

"How about we take a break at the coffee shop for brunch before we head our separate ways?" He'd been in a rush that morning and missed breakfast. His growling stomach produced evidence of his lack of nourishment.

Honey held a hand over her half-hidden smile. Her blue eyes looked like they held a twinkle after hearing the rumbling complaint from his gut.

Loretta shook her head. "I better go home and get started on redoing the portrait. Pray for me. I'm going to need every petition you can offer to get a recognizable image completed in the limited time I have. You and Honey go have a nice time."

Her smile hinted at something Jonah wasn't sure he wanted to address. Honey looked bewildered.

Chapter Four

"Would you like to go with me? I mean to the coffee shop for some brunch?" Jonah bit his tongue to keep from uttering another embarrassing comment.

"Sure. You know I can't resist their lemon-filled donut." She fell in step beside him as they strolled down the sidewalk toward the shop.

Jonah often brought donuts to their business meetings and made sure to include a few of Honey's favorite treats. A ripple of something akin to hope filled his chest as they entered the establishment. Maybe he should take a hint from Loretta. He led Honey to a table for two near a window and pulled out her chair. "What would you like to drink with your donut?"

"I'll have a hot chocolate in honor of the Christmas season." Her smile warmed his heart as headed to the front of the shop to place their order. Honey sure was a sweet woman. He wondered why he hadn't noticed how appealing she was until recently.

~~~~~

Honey shifted in her seat and noted a couple from church chatting as they sat a few tables away. She gave a friendly wave before turning to focus on Jonah while he waited in line. Usually she came to the cafe with either her lady friends or the worship band. Sitting alone with Jonah would be a new experience. The feeling both intrigued and worried her, especially since their table sat where everyone could see the two of them.

"Here you go. Bon appétit." Jonah set the tray between them and reached for her hands. "Let's give thanks."

Honey stared at the top of his bowed head for a split-second, then quickly closed her eyes and tried to concentrate on his words of gratitude. Her mind should be following his petition, but all she could think about was how her hands felt at home in his, an emotion she hadn't experienced since the passing of her husband.

After saying "Amen," Jonah looked up but didn't release her hand. "How long has it been since your husband passed?"

Could the man read her mind? Honey pulled her hands away and reached for the stirrer sticking out of her cup of chocolate. Looking out the window, she slowly calculated the years. "Disease took him away about sixteen years ago. He was a good man like you." Honey turned her gaze back to Jonah, reminding herself that he was her minister, not a potential date.

"My wife left this world ten years ago, but you probably remember that from when I started my position with The Rock Church. I came here to be near my daughter's family. I don't know what I'd do without those grandchildren to love."

"You would do what my husband and I did. We took in every stray from young to old and loved them as family." Honey's thoughts turned to Scott and Ginny Hallmark who'd been one of her more recent unofficial adoptions. They'd become a nice family and she loved their children like a grandmother.

"I've adopted members of my church family, too, but there's something special about my grandchildren. Maybe you could add my family to your adopted ones." He winked as he lifted an iced muffin with Christmas sprinkles on top.

The minister winked. *Oh, dear.* Honey didn't know how to react. Her body gave her no choice, letting her know that wink was tastier than her sugary lemon donut. She lifted her treat in the air, hoping for a distraction. "I will give that some thought." As she took a bite of the pastry, she noticed the couple from church raising their thumbs and grinning.

Honey turned her gaze back toward Jonah, who held his coffee in the air with a Santa Claus smile. She fought the urge to grab a napkin and brush green and red sprinkles from his soft looking beard.

~~~~

Later that day, the trio of friends sat around Annabelle's table. Her husband, Gerald, sat nearby with a smile on his face, nodding in agreement with all they said.

"It doesn't look like the police are going to be much help until after the holidays, if at all." Loretta wagged a finger in the air. "We need to make a list of suspects, like they do on television."

"Shouldn't you be working on the new portrait?" Annabelle faced Loretta.

Loretta crossed her arms. "I've covered the canvas with an undercoat. The oil paint needs to dry before I can start putting in details. I still have doubts about making the reproduction resemble the original." She let out a dramatic huff.

Honey took a yellow legal pad out of her bag and laid it on the table. "Then let's get started with a list. Who are our main suspects?"

"I don't like the person working the front desk at the college. He didn't seem to care. That makes me wonder if the man knew what happened to my art and cash." Loretta thumped her hand down on the table. The other women and the older man jumped and looked at Loretta in surprise.

Honey cleared her throat and tapped her pen on the pad of paper. "Who else?"

"The custodian is always around. She seems friendly enough, but you never know what people may do when they become desperate." Annabelle looked embarrassed. Honey knew it was hard on the woman to even think of accusing another person of a crime.

Honey shook her head, doubts ebbing and flowing through her thoughts. "I like Mary. She's always pleasant and seems to love her job. I don't think she would steal."

"Put her on the list anyway." Loretta placed a finger on the paper tablet.

Annabelle leaned forward. "What about Tillie? She left the pool before we did. Her attitude has been worse than usual, if that is possible."

Her husband's head bobbed in agreement. Gerald's smile held a pleasant memory of the man he once was.

"Do we have more suspects?" Loretta asked.

"None that I can think of at the moment, but anyone on campus could have entered the lockers while we were in the water. The only other people who left early were Melody and the twins. There's no way they would steal from anyone." Honey leaned back in her chair. She knew Melody quite well. Did she really know the twins? She pushed that thought to the side. If one of the youngsters did something questionable, Melody would have brought it to their attention by now.

After a thirty minute discussion, Loretta stood and grabbed her

15

purse. "We need to start our investigation before the crime scene gets cold."

Honey gave Annabelle a hug and headed out of the room, passing by the woman's husband who lightly snored in his chair. "Take care of your mister. We'll keep you up-to-date."

Annabelle waved goodbye. "Try to keep Loretta under control." The sound of her laughter remained in Honey's ears as she hustled out to jump in the car with Sherlock Loretta.

Honey gripped her arm rest as Loretta swung the car out of the driveway and barreled across town. Several beeps accompanied them as they zipped around another vehicle.

"Slow down, Loretta. You're going to get us killed if you don't get control of yourself." Honey fanned her face, praying for her heart to stop racing after a near collision as they circled a recently constructed round-about.

Loretta's knuckles were white as they gripped her steering wheel. "The college buildings are closing down for the holidays tonight. I don't want to take a chance of missing our suspects."

Honey clasped the passenger seat armrest as her companion whipped into a parking space. "Loretta, calm down. Anger isn't going to solve a thing. Remember what Jonah preached about last Sunday. Using harsh words isn't going to solve anything."

Loretta jumped from the car, seeming to ignore her passenger's words.

Honey rushed to join her fleeing friend at the building's side entrance, near the indoor pool. Loretta barged ahead like a freight train, muttering something about Jesus overturning tables at the temple.

After entering the building using their keychain pass cards, their footsteps echoed down the empty hallway. In the distance, a radio played Christmas songs, while a woman sang along using an out-of-tune voice. Loretta zoomed ahead like a heat-seeking missile with her sights set on the cleaning lady. They rounded a corner and startled the woman who lifted her mop in defense.

"Did you take my painting and Christmas money?" Loretta blurted out the question before Honey had a chance to use a calmer approach.

The custodian's mouth fell open, and then closed. She shook her head and frowned. "I have no idea what you're talking about. I was in the building the other day when there was a big commotion, if you're asking about me hearing a lady hollering about somebody dying. I figured she lost a relative or something, but I don't know about any money or a painting."

Loretta's voice shook. "It wasn't just any lady. It was me. I lost an expensive portrait that day and all the money in my wallet. I saw you out in the hallway afterward. Maybe you took it."

The woman gasped and placed a hand near her nametag. Mary didn't appear guilty, she looked upset and steamed.

Honey spoke up. "Perhaps you saw someone different in the hall or in the shower room, Mary. We don't know who took the items. Our apologies for hinting you were involved in any way." She zipped fingers across her lips and gave Loretta a look to hopefully squelch another outburst.

Mary crossed her arms and leaned her hip against the rolling container holding cleaning items. "I don't recall anyone new or different. There are cameras in the hallways. You could ask about those with the bosses." She turned away and started mopping the hallway leading to the locker room.

Honey grabbed Loretta's arm and pulled her in the opposite direction.

"I don't think we'll get much more help from her, Loretta. Try a little tact next time we attempt to interview someone." Honey knew about frustration. She also knew compassion and patience were better than anger. "I am sorry we can't figure out what happened to the missing items. Maybe we need to go back to your studio and see if you can concentrate on using your wonderful abilities by making the new painting."

"Not before we ask about those hallway cameras. I'm heading to the front desk." Loretta forged ahead like a dog after a bone.

The same bored attendant sat at the desk reading a crime novel. He frowned when he saw Loretta marching his way. Honey pushed in front of her friend and smiled at the man. "Hi. We wanted to thank you for helping us the other day."

Loretta gasped. "He did no..."

Honey grabbed Loretta's wrist and squeezed hard.

"Ow."

"As I was saying, we appreciate you listening to our complaint the other day. We were chatting with Mary, the custodian, and she mentioned the possibility of checking the footage of the hallway cameras. Would you have access to those?" Honey's voice sounded so syrupy sweet she wondered if she would fall into a sugar coma.

The man's frown relaxed into a grimace. "I'm sorry, ma'am. I'm just filling in. My regular job is cleaning the engineering building. It isn't open for the holidays and I drew the short straw for holding down the desk here while everyone else got a long Christmas break. You'll have to wait for someone with more pull than me, who actually is on the staff for the recreation center."

Loretta snorted. "Maybe you sneaked away from the desk to go raid the women's locker room and steal my painting."

The man glared at Loretta. "See that camera over there? If or when you get your chance to see any footage, you will discover I sat at this desk the whole time during my four-hour shift. I read most of a novel that morning. I almost solved the mystery, and then you came barreling up here with your complaints."

Honey wrapped her arm through Loretta's elbow. "Thank you for your help." To Loretta she whispered, "Calm down," as they headed back toward the side door where they'd parked their vehicle. She stepped to the driver's side of Loretta's sedan. "Let me have your keys. You are not driving."

Loretta reluctantly handed over her keys and slouched into the passenger seat. "Sorry. I really lost my cool back there." A few minutes later, she straightened and a smirk exploded across her lips. "I did a pretty good angry detective imitation back there, just like my favorite TV sleuth."

Honey couldn't keep from laughing. "You were a ball of fire for sure, but I don't think a real-life detective would get away with what you see on a crime show. Maybe you should let me do the next interview on my own."

"I do need to get back to painting. Promise me you will take someone with you so you have a witness or someone who can protect you, like Preacher Jonah."

Honey opened her mouth in protest and accidentally revved the engine of Loretta's sedan.

Loretta laughed as Honey drove the sputtering car away from the parking lot.

Silence reined until Honey pulled into her driveway and handed the keys back to her friend. "Drive carefully, Loretta. I'll see if Annabelle and I can catch Tillie tomorrow morning at the senior center during the quilting craft class. There's no need to further bother the preacher with our troubles."

Honey often quilted with a group that met at First Church in the downtown area. She'd joined the women after meeting Ginny's mother during the musical, *Incident at Woodson House.* The ladies helped sew costumes for the musical's production before returning to their usual quilting, which Honey found relaxing.

When she saw the senior center's craft class about quilting a Christmas table runner during December, she signed up because of the unique design. Tomorrow would be their last class, where they would finish attaching the binding around the outside edge. Both Tillie and Annabelle were in the class.

Chapter Five

The next morning, Honey waited while Annabelle checked Gerald into the dementia day care. Once he waved goodbye, the two women headed for the classroom with their tote bags over their shoulders.

Honey walked next to Annabelle down a hallway decorated with completed jigsaw puzzles encased in frames. "Let's try to grab a seat near Tillie today. I want to talk to her after class about what she might have seen when Loretta's painting disappeared."

When they entered the room the woman in question sat alone at the far end of a table in the back of the room. Her quilted craft lay in front of her. She frowned while pinning a red binding into place.

"Mind if we join you?" Honey opened her tote and sat before the woman had a chance to disagree.

Tillie shrugged as Annabelle unpacked her bag and lined up her sewing materials at the other end of their table. Several moments of silence passed as they each began working on their pieces. The instructor walked around the room encouraging each woman and admiring their work.

"You did a nice job choosing your material, ladies." Miss Hope from the fabric store stopped at their table to check their progress. Annabelle smiled at the sweet lady. The shop owner had been very patient as she instructed the senior women in the art of quilting.

Honey held her work up for inspection as she nodded to their teacher. "Thank you for having a great selection of Christmas cloth in your store."

"There's always a demand for holiday themed prints. I'm glad you had first choice before my regulars thinned out your options. Seeing your projects almost completed makes me proud. When I do a class like this, often people get distracted and don't end up with the hoped-for result. Super job, my friends." Miss Hope moved on to another table.

Honey looked over at Tillie's quilting. "Your stitches are beautiful, so tiny and even. You must be an experienced quilter."

"My grandmother taught me how to quilt." A frown crossed Tillie's face as she paused. "I haven't done any sewing in a while. I've been too busy helping my daughter with her little ones."

"Is there something wrong with your grandchildren?" Honey hadn't expected Tillie's unhappy expression when talking about the younger generation.

"Not really. Nothing a little money can't solve, according to my son-in-law." Tillie's air quotes and rolled eyes expressed her opinion about her son-in-law's suggestion.

"Speaking of money, do you know anything about Loretta's robbery at the pool?" Honey kept her voice casual as she poked a pin into her project.

Tillie looked down at her hands. She jabbed her needle into the binding, avoiding Honey's inquiry. Honey reworded her question and spoke in a softer voice. "Did you take Loretta's money and painting, or see someone who might have committed the crime?"

"I didn't take the painting." Tillie crossed her arms and looked up.

"What about the money?" Honey had noted the omission.

The woman shrugged. "What if I did? I pay good money for those classes and I was shorted time from our last class by Melody not doing her job. When I got to the shower room, stuff was scattered all over the place. I saw money lying on the floor. I couldn't tell who it belonged to, so I figured the cash sitting in the middle of the room was payback for missing time with the swim instructor. Some of us don't have good insurance paying for the senior fitness program. It was only a twenty." She reached for her wallet and slapped the bill on the table. "Take it. We're done." She stood and started to gather her things.

"Wait." Honey recognized the pain emanating from the woman. "You're forgiven. I'll get the money to Loretta. Now, let's talk about what you did see that day."

Tillie huffed, but returned to the seat she'd vacated. "There really wasn't much to see. It looked like the clothing and towels had toppled onto the floor along with the wallet and money." She bit her lip. "I might have given things a kick. My day didn't start out too well. Anger took over when I saw you three friends chatting like a bunch of mother hens about *poor* Melody when she left the pool early."

Choosing to ignore the woman's cutting remarks, Honey laid a hand on the woman's wrist. "What made you upset that day?"

She slumped back in the chair. "My daughter stopped by to tell me about her husband's new job in Atlanta. They'll be moving away as soon as their house sells. I always thought they'd be here for me in my old age. Now it looks like my son-in-law is moving up the ladder and across the country. He talks about all the big money he'll be making. They'll live in Georgia for two years. Afterward, depending on open positions, they may end up in Seattle or New York."

"Do you have any other family close by?" Annabelle joined the conversation and moved to sit closer to Tillie.

"No one." Tillie fingered her quilted work and shook her head.

"Do you have a church family?" The urge to share God's love entered Honey's heart.

"I haven't attended anywhere in a while. After my husband's funeral, going back into The Rock Church building only reminded me of his passing." Tillie's face sagged.

Honey placed a hand on the woman's shoulder. "We have an active seniors group at our church. They meet in different people's homes so you wouldn't have to start by going into the building. I'm sure everyone would be happy to have you join us."

"I don't think I'd fit in." She picked up her needle and appeared to be concentrating on her stitches.

Annabelle placed her hand on Tillie's. "You never know until you try. There's quite a few in the group who are widowed or chose to stay single. Many members are without family in town, so we support each other as brothers and sisters in the Lord. They've been helpful during Gerald's recent decline."

The woman shook her head. "My apartment is here in the downtown area. I don't drive anymore. I rely on my daughter to take me places. Traveling around to different homes won't work once they move."

Honey ran a finger over Tillie's quilting. "First Church is right around the corner from here. I go to their quilting group a few times each month. You could start with them and go to their church services when you're ready. They would love to have someone who can stitch like you."

"I don't know." Tillie's voice wavered.

"Miss Hope is a member of the congregation and brings the quilters scraps of material from her shop. What we don't use, some of the women take home and make into crafts to sell. Ginny Hallmark's mom often sells items for the ladies when she goes to craft fairs with her husband." Honey added the enticement, hoping she read the woman's indecision correctly.

"Really? I'll have to give joining their group a thought." A rare smile crossed Tillie's face. "Now, let's not waste our time, gals, we need to get these quilted runners wrapped up."

Honey chuckled to herself. The woman was back to being her serious self, but maybe a seed had been planted that might bring Tillie some hope.

Now, if only they could find good hopeful news for Loretta since they'd eliminated all the obvious suspects. At least they'd recovered some of the lost money. She'd give Loretta a call and give her the cash when they met the next day.

~~~~~

Honey knocked on Annabelle's door and waited. She scanned the crowded driveway. She knew Loretta's sedan, but couldn't place the newer SUV. The home's door opened and Annabelle greeted her with a warm hug.

"Come in. I think I have a way to get the news out about the robbery." She led the way to her kitchen. "You probably remember my grandson. He helps me record my podcasts."

Honey shook the young man's hand, taking care to avoid knocking over the large microphone sitting in the middle of the table. "Yes, we've met before. You must have a new vehicle."

21

"The SUV is at least new to me. Have you ever thought of trading in your Mustang?" His raised eyebrows showed interest in her vehicle.

"No. My car and I have a long history." She shook her head. The young man nodded, and then focused on connecting wires to his laptop. Honey sat down and slipped the envelope with the twenty into Loretta's hand.

"Thanks for handling the situation better than I would." Loretta leaned over to stuff the money in her purse.

Honey turned to Annabelle. "I'm guessing you figured out a way to work the theft into a podcast."

Loretta sat back up and snorted. "I hope we can keep Edmund's name out of this. I don't need to make him any more upset with me than he already is."

"No worries, my friends. I've written a Christmas skit that will act as a parable about a stolen item. I combined the lost sheep and King Solomon's decision about the stolen baby. I'll add a comment hinting about a similar situation in the locker room at the college pool. We can ask people to let us know if they saw anything suspicious."

"That sounds like a good idea, but aren't many of your listeners out of town?" Loretta sounded doubtful.

"True, but most of our fellow swimmers follow my podcasts. Maybe they will give us a break. If the play doesn't help with our case, I hope the theme will touch at least one person's heart." She passed out scripts for Honey and Loretta to study before giving her grandson the nod to start the recording.

"Welcome to Annabelle's Answers, season seven, episode five. Today I have some friends here to help me present a short skit for your enjoyment and edification. Here is *The Lost Gift*, performed by my friends Honey, as Faith, and Loretta, as Charity, and yours truly, Annabelle, as the narrator.

The Lost Gift by Annabelle, for this year's Christmas week podcast

Narrator: Once upon a time, two older women lived in side-by-side cabins at the edge of a forest, near a small village. They were great friends. One woman was an artist of great renown, named Charity. Her neighbor, a famed musician, went by the name of Faith. As Christmas approached the artist approached the musician with a request.

Charity: Hi Faith. I wanted to show you a painting I created as a gift for someone very special. Do you think you could write a song to accompany my gift?

Faith: The painting is beautiful, Charity. I love the way the snow is coming down on the cabin. Does the handsome man you painted on the porch resemble someone we know?"

Charity: He is someone I've always admired. Jonas used to live here but moved away several years ago.

Faith: Was he the one you liked before you met your husband?

Charity: Jonas and I went together during high school, then he left town and never came back. I often think about him and wonder what happened after he left.

Faith: To whom will you gift the painting and the song once I finish?

Charity: I will let you know when the time is right.

Faith: Let me borrow the painting and I'll see what I can do.

Narrator: Faith took the painting home with her and studied the scene and the likeness of Jonas. She thought back to her memories of the man she and Charity both admired. Soon lyrics began to flow about a love lost to time and distance. She shared some of the lyrics with Charity, who praised the words and encouraged Faith to keep going. One day Faith took the painting and her work out on her deck to reflect on both in the natural setting. As she admired the painting, she lifted a sheet of staff paper from her folder and composed a beautiful melody for her lyrics. She liked it so well she started singing the piece aloud and lost all thoughts of traffic on the road or sounds near her home, until she finished performing the song for herself.

When her doorbell rang inside the house, she left the painting, and her music folder behind. She spent a good half-hour engaged in a conversation with her former talent agent, who tried to convince Faith to write songs under a pseudonym for a new and upcoming singer. This wasn't the first time the agent begged her to compose for the new talent and give that person credit. She didn't like the idea of lying to the public and refused the man. After ushering him out the door, she returned to her deck. She discovered the painting and her folder containing the lyrics and staff paper were gone. She dreaded breaking the news to Charity, but knew she had no other choice.

Faith: I'm so sorry, Charity. Someone took the painting and my nearly completed song.

Charity: I trusted you with my work. Now I won't have a Christmas gift for my friend.

Faith: Give me some time to search for your painting. I promise to look everywhere until I find it.

Charity: What about the song? Do you think you can re-create the music?

Faith: I promise to try. I might be able to remember the words of the early verses. The tune was too fresh for me to recall exactly what I put down.

Charity: Do your best. I will help you search for the lost pieces.

Narrator: Faith and Charity spent several weeks scouring the forest and nearby town, searching, but not finding the missing items. Neither felt like exchanging gifts that Christmas and sadly mourned the loss of their creations.

"This is Annabelle. Allow me to interrupt our little skit to let you know that someone had a very special gift planned for this Christmas, right here in my hometown of Forest Glen, Ohio. If you happened to be over at the college when someone took a certain something from the ladies' locker room located by the indoor pool, please let me know if you have any clues about where it is. We won't prosecute. We just want it back. Now let's return to the rest of our story."

Loretta frowned as Annabelle returned to the script.

Narrator: The two friends searched for almost a year until Charity finally found a clue.

Charity: Open up your door, Faith...You won't believe...what I just saw on...television.

Faith: What's the matter, Charity? You look about ready to faint. Take a deep breath and calm down.

Charity: There was an ad...for a new album... called 'Hoping for Love'...it looked like... The cover looked like my painting and the lyrics playing in the background sounded like what you shared with me over a year ago. I loved the words then and committed a few phrases to memory.

Faith: Do you remember the name of the singer?

Charity: I think it was Jeritta Malitta. I never heard of her before.

Faith: Unfortunately, I know who the singer is. I have a feeling I know how she got our painting and song. We're going to make a phone call to my former agent and I need you to listen in as my witness.

Narrator: The case of the stolen music and painting headed for court and made big news in the music world. Faith and Charity and the 'Hoping for Love' album filled entertainment pages across the nation. The judge found Faith's agent and his partner guilty of stealing the song and painting. The agents had planned a visit to Faith so they could beg one last time for the rights to her song. When they heard her singing the new song on her deck, Faith's former agent decided to distract Faith with a visit, while his cohort stole what she left outside her home.

They also faced judgment for lying to Jerrita about where the song came from. In his private chambers, the judge placed the song and painting on a table and met with the creators and performer to discuss the future of the hit album. In the end, all parties agreed to share the royalties. The singer returned Charity's painting, along with a request for the artist to create another cover. Faith agreed to compose a few new songs for Jerritta Malitta as long as Faith's name appeared as the composer. Their fame brought the long-lost gentleman, Jonas, back into their lives. He stood by them as they endured the court case and moved back to town a few months later. The following Christmas, Charity finally gave her gift to someone special.

Charity: Merry Christmas, Faith. I painted this picture for you a year ago. I hoped when you wrote the song you'd realize Jonas and I were never in love. We broke it off when we came to understand he only had eyes for you. When you didn't show any interest in him, he left town. Now you and Jonas can put this painting above your mantlepiece and celebrate your new life together as you listen to your song. Merry Christmas.

Narrator: And they all lived happily ever after.

"This is Annabelle signing off. Make someone's Christmas brighter this year by doing the right thing. Merry Christmas, and I will see you in the New Year." Annabelle held a hand in the air until her grandson nodded. "Great performance, ladies."

"Do we have to keep the part about not prosecuting the person who took my painting in the podcast? Maybe your grandson can edit that out," Loretta groused.

Annabelle shook her head. "Maybe the culprit will feel some pressure to come clean with the threat of prosecution."

Honey hesitated for a second before adding a suggestion of her own. "I'd be glad to redo the whole thing if we could use the name John instead of Jonas. I almost said the preacher's name, instead of what you wrote, whenever Jonas appeared. I hope I didn't stutter."

"So Jonah makes you stutter? Is there something we should know about the two of you?" Loretta giggled.

"No. I don't know. Well, maybe I'll know more after our first date tomorrow night." Honey felt like a mouse held under a cat's paw.

Annabelle's grandson stood and gathered his gear. "Excuse me, ladies. Let me wrap up my equipment and I'll be on my way. I don't think I'll need to do much editing on this one. I'll post it later tonight. Does that work for you, Grandma?"

Annabelle nodded.

Honey stood to make a quick exit.

Loretta grabbed Honey's arm and motioned for her to sit down.

No one moved again until the grandson cleared the table and left to speak with Gerald in another room.

"Out with it, girlfriend." Loretta still held onto Honey as she grinned like a Cheshire cat.

"Do tell..." Annabelle looked at Honey with a pleasant expression.

"I really can't explain what is happening other than to say I seem to be getting extra attention from Preacher Jonah in the last few weeks."

Loretta snickered. "Only in the last few weeks? He's admired you for a long time and everyone but you two seem to have noticed."

"Oh." Honey didn't know what to say. She hoped her face wasn't turning all shades of red. She was too old for this kind of thing.

"We might have gathered that you like Preacher Jonah too." Annabelle laid a comforting hand on Honey's arm. "I don't think anyone would be upset if you date or even become more than friends with him."

Honey's shoulders lowered. "Do you really think people won't mind if we have a date tomorrow?"

"I think most people would be happy for you. Though, it shouldn't matter what anyone else believes." Annabelle's words comforted Honey.

She jumped when Loretta clapped her hands. "We need to find you something special to wear. I've got some really fancy dresses in my closet."

"We're going somewhere casual. I want to go there looking and acting like myself." Honey appreciated Loretta's offer but knew she would never look right in the artist's flashy clothing. She didn't want to send a wrong message to Jonah. either.

"Good for you. We'll pray the best for both of you." Annabelle reached out and gave her friend a hug.

Loretta joined them.

Honey prayed she was doing the right thing.

Chapter Six

Jonah adjusted his plaid tie before knocking on Honey's door. He'd said casual, but the urge to take Honey to a special place overruled his good sense. It didn't matter. If she opened the door wearing a tee-shirt from the Senior Center Bash last summer, he'd make a quick adjustment to his plans.

He heard her footsteps and stood a little taller. When she opened the door, he smiled in relief. The red and green top almost matched his tie. Her black pants looked freshly pressed and ready for an evening at the town's nicest restaurant. He stepped in to assist with her coat and inhaled a soft lavender scent. The woman was sweetness personified. Tonight he would be blessed by her presence.

"Would you like to take my car?" Honey offered him her keys.

He covered her hand as he reached for her key chain. "You have truly shared a great gift with me."

She laughed. "If I didn't know better, I'd say you liked my car better than me."

He sobered. "There is no comparison to the sweet Honey in front of me."

He watched her face turn pink and prayed he hadn't overstepped. "Thank you for the honor of driving your car. I am thrilled to take you to Francine's for dinner tonight. I hope you will enjoy our outing."

Honey's smile reached down into his soul. He held her door and then attempted to whistle a happy tune as he walked to the driver's side. He hadn't whistled in a long time and no true whistles passed his lips. A practice session of lip puckers was long overdue. The exercise might come in handy for something else if... He closed off his thoughts and concentrated. He might need some lessons on using a gear shift again.

A few minutes later, they coasted into the parking lot for Francine's Restaurant. Honey giggled the whole way there as he struggled to keep the car moving forward at an acceptable rate of smoothness and speed.

"We made it." Jonah chuckled. "I won't object if you want to drive once we finish our meal. I thought we might go see the lighthouse along the lakeside tonight when we're done."

She kept laughing as he handed her back the keys and walked around to open her door.

The hostess seated them right away, thanks to arriving promptly at the time of their reservation. The window next to their table overlooked the creek streaming its way toward Lake Erie. A garland of evergreen surrounded the window, sharing seasonal scents. Their tabletop candle reflected in the glass. Honey's eyes sparkled from the same light. Soft Christmas carols played in the background, making his heart sing. He heard Honey humming along too. She was a beautiful woman. He wondered why he hadn't noticed her before, as more than a co-worker. He knew why. God's timing was always for the best. He hadn't been ready. Perhaps she hadn't either. He prayed tonight changed everything.

The waitress brought menus and they both ordered the special, Amish ham loaf, scalloped potatoes, and grilled asparagus.

"Thank you for coming tonight, Honey."

She smiled back. "I'm glad to be here with you."

He reached for her hands and squeezed them gently as he prayed. When they lifted their eyes, their hands remained joined. Warmth coursed through his whole body. "I'm just going to blurt this out. I would be interested in dating you, Honey. I haven't gone out with anyone in a long time so I might be a little rusty."

She clasped his hands tighter. "I'm pretty rusty myself. My late husband was the only person who ever courted me, so I'm not sure I even know what to expect. If you can put up with my bumbling along, I can give us a try."

Jonah's heart thumped in his chest. "I've put up with you during church committee meetings, I'm sure we can manage to get along."

She pulled back, her hands and eyebrows rose. "Really?"

Had he blown their relationship already? His mouth gaped open as he tried to think of a way to repair the situation.

"Did the grandkids steal your tongue, Mr. Preacher?" She half-hid a smile behind a hand, but her body started shaking as laugh lines crinkled beside her eyes.

Jonah joined her mirth as he reached for one hand. "You had me scared there for a minute, sweet lady."

They spent the rest of their evening enjoying the meal, speculating about the lost painting, laughing about humorous situations at church, and talking about his grandchildren. Later, Honey drove them to the lake shore where a lone lighthouse illuminated the night sky with its beacon of protection and light. When Honey shivered, he wrapped her in his arms and placed a kiss on her forehead. A feeling of lightness lifted his thoughts to God, the one who knew the right time to bless those who served Him and open their eyes to possibilities for the future.

Chapter Seven

On Christmas afternoon, Annabelle picked up Honey in her small SUV with front-wheel-drive. Snow covered the ground, creating the classic Christmas look. Snowmen stood in yards and sleds slid down the only hill in their northwest Ohio town. Gusts of flurries still dusted barely plowed roads. Leaving the Mustang safely secured inside the garage sounded better than skidding across town. Honey gladly accepted her friend's offer for a ride.

Annabelle left her grandson back at their house 'man-sitting' Gerald, providing a window for the three women to celebrate their own Christmas at Loretta's bungalow. Honey balanced two small gifts on her lap, listening to Annabelle chat about seeing many members of her family during Christmas morning breakfast.

"It seems like they're all growing so fast." My 'man-sitter' is the oldest of the bunch. I've given up on picking out a gift for each of them. With Gerald needing so much of my time, I decided to just give money to each of them this year."

"I'm sure they understand and you shouldn't feel guilty. You're blessed to still have your husband around." Honey stared out the window, her thoughts a jumble of the past and present. "I did have fun picking out a book for Ginny and Scott's Melissa and a stuffed bear for their little Treasure Hope. They invited me to their house this morning and we had a great time."

"I wonder how Loretta fared without Edmund's extra money to use for her niece's and nephew's presents."

"We'll have to ask her in a few minutes." Annabelle parked her car and grabbed a tote from the back while Honey rang the doorbell.

"Come in, you two." Loretta sounded cheerful. Honey sighed in relief. She prayed her friend finally found some peace about the situation with the missing money and the portrait of Edmund's wife.

Loretta hung their coats on a small hat tree standing near the door. The scent of fresh oil paints and pine air fresheners entered Honey's nose. She fought back a sneeze.

Loretta handed her a tissue box. "There are plenty of these if you need them. I know the paint odors make you sneeze, but I've been busy the last week. Come and see what I've been doing."

The women walked past a small combination living room and bedroom, boasting a sofa and cushion-filled daybed sitting across from each other. They followed their host down a short hall to the former bedroom in the house, which currently served as Loretta's studio. Drying racks holding multiple paintings lined one wall. An easel sat in the middle of the room with the portrait of a beautiful woman's smiling face looking their way.

"I finished Edmund's Lorine last night. What do you think?" Loretta posed beside the canvas.

Honey clapped her hands."I love the way you used his cabin as a background. He should be pleased with what you've done. Her face is so life-like."

"She looks like a very happy woman and so do you. I'm glad to see your joyful personality has returned." Annabelle stepped forward for a closer look. "Your details are amazing. I'm proud of you, my dear friend."

"Come, there's more to see." Loretta walked to one of the drying racks and held up a watercolor of Annabelle and Gerald's faces. "I don't have the money for a frame this Christmas, but I made this for you and Gerald to have as your gift."

Annabelle carefully took the painting and held it under the light in the center of the room. Tears rolled down her cheeks. "Don't worry about a frame. We will cherish this forever. I'm sure it will become a family heirloom when life is over for us. Thank you, Loretta. This is the best gift I've ever received."

"I made some quick paintings for each of my nieces and nephews. They aren't coming until a couple of days from now, so those paintings have time to dry. I used watercolors for the two of you so we could share our gifts today." She turned and leaned over to pluck another painting from the rack. "Here is Honey's gift. I hope you appreciate the thought behind the art."

Honey stared in awe at the sunset painting her friend had created. The colorful sky and summer countryside were beautiful and would match her living room colors perfectly. In the center of the painting, a red Mustang, with its convertible top off, traveled toward the setting sun. Two windblown heads of gray hair appeared above the back of the car's seats. What?

"Your painting is astounding, but I'm not sure I understand about the two people in the car. I usually drive alone unless I have a carload of ladies with me. The driver looks like a man in my driver's seat." Heat rose in Honey's chest. She didn't know how to react to the obvious attempt at matchmaking.

"Maybe the time to let a man drive your car has arrived." Annabelle's soft whisper warmed Honey's ear.

"He didn't do so well when I let him try the other day." Honey snickered.

"What are you talking about?" Loretta raised her eyebrows higher than Honey had ever seen before.

"Did you let Jonah drive the Mustang? You must be getting

serious."A smile spread across Annabelle's face.

"I don't know about serious. We agreed to date and that is all. I don't know if I'm ready to be the minister's girlfriend, or wife." Honey closed her eyes, hoping her companions would change the subject.

Annabelle laid a strawberry-scented hand on her shoulder. "You minister more than any woman in the church between leading the band, the senior group, adopting families as your own, teaching lessons, what have I forgotten? Your life is a witness to those who are struggling. Look at how you dealt with Tillie the other day. I wouldn't be surprised if she went to the Christmas Eve service at First Church last night."

Honey shook her head. "I don't know. Last night at our own service I noticed people looking at me and talking behind their hands."

"Did you see anyone frowning?" Loretta asked.

Honey answered slowly. "No. They appeared to be smiling, but I couldn't tell if they thought I was being a funny old woman or what. I wouldn't want to ruin Preacher Jonah's ministry."

Annabelle squeezed Honey's shoulder tighter. "I'll tell you what I heard. The people near me said it was about time you two noticed each other."

Honey waved her hands in front of her heated cheeks. "Well, we will have to see what happens. Until then, Jonah and I are just having a few dates. Annabelle, did you bring the Christmas cookies?"

"I sure did. With everything that is going on in your life, did you remember the sausage and cheese?" After giving Honey a hug, Annabelle stepped away.

"I have them and some crackers in my bag, along with some sensible gifts for both of you." Honey headed down the hallway to grab her tote.

Loretta grinned. "I made some lime punch this year. I got tired of having red every Christmas and decided to do something different. I'll be in the kitchen setting up. You two get your treats and gifts and let's get this party started."

After snacking from the trays of goodies, Honey gifted Loretta with a box of special-order paints and gave Annabelle several gift cards to restaurants with home delivery services.

"I hope you can use my gifts." Annabelle passed out small flat gift-wrapped packages. "I created these while sitting with Gerald."

"They're adorable." Loretta put a quilted oven mitt on each of her hands and waved them in the air.

Honey held up a pair of hand-quilted pot holders. "These will be perfect for carrying in my pot of meatballs for Ginny's party in a few days."

"Is Jonah going to pick you up for the party?" Annabelle winked at Honey.

"No, he has some other places to be earlier in the evening." Honey didn't mention that Jonah promised to join her after he made his rounds to other church-related activities.

Chapter Eight

Honey climbed the steps to Ginny and Scott's home with several holiday-themed bags hanging from one elbow. She carried her pot of meatballs with both hands gripped around the gifted pot holders. Annabelle followed her with a stack of small packages tucked under one arm, while clinging to her bewildered husband's elbow on her other side. Gerald's free hand held the handles of a clear plastic tote holding a plate of frosted cookies.

Loretta parked her car behind Honey's and dashed up to the porch, balancing several flat boxes and a plastic wrapped cheese ball plate. "Merry late Christmas and Happy New Year, everyone."

The three women hugged Ginny when she welcomed them inside. They thanked the part-time teacher and full-time mom for inviting them to the party celebrating two holidays and Melody's relocation. They placed their food items on a table in one of Ginny's front rooms across from where noisy partying sounds filtered out into the hallway.

Loretta sagged into Honey's side. "I hope this party and my redone portrait don't ruin Edmund's life or my reputation as an artist."

"I'm sure he will be happy after getting a preview the other day. Edmund seemed understanding when we told him what happened to the first painting. Now, I don't know about you, but I'm going to grab some of Annabelle's iced cookies, before the rest of the crowd discovers them." Honey placed a cup of punch on a saucer with a couple of the delicious sweets.

As they neared the entrance to the room where people gathered, Honey noticed Edmund seated on the floor, chatting with the twins about their trip to Florida. She realized her friend saw him when Loretta stiffened beside her. One of the flat packages must contain the redone portrait of the long-lost wife.

Linking arms, the two women followed Annabelle and her husband, Gerald, into a large living room. Melody sat at her piano playing arrangements of Christmas carols. Other people in the room snacked on cookies and punch, or sang along with the music.

Edmund waved them over to where the twins sat shaking presents. "Look, Lorie and Lincoln. These ladies brought more presents to sort."

"Yay, Grandma Lorna said she would bring presents, too, once she gets her nail glued on." Lorie bounced to her feet.

"I didn't know you could glue a nail." Lincoln wrinkled his nose.

31

"That's because you're a boy." Lorie stretched out her arms for presents.

The youngsters fussed good-naturedly as they relieved the newcomers of their packages and placed them in the piles amassed at the bottom of a tall spruce tree. Between the tree's fresh aroma and cinnamon spices simmering from warm punch, scents of Christmas filled the air,

Edmund chuckled as he edged his way onto an easy chair near where Honey and Loretta sat. Lights twinkled on the tree. Multicolored ornaments mingled with homemade children's decorations. Ginny's husband, Scott, perched on a loveseat with an arm wrapped around Treasure Hope. As he hugged his tiny girl, he read a story about a young creature named Lucy being afraid of a thunderstorm. Lorie and Lincoln joined the children at his feet after the Hallmark's adopted daughter, Melissa, waved to them and patted the space next to her.

When the story drew to a close, with Lucy learning to face her fears, the children laughed at the comical ending. Moments later, Ginny led the group in applause as Melody played the final cadence of "Joy to the World."

"Thank you all for coming tonight. I really appreciate Melody providing the musical entertainment for our party. I'm sure the children in the room are ready to open some gifts."

"Shouldn't we wait for Grandma Lorna's presents?" Lincoln put his hands on his hips.

Groans came from the corner where the youngsters sat near Scott.

Melody waved her hand. "I'll give her a text and see what the delay is. There's no need to disappoint the children."

"What about the adults?" Several grown-ups laughed at Edmund's question as the kids cheered.

"Maybe Mr. Bradley should open his first." Lincoln brought a flat square-shaped gift to the older man. Cheers erupted. Edmund held the package high and pretended to shake it and peep inside a torn corner of the wrapping paper.

Loretta squirmed in her seat, making Honey's punch slosh out of the holiday teacup. Providentially, she had chosen to use a saucer underneath her cup for cookies. "Thanks, Loretta. I've been fighting the urge to dunk a cookie into the punch all night. Now I have an excuse." She lifted a soaked cookie from the saucer and dipped it into the overflowing drink. "Mmmmm."

Loretta looked down at her wringing hands. "You always try to see the good in things."

Honey leaned closer to her friend's ear. "When I don't look for something positive, life only gets worse. Perk up. I'm sure your painting will be fine." She dipped her cookie and lifted it toward Edmund. "What are you waiting for? Open your present."

Paper fell from the painting. Edmund held it at arm's length and then hugged it to his chest. "Thank you, Loretta. My memories have faded, but I believe you captured the spirit of my sweetheart."

Several people gathered around Edmund to look over his shoulder at the painting. Loretta sagged back in her seat, bumping Honey again.

"I'll take that as my cue to go take another look at the painting." Honey stood, only to have Lorie knock her to the side, as the young girl rushed across the room.

"Santa brought me a painting too." Little Lorie lifted a gift bag from one of the boxes marked 'Christmas presents to be opened at Ginny's house.' "I made sure Santa found me." She pointed to the tag saying 'L-o-r-i-n-e.' "Santa left me an early Christmas gift before we left for vacation. I peeked inside to make sure he had the right Lorie since he didn't spell my name right. He put an n in my name. Then I saw a picture to help me remember my first mom. Isn't she pretty? Santa is the only one who could have known my wish about seeing her face again."

Loretta stuttered.

Edmund stared.

Honey watched the girl reach deeper into the gift bag and pull out a money clip. "Santa left something for Mama Melody too. Maybe she won't need more jobs." She pushed her hand in the bag and pulled out a bag of chocolate-covered peanut butter cups. "These must be for Lincoln. Santa didn't forget him either."

Melody rose from the piano bench and kneeled next to Lorie. "Where did you get this?"

"Right before we left to meet Grandma Lorna in Florida, I found the bag in my locker when we got out of the pool. There was a bunch of other stuff inside. I pushed the other junk out of my way so I could get to my bag at the back. Santa must have left those things for someone else. There was some really strange underwe..."

Melody laid a finger over her niece's lips. "Did you stop to think that the locker was someone else's?"

Loretta gasped.

"My bag was there first. I figured the other stuff was Santa's gift for someone else since the lock was open. I decided to get my stuff out and found the presents."

Edmund looked from the painting in his hand to the one the little girl held. Tears formed in his eyes.

The child shrugged. "I saw my name on the bag. You told me Santa wouldn't be coming until we moved here. I worried about him finding us. I guessed he left it for me at the pool since it looked like Mom."

Loretta mumbled something about a baby burglar.

33

Honey grabbed her friend's knee and squeezed hard. "Wait."

Lorie pouted. "You said to hurry when you got out of the shower. I stuffed everything in my big swim bag and ran out the door to meet Lincoln in the hall. I'm sorry I didn't put Santa's other gifts back in the locker. When we picked up our suitcases to go say hi to the mouse for Miss Loretta, I dropped Santa's present in that box." She pointed to the cardboard box where the bag formerly sat. "You said it was for Christmas gifts that we would open when we moved to Mrs. Hallmark's house."

Edmund's commanding voice filled the air. "Let me see your painting."

Lorie's eyes widened, but she obeyed.

The older man held both canvases side-by-side. His frown turned into a smile. "Why Miss Loretta, I do believe I owe you double for the fine job of capturing my dear Lorine's image in both these paintings."

Loretta nodded, but wisely managed to keep her mouth shut for once. Honey hoped she wasn't bruising her friend's knee, but knew better than to stop squeezing.

"That's my mom, Mr. Bradley? She's mine, not yours. This is a picture of her. I think..." The little girl looked down and shuffled her feet.

Melody moved closer and wrapped her arms around Lorie as she sat down next to Edmund. "One time when I visited you in Chicago, your mother showed me pictures of Grandma Lorna when she was young. She looked like your mom. It's possible you're both right. I'm beginning to think more than a broken nail is making Grandma Lorna delay getting here tonight. Maybe when she arrives we can find out if there is a reason for this confusion."

"Do you think we're talking about the same woman?" Edmund's confusion turned to a wistful expression.

Melody seemed deep in thought for a moment before speaking what was on her mind. "She was the one who pushed for me to take the Forest Glen Elementary music teacher's position when I graduated from college. When I was part of the musical she suddenly became very interested in finding out about the producer, which would have been Edmund."

"If it turns out that Grandma Lorna is who I think she might be, I happen to own an empty downtown storefront next to the new art store. The place would make a perfect rent-free piano studio for the woman who adopted some twins, who might be my grandchildren. Would you be interested in the space, Melody?"

Surprise registered on the young woman's face as she turned to Edmund. "We'll find out if you're right soon enough. Then we can talk about whether I pay rent or not. The children's grandmother, Edie Lorna, decided to visit for a little longer after we got back from our trip. She rented a room at the Forest Glen Bed and Breakfast. She should have been here by now but seems to be delaying over a problem with her nails. I think I may understand why now. Let me give her one more call."

Melody stepped from the room to make her call. Ginny clapped her hands and lifted two presents from the children's gifts. "This tag says Melissa and this one is for Lincoln." The sound of ripping paper and giggles filled the air.

Fifteen minutes later a ringing door bell interrupted the celebration. A hush fell over the crowd.

Melody checked her cell. "This should be her."

Ginny nodded to Edmond. "Would you like to have your conversation in the study?"

"No. I want witnesses, whether the answers are good or bad."

Ginny left the room and returned with a silver-haired woman beside her.

"Lorine?" Edmund's gaze followed the well-dressed lady as she walked across the floor. Melody and Lorie vacated the seat next to Edmund.

Honey touched her heart, hoping for a happy ending for the lost lovers.

Loretta grumbled about lost chances.

Annabelle whispered in her Gerald's ear and his smile reflected understanding, for the moment.

"Yes, Edmund. It's me. I should have come sooner." Edmund's former wife, who was also Lorie's grandmother, bowed her head. Then she looked up with a sad expression. "I have to confess a few things. My parents were devastated when their only daughter married a penniless man at a very young age. They were totally embarrassed to find out several months later that our short marriage resulted in a pregnancy."

Edmund held out a hand. "I had no idea."

She took his hand and tears slid down her powdered cheeks. "My father wanted me to end the pregnancy or face the fact he would cut me off from his riches. Mother intervened and we agreed on a compromise. I would change my name and move far away to raise my baby, so I didn't embarrass them further. I used Lorna as a last name and Edie for my first name as a tribute to our love and a subtle hint of Edmund's and my names. I agreed to no contact with my former husband." She swallowed before continuing.

"In exchange, my parents gave me a small allowance that provided food and housing. My baby girl and I survived on the allotted funds until I managed to make my own way in the business world. I suppose being a businesswoman was one gift my father gave me that he couldn't take away. Success came easy and my daughter and I were happy together. She grew up understanding that all the men in her life were gone."

Edmund frowned.

"Mom took us on an annual vacation and we met at their oceanfront cabin when we went to her 'home.' I dated some, but didn't feel right about going beyond a first date. I still felt married to Edmund, despite the annulment. Once the internet became part of life, I searched his name and discovered he'd done well for himself and lived here." Edie Lorna waved her hand to those sitting around the room.

Edmund leaned back with his arms crossed, his expression sad.

"When I heard through my daughter about Melody and her friends looking for teaching jobs, I mentioned the opportunities available at Forest Glen Elementary School. I figured I could pump Melody about Edmund, especially after she planned to be in the musical he supported. Now my grandchildren live here. My daughter and parents are gone. Melody and the children are all I have."

"No, dear. You have me." Edmund leaned forward and again reached for his former wife's hands. "I don't think your father would be ashamed of me anymore. I managed to make more money than he ever did. One thing I learned from his mistakes is to share the wealth. Where he was stingy, I've chosen to be a benefactor of camps, the arts, and more. If you are willing to put up with that kind of generosity, then I'd love to have you in my life, forever this time."

Cheers and words of congratulations erupted from around the room. As the noise subsided, the doorbell rang several times. Honey was the first on her feet. Hurrying to the door, she saw Jonah's profile through one of the glass side-panels lining Ginny's front door. A thrill tickled her chest with a glimpse of hope for her future.

"Hey, Jonah. You're just in time for some fantastic news." Honey waved him inside as a gust of winter wind blew into the entranceway, ruffling his silver hair.

He chuckled as he shrugged out of his coat. "That must have been the racket that covered up the sound of my first four attempts at ringing the doorbell. Sorry I'm late. After I dropped my grandkids at the church's youth party, there was a family at the hospital needing my prayers."

Honey hung his coat in the closet and turned to notice how the green shirt he wore brought out the color in his eyes. Her attraction to the man grew as he took a step closer. "So, tell me about this good news."

He placed an arm around her waist and pulled her close as they walked toward Ginny's living room. Honey's tongue seemed to be momentarily frozen. Heat made its way through her body and up her neck. "I...um...they...that is... Edmund and the twins' grandmother were once married. I wouldn't be surprised if you might have a wedding in your future."

The living room conversation stopped. All eyes turned their way.

"Are you getting married too?" Little Lorie skipped across the room to where the older couple stood in a wide pocket door entrance to the room. "Tonight Santa got me a grandpa. Preacher's grandkids can get a grandma if you—"

Melody hurried forward and clamped a hand over the girl's mouth. "Sorry, Honey and Preacher Jonah."

Honey wanted the floor to swallow her right down to the basement. Poor Jonah didn't need this. She tried to move away from his side.

Jonah's arm tightened, pulling her closer. "How about we start with a few dates, then we can talk about marriage when I've had time to figure out a decent proposal, if Honey agrees."

He looked at Honey. All she could do was nod. Their friends applauded.

Loretta's voice lifted above the commotion. "Is that a bunch of mistletoe above their heads?"

Honey looked up. Sure enough, they stood right under a round ball covered in the kissing plant.

"Give her a kiss!" Gerald shouted with a huge grin on his face as he turned to his wife. "Do I know you, sweetie?"

Annabelle's mouth opened wide in amazement. "You sure do, dearest." She puckered up her lips as she placed her hands around her husband's wrinkled cheeks and gave him a big smooch.

Jonah pointed to the mistletoe as he faced Honey. "What do you say, sweetheart?"

"Yes." Honey kicked one leg back as their lips met and he lowered her into a slight dip.

Loretta released a gigantic sigh. "Maybe next year..."

Bells rang, bringing in the New Year and a new season for love.

The End

Dear Reader,

I hope you enjoyed Honey's adventures with her senior friends and finding romance. You may recognize her from *On Cue* and *Hoping for Treasure*, along with Ginny and Scott. I hope you have read those books along with the other part of that trilogy, *Free to Love*. This story also mentions one of my children's books, *Lucy and Thunder*, which is a great story for helping the little ones overcome fears. I am thankful to Mt. Zion Ridge Press editors, Michelle Levigne and Tamera Kraft, for giving life to these stories and for providing encouragement to keep going as a creator. I am also thankful to my wonderful critique partner, Ann Cavera. The ultimate glory goes to God, the true creator of all things.

Blessings,

Bettie Boswell

https://sites.google.com/view/bettieboswellauthorillustrator/home

HOME FOR CHRISTMAS
Penny Frost McGinnis

An Abbott Island Novella

Characters:

Sadie Stewart Grayson: Moved to Abbott Island to live in her grandparent's home. Owner of Sadie's Rental Cottages and Joel's wife.

Joel Grayson: Abbott Island police officer who grew up on the island. Sadie's husband.

Lucy Grayson: Owner of The General Store and grew up on the island. Joel's sister.

Marigold Hayes: Owner of Kayak Rentals, entrepreneur. Thirty-year island resident.

Johnny Papadakis: Owner of Johnny's Place restaurant. Ten-year island resident.

Alexa Papadakis: Works at the Natural History Museum in Cleveland. Johnny's daughter.

Levi Swenson: Island police officer. Two-year island resident.

Charlotte Mercer: School teacher who spends summers on the island and works for Marigold.

Henry Marin: Johnny's sous chef. Six-year island resident.

Emmett Grant: Life-long resident lives as a bit of a hermit in the island woods.

Miss Aggie, Miss Flossie, and Miss Hildy: Abbott Island church ladies.

Owen Bently: local farmer.

Chapter One

"Charlotte?" Levi Swenson hustled down the cement steps in front of the Abbott Island police station. Across the street, the woman his heart had missed since summer stood in front of Johnny's Place. Her blond, chin-length hair gleamed on the sunny December afternoon. A pine wreath adorned with red ribbons and white poinsettias decked the restaurant's wooden door with holiday spirit. *Away in a Manger* filled the air from the loudspeaker, and a flurry of snow sparkled in the sunshine as it tumbled to the ground. One week until Christmas, and the gift he longed for most stood before him.

Focused on Charlotte, he sprinted across the street. Within a foot of her, the sidewalk snagged his shoe, he stumbled to his knees, and landed at her feet. Not his best moment.

Charlotte Mercer reached her hand to his elbow and helped Levi stand. "Are you okay?" Her eyebrows arched and her lips quirked into a half smile.

He brushed snow from the knees of his pants. "I'm fine, embarrassed, but fine. At least the snow cushioned my fall, and I didn't tear my uniform." Why did he have to stumble in front of her? When they had spent time together last summer, he had attempted to hide his clumsiness. Not today. Today, he humbled himself before the most beautiful woman he had ever met.

A full-toothed grin split Charlotte's face as a giggle escaped.

"Are you laughing at me?" Levi's fists rested on his hips as he teased his friend.

Her cheeks pinked. "I'm not laughing at you, but I didn't expect you to fall at my feet."

"What can I say?" He ducked his chin, then moved his gaze back to her. "I got excited when I saw you."

"That's sweet." She rubbed her mittened hands up and down her arms. "Do you have time to go in Johnny's for a coffee and baklava?"

He checked his watch. "Let me pop into the police station and check if Joel is there yet. If he is, I can clock out. Otherwise, I can meet you in about fifteen minutes, when he shows up for his shift."

"Sounds good. I'll get a table." Her gaze locked on his as if she didn't want him to leave.

"I'll be there soon." He lifted his leg to sprint across the street, then stopped. No falling a second time.

Inside the station, Joel Grayson was hanging his jacket on a hook when Levi entered.

Levi swept snow from his coat. "Hey, Joel."

"How's it going?" His fellow police officer stood behind his desk.

Words poured out of Levi like a flood. "I'm great. Charlotte's here. I didn't know she'd arrived already, and I ran into her a few minutes ago in front of Johnny's Place. Would it be okay if I took off now?" He caught his breath.

Joel rolled his chair from his desk and sat. "Slow down, buddy. Of course you can leave. It's almost 3:00, and no doubt you arrived early this morning." He lifted a pen from the desk and twirled it between his fingers. "Did she tell you she was coming?"

"Yes. She called me last week and told me she and her family decided to do Christmas on the island."

Charlotte and Levi's texts and calls kept them connected, but her job, teaching first grade, left little time for her to travel to Abbott Island from the mainland. Plus, the past few months, Levi had filled in for Joel several times while Joel and Sadie visited the OBGYN in Sandusky. With baby Grayson due January 2, the appointments had been scheduled closer together.

Joel stuck the pen in a Marblehead Lighthouse cup. "Is there anything I need to know before you go?"

At his desk, Levi straightened papers and shut down his computer. "The streets have been quiet today. I doubt you'll have trouble this evening. How's Sadie?"

"According to her, she feels like a beached whale. Her words, not mine. To me, she's beautiful, but she's uncomfortable." He booted up his computer. "You better get out of here. I'll see you later."

"Thanks." With a nod, Levi hurried out the door.

~~~~~

Inside Johnny's Place, a jazzy *Joy to the World* spread cheer through the dining room. From her table, Charlotte watched the front door open, and her heart leaped at the sight of Levi. His uniform, even with the wet knees, imparted a look of authority. His handsome face gave her stomach the flutters. She'd missed him. From May to August the previous summer, they'd dated. If the old saying her grandma had recited held weight, absence did make the heart grow fonder. His easy smile and laid-back personality kept her at ease. Unlike when she taught first graders and the days slammed into each other.

Time on the island, before Christmas, gave her time to settle her nerves before she met with her parents and brother for the holiday. Mom and Dad planned to arrive on the island in two days with her brother, Peter, and his daughter, Lottie. She'd not met her three-year-old niece yet, since Peter had refused to come home for so many years.

Levi pulled out the chair opposite Charlotte. "I'm happy you're here." A grin spread from ear-to-ear. He tugged his arms out of his jacket and draped it across the back of the chair. "You look great."

She tucked her napkin onto her lap. "Thank you. I slept well last night. This semester has been stressful. I needed to come to my happy place." She lifted her hands.

Frannie stopped by the table. "Charlotte, it's good to see you. What can I get you two?"

They both ordered coffee and baklava.

"Your happy place, huh? I've been thinking I might want to move to the mainland." Levi unrolled his napkin and lined the utensils in size order.

"Move? Where to?" She bit the inside of her lip.

He shook his head. "I don't know. Where you live sounds nice." A lazy smile crossed his face.

The waitress poured steaming coffee in festive mugs and added a pitcher of cream and bowl of sugar packets to the table. She placed a plate of the rich Greek dessert between them, with saucers. "Can I get you anything else?"

"We're good, thanks." Levi served Charlotte a slice of the flaky pecan pastry.

Charlotte forked a piece into her mouth. "I'd forgotten how good this tastes. I'm not sure I'd want to leave such yummy food."

Levi sipped his coffee. "Truth be told, I missed you." He stretched his arm across the linen tablecloth and held her hand. "You're on my mind every day. We've kept in touch, but it's not the same as being in person."

"My days are lonely without you. I came to relax, but I also wanted to spend time with you." She pulled back her hand and dabbed her lips with her napkin. "Plus, my class has been difficult this semester. The little ones are dear to my heart, but something is off. The last few years have been different for the kiddos with more online learning than normal. I'm not sure they understand how to function in a classroom setting. Then there's my brother, but I don't want to talk about him." She tightened her lips.

"Sounds like you needed a break. When does your family arrive?" He ate a bite of baklava.

"Mom and Dad are coming Christmas Eve, so I plan to spend the next couple of days getting ready for their visit and visiting with Marigold."

"I'm off duty Friday. I'd love to spend time with you, and help you get ready for your family. Where are you staying?" He finished the last bite.

"At the cottage I rented last summer. The Masons gave me a great price and there are three small bedrooms, so my folks will have a place to stay and um... never mind." *No point talking about Peter.*

A frown crinkled his forehead. "Okay."

After they finished their coffee, Levi stood and held Charlotte's coat for her. She slipped her arms in and buttoned the front.

On their way out the door, Levi and Charlotte spotted the three church ladies, Miss Aggie, Miss Flossie, and Miss Hildy at a corner table. The ladies grinned and waved.

Outside, Charlotte wrapped a teal scarf around her neck. "Those three women love matchmaking. By the way they grinned, they approve of us being together."

"They're pretty perceptive, aren't they?" Levi held her hand and walked her to her car.

~~~~~

Snow sprinkled from the clouds like salt from a shaker. Evening shadowed the island as a rainbow of lights adorned simple cottages. Charlotte drove her Kia Soul along Melody Drive, with Levi in the passenger seat, and maneuvered into a gravel parking spot in front of a quaint, fern green cottage. "I haven't been to the cottage yet. I wanted to find you first." She shifted the car into park. "Look, the owner put lights up."

"The Masons had one of the high schoolers on the island decorate their place and this one. I saw Nick hanging the twinkle lights the other day." Levi unhooked his seatbelt.

"It's adorable." Charlotte leaned against the head rest. "Thanks for coming with me to get settled. I'll make us some sandwiches later?"

"Sounds good to me." Levi released his door, then trod around the car to open Charlotte's.

Once inside the house, he carried her bags to the hallway, then flicked on a lamp. She hung their coats in the closet before she sank into the couch. "I love the way the cushions hug me."

"I remember this couch being comfy last summer." Tucked in beside her, he wrapped his arms around her and pulled her into an embrace.

When they pulled apart, she rested her head on his, then kissed his cheek. "Levi, I'm... " Her voice choked.

"What's wrong?" He raised his hand to her chin and lifted her face.

Her gaze met his. "My brother. I didn't want to talk about it at Johnny's, but I'm so upset. I've tried to forgive him and I can't. I talked to Marigold about him last summer and believed I had it handled, but I didn't. One reason I came here, besides for you, is to gain clarity."

He wiped a tear from her cheek. "You mentioned him a few times last summer, but you never told me what happened to make you so upset with him. Did he hurt you?"

Levi's eyes spoke anger.

"No, not what you're thinking. He never physically hurt me or anyone else." She lifted a tissue from the box on the table. "He deserted our family and left me to deal with too much stuff. At fourteen, all I wanted to do was be a teenager. I'll never forget the sorrow, and how the note he left broke all of our hearts. I still remember what he said, because I read it so many times."

Dear Dad, Mom, and Charlotte,

*By the time you read this, I'll be long gone, on my way to Nashville.
I have to see if I've got what it takes to be a star, or at least a
musician. I've dreamed of this since I picked up my first guitar. I'll
call or write soon.*

Love,
Peter

"He never called, and no letters came. He just left." Charlotte laid her
head on Levi's shoulder.

~~~~~

Wind whistled through the old farmhouse in Paris, Kentucky. A
scraggly cedar tree stood in the corner, decorated with red and green
paper chains Peter Mercer had helped his little girl tape together. He and
Lottie had added hand-strung popcorn the mice might eat, and a dozen
shiny baubles. Three-year-old Lottie huddled on the floor and watched
the single strand of lights flash off and on. So much for a merry Christmas,
yet little Lottie hummed *Jingle Bells* and didn't appear to miss her momma,
who had disappeared with another man.

A picture of his own mom flashed through Peter's mind. He'd
deserted her when she needed him most. Dad, too and Charlotte. At
eighteen, he set out to chase his dream. A year later, he had hocked his
guitar for money to buy a sandwich and a hotel room. At least he had
found a job selling records and CDs in a Nashville shop. Even if he didn't
cut his own album, he had kept a steady job. Then last year the little shop
closed, and he was out of a paycheck.

"Lottie, you hungry?"

She toddled to him and climbed on his lap. "Roni or hot doggies?"

Her blond curls felt like silk as he wrapped a ringlet around his
finger. "I'm thinking macaroni." Since the near-empty shelves held the last
box.

"Yummy!" She hopped off his lap and ran to the kitchen, where a card
table and folding chairs waited for them.

While Peter stirred the box mix cheese and some milk into the
noodles, Lottie's chubby hands stacked wooden blocks.

After the record store had shuttered, he had packed his little girl's
bags, loaded his truck, and drove as far as the gas in the tank lasted. His
friend Bo, in Paris, Kentucky, let them stay in the old farmhouse on his
property. Peter worked with his horses and mucked the barn stalls. Bo's
wife babysat Lottie for free as long as Peter took his little one to church on
Sundays, a place he'd avoided for years. The last sermon he had sat

through at his mom and dad's church mentioned the prodigal son. The person Peter saw when he looked in the mirror.

Chapter Two

The wind chime on the cottage porch sang a mournful melody, and the Christmas lights tapped against the windows. Charlotte poked her fingers between the blinds in the bedroom, then pushed them apart enough to peer at the snow-covered ground. Before she trekked to the kitchen, she tugged on a sweater, flannel-lined jeans, and her fleece-lined boots. Winter on Abbott Island bore a great contrast to summer. A blustery wind replaced the gentle breeze and cold temperatures invited snow. Growing up in northern Ohio, Charlotte understood the respect northerners had for nature and weather changes. The Erie Islands, often affected by lake effect snow, reminded her to bundle in her warmest clothes. Would Peter pack winter clothes for Lottie? Did the little girl own a coat?

Her brother, Peter, had traveled to Nashville to make his mark on the music industry over fourteen years ago. Not one word from him until last month. When he called Mom, she'd begged him to come home for Christmas.

In the cottage's cozy kitchen, a small evergreen perched on the counter, decorated with blue and white beads and tiny snowflakes. A snowman in a cherry red and light blue hat and scarf stood on the white and silver Formica-topped kitchen table. The chrome on the legs were reminiscent of a distant decade.

Charlotte sloshed a bit of creamer into her peppermint flavored coffee. She carried the cup and an iced Christmas cookie into the living room where the owners had set up a six-foot silver tree, adorned with vintage ornaments in pinks, greens, blues, and reds. Settled on the couch, she pulled her cell phone from her jeans pocket and saw a missed call from Marigold. With a tap, she connected to her friend's phone.

On the third ring, Marigold's voice sang through the line. "Hello, Charlotte. I hear you've arrived."

The woman's joy slid across the phone line. "I have. I rode the ferry over yesterday. The Masons decorated the cottage. It's adorable, and they left me a plate of Christmas cookies. I'm indulging in one for breakfast."

A chuckle sounded. "Tis the season for all things sweet. When can you come over?"

After a sip of coffee the young woman answered. "I was hoping you'd have time later today. I'd love to see the crafts you've been making and the changes in your house since you married Johnny. I wanted to visit with

Lucy and Sadie, too. Do you know if they have time to stop over?"

"I was hoping you'd say today. I already invited them for lunch."

"I can't wait to see you. I'll come around 11:30, if that's okay. I have food prep to do for our holiday dinner. Mom's bringing most of the food, but I told her I'd make dessert and appetizers." She walked to the kitchen. "See you soon. Bye." She clicked off the phone and savored the last bite of sugary goodness.

~~~~~

Once Peter passed through Cincinnati and Dayton, he anticipated acres of flat snow-covered farmland. They'd meander through the occasional small town on their drive, but in the winter the landscape would look the same, brown and white.

"Daddy, where we going?" Lottie's tiny voice called from the back seat of the rusty Ford-Ranger. "Is it a long way?"

Hands on the wheel, Peter let out a sigh. "About six hours, bug. We've driven two already, so four left."

Before he had loaded Lottie and their few belongings into the truck, they'd undecorated the pitiful little Christmas tree and carried it outside for the animals. At least his little girl believed she'd offered the squirrels and skunks a gift, but he knew the truth. He'd hit the bottom of the pit and needed his family.

After another hour of *Jingle Bells* and *Feliz Navidad*, he rolled the truck into a gas station to fill up, take care of personal business, and grab a snack. Lottie climbed out of the back of the cab and tucked her hand in his.

"Little one, you stick close to me and don't let go."

"Okay, Daddy."

Inside, the two of them picked out snack cakes, milk, and a ham and cheese sandwich. In the truck, Peter buckled his little girl in her car seat, then crawled onto the seat beside her and spread their food between them like a picnic. A faint memory of a quilt laid out on a grassy knoll tugged at his heart. The idyllic childhood he'd shared with Charlotte didn't keep him from abandoning his family. His shame of failure had dug a chasm between them, yet who did he turn to in desperation? The people he had hurt most. His blond-haired, blue-eyed sister's face flashed in his mind. She'd been left to help Mom after Dad's heart attack. Charlotte worked at the local grocery as soon as her age allowed. Not much fun for a teenage girl, and he'd never bothered to check on her. He missed the little girl who had followed him like a puppy. Now she taught school, so his mother said.

Would she remember anything good about him or speak to him?

~~~~~

A white blanket of snow diamonds sparkled on Marigold's flowerbeds, with blooms replaced by winter's comforter. Charlotte tapped on the front door, with a bag full of gifts for her friends. White icicle lights hung from the porch and swayed in the wind.

The door flung open. "Charlotte, come in." Lucy ushered her into Marigold's cozy home. The scent of pine trailed from the Christmas tree near the window, and the smell of homemade bread drifted from the kitchen.

"Can I help you carry something?" Lucy reached to her friend.

Charlotte gave Lucy a bag dressed in the colors of the holiday. "If you want to take the gifts out and place them under the tree, I'd appreciate it."

"Hey, girl." Marigold bounded to her and squeezed her in a hug, then let go. Sadie trundled behind with a hand on her abdomen.

"Hi." Charlotte hugged her pregnant friend. "How are you doing?"

The new momma-to-be glowed. "I'm good. Uncomfortable, but good." She wore a red and white striped top with "Santa's Little Helper" printed across the middle of her baby bump.

"Let's gather in the kitchen." Marigold herded them to the table. "Johnny made his chicken and rice soup, and I baked homemade rolls. I hope you're hungry."

Sadie rubbed her back. "I'm always hungry." After a prayer, they ate, too busy enjoying the delicious food to talk.

Charlotte rested her spoon on the table. "Looks like Johnny's remodeling the kitchen." A pan wall filled with copper bottomed pots stood alongside a new pantry.

"He did. Not long after the wedding, he and Henry sketched out the perfect home kitchen. Johnny is about half finished with the remodeling. As long as he cooks, he can make the kitchen into whatever he wants. Leaves me more time for arts and crafts." Fifty-something Marigold tucked her long white braid behind her. "By the way, I have crafts to share with you. Let's relax in the living room. We can have dessert after a bit."

Settled around a cozy fire, the four friends shared small gifts.

"Marigold, this scarf is gorgeous. I can wear it when I teach. Our building is cold, and I love the pinks and aquas." Charlotte wrapped the delicate crochet around her shoulders.

"I love mine, too. The reds and golds are stunning." Lucy modeled hers.

Sadie burst into tears, then waved her hand in front of her to calm herself. "Sorry, prenatal emotions. The blues in mine are gorgeous." A half-laugh escaped her lips.

Charlotte edged over to Sadie. "You have another gift. Since I couldn't make it for your baby shower, I wanted to get something for your little one."

"You didn't have to bring a gift." Sadie unwrapped the package and lifted a baby quilt with a sailboat on a lake complete with a sunrise.

Seagulls swooped across the top. "This is beautiful. Did you make it?"

"Yes, on the weekends. My grandmother had taught me how to sew, but it's been a while since I've stitched anything. I visited a quilt shop near me and they helped me design the pattern and finish the quilt. I hope you can use it."

Sadie hugged her friend. "I love it, and so will Joel. This is perfect for the nursery. We did blues and yellows, since we decided not to find out the sex of the baby until he or she is born." She held the quilt up one more time and admired it. "Beautiful."

Lucy touched the fabric. "I'm impressed. Did the work you put into this keep you from missing Levi?" She winked at Charlotte.

"Probably. I admit, I've missed spending time with him. We've had great conversations, but it's not the same as seeing him in person."

Marigold carried a tray of tea and cookies to the coffee table. "You could move to the island."

"The timing isn't right. I'm happy to be here for Christmas, though." A move to the island meant uprooting her teaching and adjusting to a life of unknowns. If the island school invited her to submit an application, the change might not support her financially. She enjoyed the little house she rented in Vermilion and her walk to work was short, plus her parents lived nearby. Not sure she had the fortitude to live out winter on an island, she'd weigh her options, but she leaned more toward mainland life. Of course, if she factored in Levi...

~~~~~

Lottie's head lolled against her car seat. One more hour, across back roads, and they'd arrive at his mom and dad's house. Thankful his parents had invited him home, he played the scenarios of what would happen when he confessed how broke he was. No money and a little girl to care for. How much forgiveness did they have for him?

After Christmas, he'd figure out a way to drive back to Kentucky and find another job. Maybe he'd get a gift he could resell for gas money, but why would his parents offer him anything after he took their car and the cash from Mom's cookie jar? When he spoke to her a month ago, she never mentioned the money or the car. Technically, the old junker had been his to drive to school, but his parents paid the insurance for a year after he left. Why they wanted him to come home puzzled him, unless they wanted to meet their grandchild. As far as he knew, Charlotte hadn't had kids yet.

An hour later, Peter's stomach growled as he pulled the truck into the paved driveway of the two-story farmhouse. A rainbow of lights twinkled from the porch, and an old sled adorned with pine swag and red ribbons leaned against the wall. A pine wreath decorated the door. In the evening light, the invitation to warmth and security about undid him. Tears

48

formed in the corners of his eyes. Home.

Before fear wrapped its hands around his heart, he undid his seatbelt and trotted around the truck. "Lottie, wake up, honey. We're at Mamaw and Papaw's." The names rolled off his tongue like he said them every day. His little one raised her eyelids and peered past him, and her mouth formed an o shape. He shifted to see what she looked at and there stood his parents. Fourteen years had aged them. Mom's white hair, the color of snow, and Dad's bald head were unexpected.

Lottie's eyes rounded as she searched her daddy's face. A question in her voice pushed out, "Mamaw? Papaw?" Peter nodded and placed her on the ground.

Her little legs carried her to two strangers, yet she hugged them like family.

Chapter Three

Friday morning, Charlotte carried her coffee to the back porch. Pinks and purples ribboned across the sky as the sun awoke the morning. The roar of the lake rolled across the island. The lake's unpredictable motion in the winter drew concern for the ferry. If the weather created choppy water, transportation on and off the island depended on the airport. She prayed the weather would allow her family to ride the ferry tomorrow morning.

Mom had called last evening to share the news Peter had arrived with Lottie. As much as Charlotte wanted to meet her namesake, she dreaded conversations with her brother. Mom made sure to tell her Lottie was short for Charlotte. No doubt to soften her heart, but how did she forgive someone who ruined her high school years with his selfish notions? After her dad's heart had failed, she took on work at the local grocery to help provide. With Mom's bad back and arthritis, she had barely managed to take care of Dad and the house. Even though her dad had recovered, she'd found her footing at the store and in school, and plugged away at both, with no time for extra-curriculars. No volleyball or softball, which played out as no scholarships for sports. At least she'd succeeded in academics and received financial help with college.

Grow up and consider what he's been through.

Okay, she'd asked God to help her view the situation through her brother's perspective, but her stubborn streak ignored answers He'd given her. She brushed the thought aside and walked to the kitchen to finish the bûche de Noël, a recipe from her French grandmother. She planned to ice the sponge cake with dark chocolate frosting, roll it tight, then ice it again. Then she'd finish the angel food cake from her mom's recipe. On

Christmas morning, she'd slice it in two and fill the middle with a cherry filling, then top it with homemade whipped cream. If nothing else went well, at least she'd enjoy dessert.

Mid-morning, a tap on the door drew her away from scrubbing the baking pans. Charlotte dried her hands on her apron and answered the front door. "Levi. Hey, come in."

He carried a bouquet of artificial flowers; red silk roses, sprigs of holly, and a few fake pine pieces wrapped in ribbon. "These are for you. I wanted real roses, but I can't get them on the island in winter. I hope these are okay."

"They're lovely." She cradled them in her arms. "Your thoughtfulness overwhelms me." She carried them to a glass jar on the table, wrapped the stems in a green napkin and tucked them in. "Beautiful." Charlotte kissed Levi's cheek and watched him blush a light shade of red. "Don't be embarrassed. I appreciate your thoughtfulness."

"Good to hear. Sometimes I wonder if I'm good enough for you."

Charlotte stepped back and stared at the man in front of her. "What are you talking about?"

He pursed his lips, then peered at her. "You're beautiful, smart, kind, and loving. I'm clumsy, not so handsome, and awkward."

"Come sit down."

He followed her to the couch in the living room. "You, my friend, are smart, handsome, and caring. I wouldn't spend time with you if I didn't think you were a wonderful man. I've met some duds, and you are not it." Her hand rested on his forearm. "I miss you more than you understand. Last summer gave me hope of a... I'll say it... relationship with you. Do you feel the same?"

His arms wrapped around her. "Yes, I do. I care about you, but I'm not good at this stuff."

"I happen to know you're great at this stuff. You brought me flowers that will never die." A laugh bubbled from her.

Levi chuckled. "You have a point. Let me start again." He stood and took her hand. She rose to meet him. "Charlotte, I'm so happy you're here. I've missed you so much." He leaned in and captured her lips with his for a sweet kiss.

She hugged him to her. "So much better." She rested her head on his chest and cherished the beat of his heart.

~~~~~

A spirit of celebration danced around Johnny's Place. The evening before Christmas Eve, Levi and Charlotte met Sadie, Joel, Lucy, and Marigold for dinner. At a table along the wall, they perused the menu. "The special sounds good." Levi pointed to the pastitsio, made with layers of pasta, meat sauce, and bechamel. The rest of the table ordered the same.

Marigold eyed Levi and Charlotte. "Are you two enjoying your time together?"

Charlotte's cheeks pinked. "We are." She glanced at Levi and squeezed his hand under the table.

"Yes. I'm thankful she's here." He bumped her shoulder.

Lucy piped up. "Be careful. Ever since Marigold married Johnny, she thinks everyone should be in love." She made a heart sign with her fingers.

"Did I hear my name?" Johnny delivered a plate of hummus and pita chips.

Levi's stomach clenched. Love meant commitment. Was he ready to say he loved Charlotte? She popped into his mind all the time, especially when she wasn't with him. She had assured him she cared about him. Every time he saw her, his heart stuttered.

"Levi, you okay?" Charlotte nudged him.

"Fine. I'm fine." As good as a man put on the spot could be.

Sadie squirmed in her chair and patted her baby bump. "How about you, Lucy? Any love on your horizon?"

Lucy squinted at her friend. "Nope. Not me. I'm free as a bird." She lifted her arms as if to flap her wings.

Levi mulled over the phrase, *free as a bird*. Was he free or falling? Charlotte's graceful movement when she lifted her water glass to her lips filled him with warmth. So beautiful. He thanked God this wonderful woman chose to spend time with an awkward man like him. Her eyes locked on his and her lips bowed into a dazzling smile. A moment of recognition caught him off guard. He loved her.

~~~~~

On Charlotte's doorstep, light snow twirled in a frenzy. Streetlights acted as spotlights on the white pirouettes. "Want to come in?" she said. "I'm going to relax this evening before my family arrives tomorrow."

Levi offered to unlock the door, then fumbled with the key in the lock until he twisted it and heard a click. "Here we go. I'd love to come in."

Inside, he hung her wool coat in the closet while she made her way to the kitchen. Then, he caught up with her and leaned against the kitchen's door jamb. He watched her draw two cups of hot water from the Keurig, then add hot chocolate mix.

"Anything I can do to help?"

She added marshmallows to two mugs, steaming with a chocolate aroma. "No. I'm good. Want to watch *A Christmas Story*?"

"You like that movie?"

"I do. It's hilarious when the kid sticks his tongue to the flagpole. My brother and I... never mind." Charlotte settled on the couch next to Levi. "We can stream it on my laptop. I'm pretty sure it's on somewhere this time of year." With the mouse pad, she clicked through until she found the classic movie about a boy who wanted a Red Rider BB Gun.

Good memories of her brother surprised her as the show played and she sipped her drink. The time they had climbed to the top of the neighbor's hill and pushed their dog down on the old wooden sled and the dog yowled the whole way. Or the time she fell through the ice while skating and he pulled her out. He'd saved her. Then he'd left. Disappeared from her life. Part of her wanted him back, but how? As the movie wound down, she peered at the man beside her. Levi's heart for people warmed her. As an officer, he helped others in ways he didn't realize, and his clumsiness was kind of cute. She cared for him more than any man she'd dated. Where might a relationship with him lead? As far as she knew, he had no relatives. She'd make sure he stopped by to meet her family, even if she and her brother were at odds. Levi needed people.

He cleared his throat. "I've seen this movie at least thirty times. Did I tell you I had a brother?"

Charlotte's mind searched for information about his brother. She shook her head. "No. You told me your parents had died several years ago and your grandparents, but you didn't mention a brother."

He breathed in. "He was two years older than me. We watched *A Christmas Story* together every year until he turned sixteen. He'd gotten his license and driven to a football game. On the way home, a drunk driver hit and killed him. That's why I joined the force, to stop potential accidents."

Charlotte wrapped her hands around his arm. "I had no idea. I'm so sorry."

"It's been several years. It's still hard, but I know he's in heaven." His fingers laced through hers. "Thanks for asking me to watch the movie. It brought back great memories." He pecked her cheek with a kiss.

"I'm so selfish. Here I am going on about my awful brother, and you lost yours."

He positioned himself to face Charlotte. "No. Everyone has a unique situation, and we each have to work through it. I prayed and drew closer to God when it happened. My parents struggled for a long time but came to peace before they died. I'm thankful for the years I had with him. I still miss him and talk to him sometimes."

Charlotte threaded her arm through his. "You are incredible. I wish I were as strong as you. Even though we went to church some when I was a child, I'm still young in my faith and need to understand forgiveness and how to live at peace in a better way. I still want to hold on to grudges and be, how do I say it? Spun up."

"Prayer has helped me step away from anxiety and agitation, because talking through situations with God brings clarity." Levi stood and pulled Charlotte beside him. "I better get going so you can rest before tomorrow.

I'm praying you and your brother can reconcile or at least find peace, and you'll enjoy meeting Lottie."

Her smile widened from cheek to cheek. "Of course I'll enjoy Lottie. I can't wait to meet her. By the way, could you stop by tomorrow sometime? I know you're working a double shift for Joel, so he can be with Sadie, Christmas Eve and Christmas, but I'd like you to meet my family." Her eyes pleaded.

He twitched his mouth. "Sure. I can come." He placed a hand on each cheek and kissed her goodnight. "See you tomorrow." He donned his coat and left.

~~~~~

A white crocheted tablecloth spread over red fabric decked Mom's holiday table. The house hadn't changed much. Fresh paint and a new couch, otherwise the place felt like the home Peter grew up in. A cinnamon-scented candle burned as his family passed a dish of macaroni around the table. Peter studied his parents and his heart ached for the sorrow he'd caused. Years of no communication with these precious people poured shame over him.

When the dish landed in front of him, gratitude for his mom, Liz, surprised him. He blurted out his appreciation. "You're spoiling us, Mom. Thank you."

Lottie piped up to her Mamaw. "Roni's my favorite."

Liz's eyes gleamed. "I'm thankful we're together again. I'd make mac and cheese every meal if you'd sit at our table and eat with us." She rested her hand on Peter's arm and turned to Lottie. "And you, little lady, are a delight. I can't believe I'm a grandma."

"Mamaw Liz." Lottie reached her chubby little hands to her grandma.

"I like being called Mamaw. Don't forget Papaw."

Lottie blew kisses to Papaw Don.

Don placed his fork beside his plate. "Son, I'm glad you're home, too. I admit, I spent several years angry, but I'm not now. Life's too short for regret. I, well we, hope you stay for a while so I can spoil this girl."

Peter chewed the meatloaf and swallowed while he sucked back tears. "I don't know what to say, except thank you. I left for my own selfish reasons, and I should've come home when my dreams failed, but embarrassment stopped me. Stupid, wasn't it?"

"Daddy not 'tupid."

With a napkin, Liz wiped crumbs from Lottie's mouth. "No, your daddy isn't stupid. Now let's get you cleaned up and tucked into bed. We have a big day tomorrow. You get to meet your aunt Charlotte."

His sister's name pierced a hole through his heart. He'd let her down. Would she forgive him or just tolerate him until he left?

53

Chapter Four

God Rest Ye Merry Gentlemen warbled from the radio in Charlotte's cottage on Christmas Eve morning. On the kitchen table, she spread a vintage Christmas cloth she'd purchased at a yard sale. She slipped dishes decked with a holly pattern from the cupboard onto the table. The owners of the cottage had provided everything. A glance at the clock told her Mom and Dad would arrive in fifteen minutes. Before she padded into the bedroom to change into a sweatshirt with Snoopy and his decorated doghouse, she sank into a chair and bowed her head.

Last night's dreams of her chasing her brother through a field and him racing away left an edge on her morning. Unprepared to see him, she sought out God's help. *"He deserves a second chance,"* echoed through her mind and heart.

Prayer finished and clean shirt on, she adorned her ears with festive jingle bell earrings. In the living room, she clicked the silver tree's lights on, and lowered the music to a pleasant hum, then she paced in front of the couch. A clock on the wall ticked off the minutes as she knelt and rearranged gifts one more time. The moment she plopped on the couch, a car's engine sounded in the driveway.

They're here. He's here.

Her hand trembled from uncertainty as she held the doorknob, then tugged open the last divider between her and her brother. On the step, a curly-headed blond with a huge pink bow stared at her. The little girl's blue eyes held a sadness mixed with hope. Lottie reached for Charlotte and her heart melted. She swooped the child into her arms and cradled her against her chest.

Liz cleared her throat. "May we come in?"

Startled by her mom's voice, she turned and carried her niece into the house. "Of course. Come in." Footsteps of three people followed. Mom, Dad, and Peter. How did her brother, who had been so selfish, create this beautiful little gift of light? Charlotte's heart pounded with disdain and love in alternate rhythm. The steady beating of her heart betrayed her anxiety. *He's here seeking forgiveness.* An unexpected, internal voice urged her to tell him she'd missed him.

"Are you my auntie?" Little Lottie drew her head back and placed a hand on each side of Charlotte's face. "You're pretty, and Mamaw said to call you Auntie C. Okay?"

A tear escaped from the many Charlotte forced back. "Yes, sweet girl." She kissed Lottie's cheek, then turned, lowered herself to the couch, and placed her niece on the cushion beside her. Charlotte's mom and dad hustled to the kitchen with bags filled with food. Peter, like a timid puppy, waited by the door.

Charlotte fingered Lottie's curls, then lifted her gaze to meet her brother's. The same blue eyes as Lottie's, but sadder, pierced her. She stood and stepped to him, then paused. "Peter. Um... you have an adorable daughter." The words she had mumbled to herself for years didn't match what came out of her mouth. *Why did you leave me? Why didn't you call? Why didn't you come home and rescue me?* Instead, she chose kindness in front of her niece.

The man stepped closer. "It's good to see you. I've missed you and Mom and Dad. I'm... "

At the words *I've missed you,* Charlotte's fourteen-year-old self took over, and she flung herself into her brother's arms. "I've missed you too."

Peter patted her back, then she stepped away.

"I'm sorry. I don't know what I was doing."

"You're being Charlotte. Remember how you used to do that when I'd come home late and you were still awake? You always acted like you'd never see me again." He sucked in a breath. "I'm guessing you thought that was true now."

She motioned to the couch when no response formed. "Sit here with your daughter while I help Mom. I'll send Dad in." She pointed to the coffee table. "*A Charlie Brown Christmas* is cued up on my laptop if you want to watch it."

~~~~~

In the afternoon, the Abbott Island streets echoed the quiet strains of *Silent Night.* A few children rolled snowmen and decorated them with wool caps and scarves and a couple of fellows tweaked their outdoor lights. Otherwise, Levi cruised through without issues.

One more hour until he planned to meet Charlotte's family for Christmas Eve dinner. He'd purchased some small gifts to take to them and spent most of the day praying for Charlotte as she reunited with her brother. From what he understood, they hadn't communicated since he left home. Fourteen years had passed. He asked God to give Charlotte wisdom and her brother an understanding heart. With no family to speak of, except an uncle who lived in Colorado, Levi longed for a brother or sister, but he'd lost the one he had. He didn't understand the dynamics of siblings who had issues with each other.

Levi showered and changed, then five o'clock on the dot, he pulled into Charlotte's driveway. Hands filled with gifts, he tapped on her door.

A man with Charlotte's light complexion and blond hair met him. "You must be Levi."

"Peter?" Levi stepped inside.

Peter grabbed his free hand and shook it. "Come in. Charlotte's in the kitchen with Mom and Dad is playing with Lottie."

Levi stacked his gifts under the tree, then followed Peter. From the vibe Levi felt, things must be going better than expected. A man rose from the floor.

"Levi, I'm Don, Charlotte's dad and this little imp's Papaw. This is Lottie, short for Charlotte. She belongs to Peter."

He bent down to greet her. "It's nice to meet you."

Lottie tugged on his pant leg. "You my unka?"

Levi's face heated. "No, you can call me Levi. I'm your aunt's friend."

The stern look the little girl directed at him caused him to hide a chuckle. With her hands on her hips, she crinkled her nose. "I hope you are a nice friend." With a hop, she turned back to the blocks she had stacked on the floor.

"She's adorable."

"Levi, you're here." Charlotte squeezed his arm. "You've met everyone but Mom." A woman the height of Charlotte, with light brown hair streaked with silver, wiped her hands on her apron.

"I'd shake your hand, but I still have stuffing on mine," her mother said. "It's nice to meet you. I'm glad you joined us."

"Thanks for having me." The scene before him could have come out of one of the women's magazines his mom used to read. A perfect holiday scene with mom and daughter preparing dinner and son and father waiting, except he sensed they walked on eggshells, as his grandma used to say. The scene reminded him of the Christmas his dad did most of the cooking because Mom had undergone chemo, and Levi had set the table and washed dishes. He'd offer to clean up here after they finished today, so Charlotte and her parents could visit with Peter and Lottie.

"Dinner will be ready in about twenty minutes. Charlotte has set a beautiful table, and I can't wait to sit down with all of you."

Liz's smile sparkled as much as the Christmas tree lights. Her joy no doubt resulted from having her son home for the holidays and meeting her granddaughter. Charlotte hadn't shared the story of what happened to Lottie's mom, perhaps she'd not been told. Not his business anyway. He came to support Charlotte and shower her with care. Knowing her heart ached over whatever happened between her and her brother, Levi set out to surround her with kindness and confidence. He'd carry her burden, in spite of her emotional strength and independence. An unexpected emotion bloomed inside him, one of protectiveness with a large dose of love.

~~~~~

Gathered around the table in the small kitchen, Peter felt anything but cozy with his family. He bowed his head while his dad asked God to bless the food. Hundreds of times, Peter had heard his dad say grace, but today those times slammed into his heart with a thud. How could he have stayed away from these people for fourteen years and lived in the wallow of his own stupid decisions? He lifted one eyelid and peeked at Lottie, sandwiched between Charlotte and Mom. The little girl deserved to be surrounded by these people, and he ached to be drawn into the circle with her.

After Dad's amen, Mom passed the serving dishes around the table. With plates filled, the sound of silverware clinking against plates filled the room.

"The ham and stuffing are delicious." Levi nodded to Liz. "I've not had a festive Christmas dinner in years. I try to work so the married guys can be with their families."

Don cut a slice of ham for himself. "That's thoughtful of you. How did you get tonight off?"

Levi wiped his mouth with his napkin. "The chief said to enjoy myself at least once through the holidays. I'll cover most of the day tomorrow, then be relieved in the evening by one of the newer recruits."

Charlotte's friend fit in better than Peter did. Like he was a puzzle piece waiting to click.

Charlotte mashed a sweet potato for Lottie. "Peter, how long are you staying with Mom and Dad?"

He set his fork beside his plate as his appetite faded. "I'm not sure. We haven't talked about it."

Liz studied her son. "Do you need to hurry back to Kentucky?"

"Daddy said we stay here, didn't you, Daddy?" Lottie chirped. "You say if Mamaw and Papaw still loved us, we'd live with them. Right?"

Peter stared at his half-eaten plate of food.

His mom's hand touched his. "Son, if you and Lottie need a place to stay, we have plenty of room. Don't worry."

Peter pushed from the table and stood, then he skulked out the front door.

Outside, he kicked a lump of snow across the driveway. The Christmas lights blinked in the dusky evening. When the door opened and closed, he expected his dad, but Charlotte waited on the stoop, wrapped in a wool coat and hat.

"Hey. Can we talk a minute?" She moved as if in slow motion to stand beside him.

He shook his head. "Not much to say. I messed up and, I'm back with a child in tow. More than me to deal with. A little girl with a broken heart whose mom didn't want either of us."

Charlotte peered at him. "I've been angry with you for years. I had no idea why you left, except to follow a dream of stardom. When I didn't hear from you, ever, I hated you for leaving me to work at the grocery through my high school years, until Dad's health stabilized enough to go back to work. In the meantime, I grew up, put myself through college, and found a job I love. I didn't understand then, but I do now. I'm sorry things didn't work out for you, but you need to realize we are your family and we love you. So stay. Stay with Mom and Dad so Lottie has support."

He closed his eyes for a moment, opened them, then addressed his sister. "How can you let me back in after I deserted you? I heard Dad had a heart attack, and I didn't bother to come home. Mom kept me updated whether I wanted to hear from her or not. She told me how hard you worked, and you gave up the sports you loved. How could I come back? You hated me." He searched her expression for acceptance.

She shook her head. "Don't you get it? We love you, you knucklehead. Mom, Dad, and I have a love unlike any other in the love of Jesus. He's taught me to forgive, and I want to forgive you. It's been hard. So, so hard. I worried over my reaction when I saw you, but then I met your beautiful little girl and my heart melted. I want to be part of her life and part of yours." She wrapped her hands around his bicep. "I don't know what happened with Lottie's mom, and you don't have to tell me, but she's losing out. Once Christmas is over and I'm back home, I want to help you find a job. We'll get through this together." Her hand rested on his arm. "Let's go eat some of the dessert I slaved over."

Peter placed his hand on hers. "Does the guy in there we stuck with Mom and Dad understand how lucky he is?"

"I hope so, because I'm pretty blessed myself." She pulled him to the door. "Let's go finish dinner."

Chapter Five

Christmas morning, Levi cruised past the cottage where Charlotte and her family celebrated. Last night, after she and her brother returned to the table, they had finished dinner and feasted on the bûche de Noël and angel food cake Charlotte had made. The gifts he'd handed out had been a hit. Lottie squealed when she tore the wrapping paper from the little ponies he gave her. She had climbed on his lap and kissed his cheek. The child tugged on his heart.

Tonight held the promise of more food and fun with leftovers and games. Levi approached Joel and Sadie's home, where Joel helped her descend the porch steps. Levi pulled the squad car along the side of the road and hopped out. "Hey, you two."

Sadie tried to hold her coat closed across her stomach, but it flapped in the wind. "Merry Christmas!" She waddled to the car. "We're on our way to Lucy's. Joel's parents are there. I can't wait to get in her recliner."

Levi opened the car door for her, then patted Joel on the back. "How are you doing this morning?"

He closed the passenger door and looked at Levi. "Better than my wife. I told her we'd stay home, but she said no. She wants to visit with my parents. Her dad is waiting to come until after the baby's born, so this is our celebration. I'm glad it's not a far drive."

Levi gave Joel a puzzled look. "Anywhere on the island isn't a far drive." He'd never seen Joel so rattled. "Have fun and tell them Merry Christmas."

Joel gave a salute. "Will do."

After a few laps around the island and a final check on the dock, Levi drove to the police station to check for alerts on his computer. Thankful for the quiet day, he locked the squad car's doors and went inside.

~~~~~

The silver tree glimmered in the morning light. Multicolored lights glinted off the aluminum branches, and Lottie stretched out on the floor with hands under her chin as she stared at the shimmering ornaments. Peter never dreamed he'd have a beautiful little girl to make memories with. Since he came clean with his family last night after Levi left, a weight was lifted from him. Mom and Dad asked him to stay with them for now, and Charlotte said she'd heard of a music store in town who needed someone to work and teach guitar lessons. Good thing Mom had kept one of his old guitars he'd had in high school.

With the quiet footing of a deer, Charlotte stepped into the room in her bunny slippers and Winnie-the-Pooh pajamas. She slid onto the couch beside Peter and gave him a cup of steaming coffee. "Milk, no sugar."

"You remembered." He took the mug and sipped.

A grin crossed her face. "I used to make it for you before school. Even though I didn't drink it, I loved the smell. Early morning classes in college triggered my need for caffeine."

Peter wrapped both hands around the mug and gave a slight nod. "Yeah, college wasn't in the works for me. My heart longed for country music stardom. Now I realize where I ignored God and raced off on my own path. A few months ago, I attended church with my buddy and his wife in Kentucky and it was like my memories reeled back to Sunday School and the teacher's words, 'God has a plan and purpose for your life, but He also allows free will. You have to decide if you want to follow Him.' I blew that."

She patted her brother's back. "You may have blown it then, but you still have a future He can help you with. This sounds simple, but start praying and asking God for help. You'll be amazed how He answers."

"Thanks, Sis. I'm still overwhelmed you want me in your life. Or is it Lottie?" He chuckled.

"When you put it that way." Charlotte swatted his arm and laughed.

From the floor, Lottie looked at her daddy. "When we gonna open presents?"

Mom and Dad padded into the room. "How about now?"

"Yay!" The little girl clapped and hopped on Peter's lap.

~~~~~

Parked along the street beside the lake, Levi watched a couple of kids race across the rocks near the churning water. As Levi opened the door to warn them about the danger of the slick stones, his cell phone chimed and the boys rushed away.

He slid his finger across the screen to answer. "This is Levi."

"Levi, it's Joel. I've been trying to reach the EMT on duty today, but she doesn't answer. Is there any way you can swing by and check if Donna is available? Sadie's legs are swelling and she's having contractions. I have a call in to her doctor, but I'd feel better if Donna is around."

"Sure. I'll go now. Is there anything else I can do?" He put the cruiser in gear and pulled into the street.

"Could you follow her here or bring her? We're at Lucy's."

"You got it." He disconnected the call, flicked on the strobe light, and drove across the island. In Donna's driveway, Levi noted three cars. *Looks like she's home.* He hurried to the door and knocked.

A woman about forty answered the door. "Levi, is everything okay?"

"Joel phoned and Sadie needs you to check on her. I can take you or you can follow me." He rubbed his hands together to warm them against the cold.

She turned behind her and said something to her husband, then turned back to him. "I'll follow you. Let me get my bag and a coat."

In a few minutes, Donna climbed into her car and followed Levi. In ten minutes, they pulled into Lucy's driveway.

The two of them hustled to the door. "Joel said he tried to call you."

"Something is wrong with my phone. I saw the missed calls after you stopped, but the phone didn't ring. Thankfully, Marty bought me a new phone for Christmas." At the door, she pressed the doorbell.

Joel opened the door and hurried them inside. "Sadie's in the front room on the couch."

Donna knelt beside the pregnant woman. "I hear you're uncomfortable. I'm going to take your vitals." She retrieved the blood pressure cuff and stethoscope from her bag and wrapped the cuff around Sadie's arm and proceeded to check the numbers. "A bit high, but not unusual for how far along you are and all the holiday busyness." She tucked a thermometer in her mouth. "Normal temp. Joel said you've had contractions. How many and how far apart? Are they intense?"

Sadie sat up. "I've had four since three o'clock this morning. They aren't close together, but they're like an elastic band tightening around my middle. I'm super tired and my head hurts."

Donna checked her pulse. "Seems normal. Your blood pressure may be elevated due to the contractions. The way you're describing them, they sound like Braxton Hicks. They're considered false labor, but you'll want to check with your doctor. I'm guessing you're tired because they woke you up last night." She put her hands on her hips and looked at Joel. "Is there a room with privacy where I can check Sadie's dilation?"

Later, Donna assured them Sadie had dilated one centimeter, and they had no danger of a delivery today. "Sorry, no Christmas baby, but I want you to go home and rest. I'd take it easy until you have the baby. Did you find out what you're having?"

"No. I want to be surprised."

"I did too, with both of mine. I better get back to them and finish fixing dinner. I'll be praying for you." She hugged Sadie and left.

Sadie and Joel met Levi and Joel's family in the living room. "I'm taking Sadie home so she can rest. Lucy, if you'd fix food for us to take, I'd appreciate it. At least we opened presents." He helped Sadie with her coat. "Levi, thanks for helping us today. You don't have much longer on your shift, do you?"

"You're welcome, and I have another hour. Then I'm going to Charlotte's."

Joel's mouth lifted in a half-smile. "Charlotte's, huh?"

"Yep. Having dinner with her family again." Heat crept along his neck.

"Have fun."

"I plan on it."

~~~~~

The sunset celebrated Christmas with scarlet streaks across the darkening sky. Most of the homes' Christmas trees sparkled through their windows, and lights on porches winked a warm hello. Levi sat in his car a moment before going into Charlotte's cottage. Little Lottie peered out the window and stared at the sky. What a sweet girl. She'd won the hearts of everyone. Peter fit back into the family, and Charlotte had said she forgave him and loved him. What a great gift for them. After they left, he'd have a few more days with her. He hoped to have time to talk to her about their possible future. He'd never been in love, but the emotion that stirred inside him must have been the love he longed to share with a woman. The time had come to add a commitment to the longing of his heart. He hoped she wanted to, also.

Inside the house, Levi shook out of his jacket and joined everyone at the table.

Liz stood at the counter. "Let me fix you a plate. I'm sorry we didn't wait on you, but Lottie got hungry, and so did I." She piled on a serving of lasagna and garlic bread and fixed a salad for him. "We do things our way for the holidays. I hope you enjoy it."

"This looks amazing. Thank you. I haven't eaten much today." He prayed a thanks for the food, then dug in. "Delicious."

Liz beamed. "I love to make lasagna. It's easy, fun, and perfect for a big meal."

Levi finished the pasta dish while everyone chatted. "I'm full. Thanks so much."

Charlotte cleared the table and loaded the dishwasher. "Want to play Uno?"

Peter grinned at his sister. "I haven't played Uno since I was a kid. I used to beat you."

Charlotte crossed her arms. "I was younger than you. Of course you beat me, but not anymore."

She dealt the cards while Peter helped Lottie set up a castle her grandparents gave her for Christmas.

Levi hadn't enjoyed time with a family for years. The laughter and joy he witnessed from this once broken, now mended group filled his heart with hope. Charlotte's quick wit and kind heart tugged at him. He loved her and the people she loved. After he had graduated from the police academy, he'd hoped to find someone to share life with, but he didn't imagine anyone would want to date him. His clumsy, shy ways tended to deflect women, yet Charlotte wanted him around. Through their letters, texts, and phone calls, they'd drawn closer and shared their dreams and hopes. Tomorrow they'd send her parents and Peter off, then spend a couple of days together before Charlotte traveled home. His heart missed her already.

Chapter Six

Ten o'clock Monday morning, a light snow powdered the island and wintry winds tossed a freezing chill through the air. Levi lugged suitcases to Don's car and helped Peter load Lottie's new toys. "Good thing your parents drive an SUV."

"For sure. Lottie's stuff alone filled up the back." Peter stepped to Levi and offered his hand. Levi shook it. "I'm glad I got to meet you, but I'm sorry you had to witness the family drama. I'm thankful Charlotte has accepted me back and forgiven me. She probably still has to work through some of the hurt I caused, but it helps she has you."

Heat crawled up Levi's neck, his normal response to attention on himself. "It's okay. I'm thankful you came home, and you'll find Charlotte is the kindest person you'll meet. She loves Lottie already, and she missed you." The two men walked shoulder-to-shoulder to the house.

Charlotte carried a bag of food for their trip in one arm and Lottie in the other. She hugged the little girl close to her. "I'm going to miss you, but I'll be home in a couple of days, then we can play and visit."

"Will Unka Levi be with you?" Lottie pointed at him.

Charlotte's cheeks pinked and she ducked her chin. When she raised her head, she regarded Levi. "No, honey. He lives on the island and has to stay here and work."

Levi stepped closer to them and retrieved the bag of food Charlotte carried. "I'll come visit. Okay?"

Lottie clapped. "Yay! Fun."

Levi's eyes met Charlotte's and they both sighed. She'd leave the island, and they'd go back to texting and calling. He'd find a way to visit her more often. Was it time to search for a job on the mainland? One with full-time hours and better benefits. Working thirty hours a week and renting a small home was fine for him, but if he ever wanted to get married, he'd need something more stable. Marriage. Was he prepared for a lifelong commitment?

"Levi, they're ready to go to the ferry. You coming?" Charlotte tugged on his coat sleeve.

"Yeah, I'm coming." He opened the car door for her, then got in and drove to the dock.

From the landing, they waited for Don to pull the car onto the ferry. Charlotte threaded her fingers through Levi's. "What a great Christmas. The peace I have about Peter and Lottie is an answer to prayer. I get to be that little girl's aunt, and I can't wait to help her learn to read and see how she grows."

"You're anxious to get home, I suppose." He squeezed her hand as they walked back to the car.

She bumped him with her shoulder. "I am, but I also don't want to leave you. What do you want to do today?"

They climbed into the car. "With the fresh snowfall, I hoped you'd join me for a hike in the park. The trails are well marked and the walking will keep us warm." He drove them to the cottage.

Inside, Charlotte moved to the kitchen. "I'll make a thermos of hot chocolate to take and a couple of sandwiches."

"Sounds good. I'm happy to have you to myself for the day." The love his heart held for this woman would keep him warm.

~~~~~

White blanketed every inch of the forest. A peaceful stillness drifted through the trees. An occasional chirp from a cardinal accented the quiet. Charlotte, dressed in a long parka, extra socks, and boots, paused and closed her eyes. The beauty she soaked in from the calm of this place filled

63

her soul with joy. She had let go of her anger and embraced forgiveness with Peter, and now she experienced the most beautiful place on earth with the man she loved. The revelation startled her. Levi stood near, toting a backpack with their picnic supplies. Did she love him? She had waited until after college to consider dating anyone more than a few times. Now at twenty-eight, she imagined herself with him for the rest of her life, but when did her feelings change? She loved their phone calls before she fell asleep at night and texts throughout the day. Now being in person with him sent her emotions into overdrive. The real problem, the one they might not solve, was where they would live.

Marigold had suggested she move to the island and teach, but no jobs came up last summer. She would check again, though she wanted to stay in the school system she worked in to keep her benefits, and she enjoyed the people she worked with. Plus, Lottie and Peter had moved back.

Levi interrupted her thoughts. "You okay?"

Charlotte laid her hand on his arm. "I'm good. Enjoying the beauty of the woods." Plus, wondering where life might take them. She planned to spend time tonight praying and reading her Bible. Those two activities always gave her a clearer outlook.

The two trekked through the trees and bushes. Their boots made a shooshing noise as they moved along the trail.

She pointed ahead. "There's a spot up here where we can lay out the blanket and eat. I've never had a winter picnic, but this is fun. I'm glad the wind calmed, so it's not so cold." A brown bunny hopped across their path and a bush rustled nearby. "Maybe the animals will join us."

Levi spread the thick blanket over the snow, and they both settled on it. Steam rose from the cups as he poured hot chocolate. "This smells good." He sipped from the mug. "Tastes good and it's warm. Thanks for making it."

She chewed a bite of sandwich and swallowed, then sipped the hot cocoa. "You're welcome." She reached for Levi's hand. "Not everyone would do this. I'm so happy you are willing. I love to hike no matter what the weather is, and this is so beautiful and refreshing."

After he finished his sandwich, Levi scooted closer to Charlotte. "I'm happy to spend time with you, especially hiking."

She caught him gazing at her.

"Do you have any idea how beautiful you are and how much I enjoy your company? I've never met anyone quite like you." He touched her face with his gloved hand.

A nervous laugh escaped her. "You're embarrassing me."

"I mean it." He leaned in and kissed her lips. When he pulled away, her heart told her what she hoped for their future.

~~~~~

The scent of pine wafted through the house from the tree perched in front of the window. Sadie rested on the couch and reminisced. She spotted a wooden owl her father-in-law made, her brother's baby booties draped over a branch, and a macrame star Marigold had given her. She'd added a first anniversary ornament for her and Joel and she'd sneaked a baby's first Christmas ornament, minus the year, on the tree in case their child came early.

Donna had checked on her this morning and told her to rest. The doctor had advised her to keep her feet elevated and relax. She sighed with relief that the contractions had stopped last night and she'd slept.

In full uniform, Joel leaned over her and kissed her forehead. "Please call me if you need anything. I imagine things will be quiet today. Lucy is stopping by later to help with Rosie, and Marigold is on alert if you need her. Johnny's Place is closed this week for the holiday. They are going to visit Mari's dad tomorrow, but plan to return by Thursday, and Alexis is going with them."

Sadie rubbed her stomach. "You worry too much. Donna is on speed dial, so I'll be okay. She's had midwife training and delivered babies."

He tucked a pillow behind her back. "Yes. You told me, but I'd rather not have to deliver the baby here."

"I agree, but it's good to have a backup. You were trained for emergencies, so I know you can help."

He zipped his jacket. "True, but let's not find out what I remember."

She wrapped a plush blanket around her middle. "I plan to cozy up with old movies today, and I have leftovers to eat."

"As long as you keep your phone with you, we'll be good." He leaned in for a goodbye kiss. "I love you."

"Love you, too."

Sadie watched him leave and listened to the click of the lock on the door. Good thing Lucy had a key.

By noon, Sadie's tummy grumbled. She lifted from the couch and padded to the kitchen. The cool floor refreshed her bare feet. From the refrigerator, she scavenged turkey and cranberry sauce. Good enough. She made a sandwich with the turkey and sourdough bread her mother-in-law had baked. At the table, she sank her teeth into the first bite. As she chewed, a pain wrapped around her middle. Not again. It let up and she finished her lunch. After a trip to the bathroom, she settled on the couch, then fell asleep.

~~~~

Stars shimmered in the darkened sky and a chilly breeze blew. Charlotte and Levi scurried into her cottage and shed their coats. He brushed the snow out of his hair. "It's colder since we left the house."

She tugged off her mittens. "With all the walking we did, I didn't realize how cold it was until we drove to the beach for the sunset." She shivered. "I've got canned soup I can warm, if you want."

He rubbed his hands on her upper arms. "Sounds good to me. I'm not hard to please when it comes to food. At home, I eat peanut butter or grilled cheese. What can I do to help?"

"You can grab bowls from the cabinet by the sink. The owners of the cottage sure went all out to supply what we needed. I hope I can rent this again next summer." She emptied the soup into a pan and lit the gas stove.

He pulled spoons from a drawer. "Thinking about next summer, huh?" At least he had that to look forward to.

"I've been thinking about a lot of things." She leaned against the counter.

Levi planted himself beside her. "Like what?" A playful grin stretched across his face.

She patted his cheek. "About you, of course. You're the sweetest man I've ever met, and I want to spend more time with you."

He leaned in to kiss her.

"No." Charlotte startled him and he backed away. "Look. The soup boiled over and made a mess."

"I guess you were distracted." Levi lifted the pan and clicked off the burner. "I'll clean it since I was the one who distracted you. Looks like there's enough for us to eat and it's not burnt."

"I must have turned the heat too high." Charlotte pulled paper towels off the roll and handed some to Levi. He dampened them and wiped the mess.

"It cleaned up easy enough." He tossed the towels in the trash with his best basketball move. "Two points."

Charlotte took a step back and tossed hers. "Three pointer."

Laughter rang through the kitchen as he pulled her into a hug and found her lips with his. He'd miss holding her when she left.

Chapter Seven

Snowflakes, as round as peppermint candies, floated to the ground the next morning. The caretakers on the island had plowed heaps of snow to the curbs from the overnight snowfall. Levi cruised the streets and stopped to check on a few of the older island folks to see if they needed help. He shoveled a few walks and sprinkled salt, but most of the people shook their heads no since they'd experienced many winters on the island. If he moved to the mainland, he'd miss this. Part of his patrol included checking on neighbors and making sure they had heat and food. In a larger town, he assumed he'd stay busy with robberies and assaults instead of goodwill. Or he'd have both. Either way, he pressured himself to figure out what he wanted to do.

The work kept him busy, but the clock on his radio dragged. Anxious for three o'clock, when he'd be off work and with Charlotte, he rolled on. With Johnny's Place closed, he planned to take her to the Abbott Island Restaurant for homemade pizza and Saratoga chips, then finish with their homemade ice cream. Charlotte loved their chocolate marshmallow. He drummed his fingers on the steering wheel, hoping to tap the time away.

At two o'clock, Levi parked in front of the police station and walked inside. Before he settled at his desk, the phone rang. "This is Levi. How can I help you?"

His buddy and coworker's voice stretched across the line. "This is Joel. How are the roads?"

Levi dropped into his chair. "Not bad. The road crew is out and they've plowed and salted. Is Sadie okay?"

"She's having pains again, but just a couple. I think it's getting close to time, and I'm concerned we won't be able to get to the hospital. Is the ferry running?"

"I saw one this morning, but now the water is churning. I expect the ferry will stop running later today. Do you want me to check?"

"No, but if you hear anything, I'd appreciate you telling me. Nate is covering for me tonight, since I don't want to leave Sadie. I asked her to go to my mom and dad's on the mainland, but she said no."

Levi twirled a pencil. "Hopefully, the timing will work out. Call me if you need anything at all."

"Will do. Thanks." The phone clicked off.

Joel sounded on edge. Marriage and a baby added stress to life. Did the positives outweigh the anxiety? All his life, Levi met people who teased him about his clumsiness. He got called Barney Fife a time or two, but he'd passed his training at the top of his class. His klutziness never impacted his career. Being in the company of a pretty lady was another story. His mouth and brain misfired, and he embarrassed himself, until Charlotte. Her sweet personality and kind demeanor brought out the best side of him. He had stumbled in front of her, but she didn't poke fun. She teased him, but in a loving way. Could someone as sweet and kind as Charlotte want to spend time with him for the long term? He hoped so.

~~~~~

At five o'clock, Levi knocked on Charlotte's cottage door. With her walk and steps cleared, the lights on the bushes shimmered under their snow blanket. The silver tree by the window twinkled. What a Christmas the two of them had experienced, and they'd celebrate again tonight.

The door swung open and revealed his beautiful Charlotte. Her peppermint pink tunic over leggings brought out the rosiness of her cheeks, and those blue eyes sparkled. "Come in."

Inside, Levi shed his coat and hung it on the rack. "Smells good in here. Have you been baking?"

"I have. Since Sadie is on bedrest, I wanted to take her homemade bread and cinnamon rolls. Do you want to drop them off on the way to the restaurant? By the way, I made enough for you, too." She strode to the kitchen.

Levi followed her and stopped beside the counter. "Those smell amazing. Joel and Sadie will appreciate them, and so do I." He picked up the plate his were on and gave them a look of longing. "We'll drop them off. I want to see how they're doing. Joel called earlier, and he was afraid she might go early."

"How about we go now?"

"Sounds good to me."

They stepped outside. "You've been working today. Did you shovel or did somebody come help you?"

She slid into the passenger seat. "Just me. I enjoy working outside, and scooping snow was invigorating. Plus, the air is so clean here. It's refreshing to breathe in the crispness."

He slid into the driver's seat and pulled out of the driveway. He'd miss the cleanliness on the island. The council worked hard to keep the place pristine. One more thing he'd leave behind if Charlotte wanted him to. His heart assured him he'd give up most anything for her.

~~~~~

In Sadie and Joel's driveway, Charlotte lifted her baked goods from the back seat. The fresh smell of the bread met her and reminded her of how much she loved the island ways. Everyone watched out for each other and helped when needs arose. Last summer when Marigold experienced a rough patch, folks responded with compassion. Charlotte's friends from her school and church showed kindness, but this small, close-knit community shared a special bond.

On the porch, Levi tapped on the door. Joel met them. Exhaustion had painted dark circles under his blood-shot eyes. "Hey, you two. Come in."

Sadie greeted them from the couch. "Hi. Excuse me for not getting up, but I've been told to stay off my feet, and Joel will get after me if I don't listen."

Sadie's golden retriever, Rosie, nosed Charlotte's package, wagged her tail, then lay down beside the couch.

"She doesn't know what to think." Sadie sat up straighter and shoved a pillow behind her back. "She's not used to me lying around all day. Thank goodness Joel's here to let her out.

Charlotte perched on a chair by Sadie. "Rosie's life is about to change." They both chuckled. "I baked bread and cinnamon rolls this morning and wanted you to have some. Since you don't feel up to cooking, I hoped you'd enjoy comfort food."

Sadie accepted the bag from her and pulled out the rolls. "Oh wow, look at these, Joel. These are bakery worthy." She took a deep breath. "Smell the cinnamon. I think these will make a good dinner." Weariness crossed Sadie's puffy face. "My appetite's not been great for a couple of days but I'll be eating these, for sure. Thank you." She held her arms up to hug Charlotte. The young woman bent and patted her on the back.

Joel slid a cushion under Sadie's feet. "Keep those tootsies elevated."

"Thanks, hon." She squeezed Charlotte's arm, then let go. "He's so good to me. I might share the goodies you brought with him." With a wink and grin, she passed the package to Joel. He and Levi carried the baked goods and their conversation to the kitchen.

"You two make a great pair."

What would it be like to be married to someone who cared so much? Her gaze lingered on Levi, through the arched doorway. She sensed he lacked the confidence Joel had, but he had a quiet assurance about him. His calmness and gratitude fueled his ability to handle situations with grace. When she and her brother clashed, Levi had stood by her and eased her pain. Then, he welcomed Peter as if he'd known him all his life. How had this man not married yet?

He's waiting for you. A voice as clear as Sadie's sounded in her head. Could he be the one?

Levi squeezed Charlotte's shoulder. "We'd better go and let these two get some rest."

Joel walked Levi and Charlotte to the door. "Thanks for the treats. Much appreciated. I'm hoping we can get a good night's sleep before this little one comes, because we won't after."

"I'm sure life will change." Charlotte waved before she stepped out. "You two take care."

On the way to the car, Charlotte grasped Levi's hand. "They're worn out and the baby isn't here yet. I hope they get to sleep tonight."

He gripped her hand with tenderness. "I hope so. I can't imagine."

Neither can I. Charlotte climbed in the car and buckled her seatbelt. *Neither can I.*

~~~~~

Heavy white flakes tumbled from the sky and piled on top of last night's snow. A half-inch of the white stuff dressed the sidewalk. Levi opened Charlotte's car door and offered to help her out.

"It's slick. A lot came down in the last hour."

The restaurant's Christmas lights blinked red and green through the window and *Santa Claus is Coming to Town* sang from the outdoor speakers. Christmas on Abbott Island lasted through New Year's Day.

Inside, the fragrance of pizza sauce swirled through the room. Round tables covered in red and white checked tablecloths hosted patrons, and candles wreathed in artificial pine and berries donned each table. The hostess's jingle bell earrings tinkled as she led them to their table in the far corner.

"Here you go. Your waitress will be with you in a few minutes." She retreated to the hostess stand.

Levi pulled out Charlotte's chair. "Smells good in here, doesn't it?"

He sat across from her and they perused the menu. "Last summer, you ate pineapple and peppers on your pizza. Which I detested until I tasted it. Want pineapple and peppers again, with ham?"

Charlotte studied the menu, then gave him a sideways glance. "With Saratoga chips and the sweet and spicy dip?"

"Sounds perfect."

They placed their order, and the waitress delivered sweet tea for each of them.

"I've never met anyone else who drinks tea with pizza. Most of my friends order pop." Charlotte sipped her drink.

"I grew up with a southern granny, and we drank sweet tea with everything. No one makes it as sweet as she did." He placed his hand over hers and prayed thanks for their meal.

By the time the pizza arrived at the table, both their stomachs growled.

"We're ready for this." He served slices to both of them.

After a big bite, Charlotte wiped her mouth with her napkin. "The ham makes this pizza better, and I already loved it."

"It's salty and sweet, with a little spice."

They each finished a slice.

Charlotte reached her hand across the table. "I'm so happy I came to the island. I've missed you."

Levi grasped her hand. "I've missed you, too. We can't wait so long next time."

"I hope you can come to the mainland soon. I'm sure Lottie will want to see her unka." She giggled.

She let go and picked up a chip and dunked it into the spicy dip and popped it in her mouth.

"I love a woman who enjoys her food."

"Then you must love me." Red rose from Charlotte's neck to her cheeks. "I didn't mean..."

Levi held up his hand and waved it back and forth. "No, no. I understand."

She released a nervous laugh.

The rest of the meal, they stuffed themselves with pizza and let the conversation rest.

Charlotte leaned against the back of her chair. "I'm full."

"No room for ice cream?" Levi patted his stomach.

She scrunched her nose. "I hate to say no, but I don't think I can eat another thing. How about we take a walk, then see if we have room?"

"Sounds good."

~~~~~

The snow clouds cast a veil over the stars and a sliver of moon hung overhead. Charlotte tucked her hand in the bend of Levi's arm and strode along Division Street to the beach area. At the top of the hill, they stopped and watched the whitecaps rip to the shore.

"Listen to the water." Charlotte closed her eyes and heard the waves crash. "It sounds angry." Island life in the winter sounded overwhelming. Levi had shared how he checked on the older folks and made sure they had supplies. As much as she loved snow, the lake effect snow on an island might not be as enjoyable.

She leaned into Levi. "How often do the ferries stop running in the winter?"

"From the end of December to the first of March, they either run when the weather is reasonable or they shut down altogether. Some years have been mild and they shut down for short periods. Other times they stop for months. Island weather is unpredictable. We are at the mercy of the lake." He patted her mittened hand.

She rested her other hand on his. "Summer is so different. The warm weather makes you forget what the rest of the year brings. I'm glad I came for Christmas to experience the winter weather here." As beautiful as the island appeared dressed in white, doubt shadowed her desire to live on the island in winter.

Chapter Eight

Wednesday morning, snow flurried and the lake churned. When Levi checked with the ferry office, they reported they had shut down for the rest of the week. Private boaters understood not to place themselves in danger, so the airport held the only transportation to the mainland. Charlotte had planned to travel home on Thursday, but she'd decided to stay a few more days. Levi's heart soared. Last night he had longed to share his feelings for her, but the words stuck in his throat. Today, he'd practice what to say and reveal his heart when he stopped by this evening.

In the squad car, he parked by the ferry dock. The lake swirled and pounded the shore. Ice floes had formed along the beach beside him.

Dangerous waters, for sure. He adjusted the rear-view mirror so he peered at his own face. With a smile, he spoke to his reflection as if Charlotte sat in front of him. "I've been thinking... I'm hoping you feel the same way about me as I do you." Lame. "I've grown to care about you." He smacked his hand on his forehead. *Why can't I say 'I love you' to her?*

By the end of his workday, Joel hadn't called, so Sadie must be okay. The only incident he'd dealt with were two boys fighting over a sled. At home, he showered, dressed in his favorite sweater and fresh jeans, combed his hair and splashed shaving lotion on his cheeks. Not too much. He didn't want to choke Charlotte with the woodsy scent. On the way to her house, the General Store's open sign invited him in.

"Hi, Levi." Lucy rearranged a stack of sweatshirts.

On a shelf by the register, he spied a box of holiday chocolates. He had hoped Lucy still stocked them. "Hey, Lucy. I'd like to buy these."

She sashayed to the counter and scanned the barcode. "Something for a special someone." Lucy's ornery grin made him want to leave the candy on the counter and go.

No doubt red crept into his heated cheeks. "Maybe."

"I saw Charlotte yesterday. She looked happy." Her grin changed to a smirk.

"Glad you saw her." His voice lowered and his heart raced. Why did talking about Charlotte set his insides to jumping? "Thanks, Lucy." He paid and bolted out the door.

By the time he pulled into the cottage driveway, his breathing slowed and his face cooled. Before he let himself think too long about Lucy's teasing, he hopped out of the car with the candy and jogged to the house. His foot slipped, but he caught himself before Charlotte answered the door.

"I saw your car in the driveway. Come on in." She waved him inside.

He followed. "This is for you." He held the chocolates out for her.

She placed her hand on her heart. "Thank you. We can eat some for dessert tonight." She carried them to the kitchen, and he followed. "I have the makings for tacos. How does that sound?"

"Perfect." His words jammed in his throat like a chewy candied orange slice. Tonight, he hoped to share how much he loved her, but he couldn't shove even the simplest words out. He cleared his throat. "Can I help?"

She turned to him and touched her lips to his cheek. A tingle moved from his toes to his head.

She handed him a cutting board, the veggies, and a sharp knife. "You can chop the tomatoes and peppers while I prepare the hamburger."

They worked together with a pleasant rhythm and had the meal ready in half an hour. At the table, Levi prayed and asked a blessing on

Charlotte and her family.

"Thank you. I talked to Peter and Lottie last night, and they're eager for me to get home." She bit into her taco.

Levi finished chewing, then placed the taco on his plate. He studied Charlotte. "Are you ready to leave?"

She pursed her lips and met his gaze. "If I'm honest, I wish you were going with me."

Levi's phone chimed. Not now. He wanted to talk to Charlotte about their future. Since he served the people, he pulled the phone from his pocket and checked the screen. "It's Joel."

~~~~~

The snow had stopped, but the roads wore a thick layer of packed flakes. Levi crawled along the icy road on the two-mile trip from Charlotte's to Sadie's. As they approached the house, he noticed a vehicle in the driveway. "I think that's Donna's car. She's delivered babies, but Joel and I have only viewed videos."

Charlotte held his hand. "I'm sure whatever needs to happen will. I wish Marigold was back. She'd know what to do."

"I'm not sure when they'll get to come back or when you'll get to leave." He hustled out of the car and walked Charlotte to the door.

Inside, Joel grabbed his arm. "We can't get off the island. No time to check the airport. She's in heavy labor. Her pains were so strong they threw her on the bed. Good thing she was standing beside it. She's in the bedroom now, and Donna is with her. You can go in, Charlotte."

"Joel, slow down." He patted his buddy's back and led him to the couch. "Donna is here and we can do this. She's delivered several babies. Is Sadie in distress?"

Joel scooped in a deep breath. "Not right now."

Donna stepped into the living room and cleared her throat. "Sadie is doing great. From what I can tell, this will be a normal delivery. Her blood pressure is good and she's dilating. The baby's heartbeat is perfect and the little one is in the best position possible. I will need towels and yes, boiled water. We want everything as sterile as possible. You'll need to keep Rosie out here. She wants to sit beside Sadie, but that's not happening."

Levi petted Rosie. The sweet dog lay down on her cushion by the Christmas tree. "Good, girl. Here's a treat." He fed her a favorite biscuit, went to the kitchen, and started water to boil, then strode back to the living room.

Joel paced in front of the couch and ran his hand through his hair.

Levi touched his elbow. "You need to be in with her, don't you?"

"Yeah. Donna said I should. I didn't think I'd be nervous. I'd be calm if I were at the hospital."

"It'll be okay. I found a pan and started the water. Where are the towels?" Levi glanced down the hallway.

Joel pointed. "There's a closet in the hall with clean towels."

"You get them and take them to Donna and I'll get the water."

A few minutes later, Levi peered into the bedroom. "Is it okay to bring this in?" He didn't want to witness anything he didn't need to.

Charlotte sat on the edge of the bed and held Sadie's hand. Joel stood on the other side and rubbed her shoulder.

Donna motioned him into the room. "Set the pan over here on the bench. If the baby waits a while, we'll need to heat it up again."

"Hey, Levi. Ugh." Sadie cut off her greeting as her expression distorted with pain and her body tensed.

Joel counted breaths with her and Charlotte breathed along with them. The woman he loved blessed everyone. He admired how her gentle manner kept Joel and Sadie calm and how she jumped in to help without hesitation.

Donna rested her hands on her hips. "It's amazing what a woman's body goes through to birth a child. Sadie's a champ. No meds to help with the pain." She patted Levi's shoulder. "You've been trained. Right?"

Levi's insides shuddered. "I have, but I lack your experience and it's weird delivering our friend's baby, but I'm willing to help if need be."

She patted his back. "That's the spirit. I'm happy you're available."

Three hours later, Levi petted Rosie as a baby's cry sounded from across the house. He'd held his vigil in the living room for the last hour and prayed for Sadie and Joel.

Charlotte bounded into the room. "The baby's here."

~~~~~

Night had fallen and the living room glowed in lamp light. Charlotte rushed to Levi and hugged him, then clapped. "The birth of a baby is the most amazing thing. I didn't watch everything, but I got to see the sweet little one as soon as Sadie pushed." She swooned to the couch. "I had no idea. I mean, I had an idea, but I'd never witnessed a mom in labor."

Levi wrapped an arm around her and listened until she finished. "Did they have a boy or girl?"

Charlotte sat straight up as if a coil pushed her from the back of the couch. "I didn't ask. I saw the baby and ran out to tell you."

"Donna didn't say?"

"She might have. I was so excited I didn't hear." She grabbed his hand and pulled him behind her. "Let's find out."

In the bedroom, Donna waved them inside. Joel sat on the queen size bed beside his wife, who held a tiny bundle. With the lights low and soft music playing, the new parents and baby looked like a painting. Joel and Sadie's smiles gleamed.

Levi and Charlotte entered with quiet steps. Joel motioned to them.

"Come take a peek at our girl."

They glanced at each other and echoed, "A girl."

Sadie held her out to them. "Meet Julia Grace Grayson. After Grammy. We'll call her Gracie."

Levi's heart melted. What a sweet face on this new little islander. "So, she'll be Gracie Grayson?"

The parents marveled at their new baby.

Rosie murmured a whimper from the doorway. Her tail wagged as if she were flying a flag.

"Come here, girl." Joel held his hand out to her.

She trotted across the room and sat at attention. "Good girl." Joel petted her fur. "We have a new family member for you to meet."

Sadie held baby Gracie so Rosie could sniff where the blanket covered her feet. The dog tilted her head to the side, then went down to the floor.

Levi laughed. "I think she approves."

Chapter Nine

Later, in Charlotte's cottage, she and Levi cuddled on the couch. Though it was late, they settled in to watch a Christmas movie. She passed the box of chocolate to him. "Dark or milk?"

"Both." Levi plucked one of each from the carton. "How about you?"

"Dark. I love the rich flavor." She savored a dark chocolate-covered cherry. "I don't know about you, but I'm having trouble focusing on the Griswolds. After witnessing a baby being born, I can't stand to watch him mess up the Christmas lights."

"Same here. We witnessed a miracle." He stretched his back. "I'll enjoy seeing little Gracie grow up on the island."

Silence blanketed the room, and Charlotte stared at the floor. Levi reached over and curled his fingers around hers. "If I stay on the island, of course." He lifted her chin with his other hand. "Want to talk?"

She gave a slight nod. Leaving the island made her heart ache, but not being with her brother and Lottie hurt, too.

Levi shifted his body to face her. "I've been praying, and thinking, and praying some more. At one time, I wanted to be a teacher. Did I ever tell you I'd been a math nerd in high school and considered teaching middle schoolers? Then I attended the police academy. I've not regretted it until now. Maybe regret isn't the right word, but I'm considering a change. I've finished three years of college and could complete a teaching degree in a short time while I work." He paused. "I'm telling you this because I, um, I love you, Charlotte, and I want to have a future together and live in the same place."

Her eyes watered and she blinked back happy tears. "You'd do that for me?"

"Yes, of course. I've never met anyone like you, and you want to be around me." His laugh danced through the room. "I'd move to a different country if it meant we'd be together."

She placed a hand on his cheek. "I love you, too. If you were a teacher, we could live on the mainland and spend summers on the island."

"My thoughts exactly. I loved meeting your family, and I believe I'd be a good teacher. As much as I love helping people as a police officer, I'm ready for a change." He kissed the tip of her nose. "I've loved working on the island, but I don't think I want to work as a police officer in a city or a town on the mainland. It would be too different. I'm willing to find a job to match my schedule, and I've checked out a couple of online programs."

She wrapped both hands around his. "We always need subs. A good fit while you finish your degree."

"We'll figure this out. I'll start searching for a job near you and a small apartment. I hope to move at the end of the summer."

"Sounds good. I'll come and work for Marigold again, then we'll have summer on the island."

He moved his hands to rest on her shoulders? "All I know is, I've found the love of my life, and I don't want to lose her. Since Sadie's had her baby and Joel comes back after his time off, I'll have free time to come visit you." He tugged her into a hug. "I love you, Charlotte."

She hugged his neck and whispered. "I love you too, Levi."

The End

Dedication

To: Sara & James, Maggie & Michael, Hannah & Stephen, Adam & Brenda, & Kati. Thank you for all the Christmas memories!

Acknowledgements:

You can't write a Christmas novella without a hundred memories flooding the heart. The joy of watching children open their gifts with a sparkle of hope, the delight of little ones in a Christmas play, the Christmas tree lit and the carols playing, all fill me with appreciation for the season of joy.

One beautiful memory I cherish is the time my husband, Tim, indulged me around the holiday and drove to Marblehead, Ohio, so I could see snow. We didn't have any in southwest Ohio that year and he knew how much I missed it. His love and understanding over the years still amaze me.

The year we celebrated Sara and James at their beautiful December wedding was pure joy. Love to all of our children and grands. Looking forward to many more celebrations together.

A huge thank you to Mt. Zion Ridge Press for including me in this collection of Ohio Christmas novellas.

Special thanks to my critique partner, Kathleen, for your eye for detail. May you have many merry Christmases.

Most importantly, I thank God for sweet baby Jesus, who came to love us. Without His love, I'd have none to share.

Books by Penny Frost McGinnis
Home Where She Belongs (Abbott Island book 1)
Home Away From Home (Abbott Island book 2)

ANNA'S CHRISTMAS PROMISE
Tamera Lynn Kraft

A Schoenbrunn Christmas Story

Chapter One

December 23, 1773, Schoenbrunn Village, Ohio

Anna Brunner kneaded dough while she tried not to notice it was almost dusk. Her husband still wasn't home.

She wiped her hands on her apron and glanced out the six-pane window. The last glint of sunlight blazed the horizon, gleaming on the dirt path. No trace of him.

After scooping some sugar, she worked it into the dough. She tried to keep her mind on the Christmas Eve Lovefeast and all the work she had ahead. She'd been honored with the mission of making the sweet buns and would be one of the *Dieners* serving the meal at their newly built church.

It did no good to fret about what was going on at the meeting down the road. She'd find out soon enough. She released her anxiety into the dough as she squeezed her fingers through and pounded it into shape.

After living in this village for over a year, celebrating the yuletide with all the fanfare it deserved would make up for everything.

Almost.

The children giggled as they finished a game of jackstraws. Belinda, eight years old, failed to remove a straw without touching the others, and Lisel, the round-faced six-year-old, smirked as she shouted out in triumph. Three-year-old Katrina's brown curls bounced as she clapped for Lisel. She hadn't managed to win any rounds, but Belinda insisted they let her play until a winner had been declared.

"Let's get the tree ready," Belinda said.

The girls threw the wheat straws in a basket and dashed to the wooden pyramid frame their father had built. Large boughs were stacked in the corner of the room. Earlier today, before John was beckoned, he'd cut them from the pine trees that lined God's Acre, the village cemetery.

Anna was glad Moravians didn't cut down trees and drag them into houses the way some did, leaving ugly stumps where the trees grew. By using the frame built from wood, and boughs cut from limbs, they still managed to build a nice Christmas tree without damaging any trees.

Once all the limbs were in place, the girls would decorate it with Scripture verses written on pieces of paper, and pure white beeswax candles with red ribbons tied around them to represent Jesus, the light of the world, who shed His blood on the cross.

Maybe this year will be better.

Anna's thoughts drifted to when her husband announced his decision to move to the Ohio wilderness. She had been livid. Many Lenni Lenape were forced to move west, but that didn't mean the missionaries from the Moravian Church needed to follow those Delaware Indians, at least, not the missionaries with families. There were still plenty of natives in Pennsylvania who needed to hear the Gospel.

John had gazed at her with his steel blue eyes. "Anna, we learned to speak Lenape and taught it to our children for this reason, to share the Gospel with the natives."

"We're already doing that. Think of the danger." She'd delivered a daunting glower of her own, meant to dissuade him. "We have children to consider."

For days, she'd tried to change his mind by pointing out they didn't need to leave their family and friends in Bethlehem to serve God. He promised her they'd be safe, that the girls would be protected.

"Stop making promises you can't keep." She had swiped at a tear running down her cheek.

"We have our duty as missionaries." His voice was calm as if his statement settled the matter.

"I won't go." The declaration had shocked her as much as it did her husband.

Now, Anna glanced out the window. Dark clouds had blown in, obscuring the rising full moon.

John should have been home eating his supper by now.

Earlier, she'd arrived from walking the girls home from school to find John huddled around the fire in discussion with Brother Luke, a village elder. Luke had been a Moravian for so long, she sometimes forgot he was Lenape.

"We can't let him face them by himself." John's furrowed brow wrinkled his normally pleasant face.

When Anna closed the door, the conversation abruptly stopped.

Luke stood. "Forgive the interruption, Sister Brunner. The elders have need of your husband's wisdom."

John had grabbed his coat and kissed her on the cheek.

Anna placed a hand over her stomach. "When will you be home?"

"I don't know, but it'll be in time to sup with you and the children. I promise." He had closed the door behind him before she could say more.

That was four hours ago.

Lisel attached another bough to the tree and scooted next to Anna, pulling on her skirt. "Mama, when do we eat? I'm hungry."

Anna reached down and gave Lisel a hug. "Soon, child. Help Belinda and Katrina with the tree." She grabbed the copper ladle hanging on the wall next to the fireplace and stirred the stew she kept warm on the embers. The aroma of pieces of roast pig, overdone potatoes, and turnips made her stomach rumble. If John took much longer, she'd feed the children without him.

She remembered the astonishment in John's eyes when she'd told him she was staying in Bethlehem. He didn't say anything, didn't chide her, or tell her she was a disobedient wife. He wrapped his arms around her and kissed her forehead.

She'd quivered under his touch.

He'd kissed her in a way that overpowered her objections as she melted against him. Pulling back, he'd said in a quiet voice, "Shall we deny the Lamb that was slain the reward of His suffering by refusing to go?"

A lump had formed in her throat, and before he'd released her, tears rolled down her cheeks. What choice did she have?

So they had set off with a group of twenty-eight Moravians, both white man and native, to settle the wilderness and preach the Gospel to the Lenape.

Anna hadn't felt safe since. She punched the dough and set it on the bread board to rise.

Since they'd moved to Schoenbrunn Village, most Lenape welcomed the Moravians, but some looked upon them with suspicion even though most of the families in the group were natives. Then there were the Iroquois, Wyandot, and Shawnee, all warrior tribes leery of the settlers. Some of them were even hostile toward Lenape.

Looking out the window, she couldn't see anyone coming down the path, only shadows of other cabins. She grabbed the flintlock on the mantle and lit the candles so they could see to eat their supper.

There'd even been an incident in Gnadenhutten, their sister village to the south. Wyandot marauded homes and stole supplies. They didn't hurt anyone, but they might next time. Or they might decide to pillage Schoenbrunn Village.

She rubbed her belly, hidden by the light blue apron that protected her blue and white striped wool dress. She'd sewn it last winter out of the material she'd bought before they left Pennsylvania.

New life growing inside helped keep her mind off the dangers. Maybe next year she could give John a son. Then things would be the way they were before. She would tell him the news on Christmas Day.

She set tin plates on the wooden table next to the wall where the children had decorated the tree. Many of the preparations for the celebration were already done and laid out. Their small cabin was crowded with the tree and extra food, but it was worth it.

They still had just enough room for the rocking chair perched by the fireplace. John had made it for Anna last Christmas. Baskets, water carriers, a spinning wheel, and various other tools were hidden away on shelves in the corner to provide more room. A straw tick where the children slept was tucked under the rope bed.

Lisel reached up as far as she could to attach a bough to a higher wooden beam. Katrina only managed to reach the lower planks. Belinda moved the papers and ink bottle from the table where she'd been writing out Scriptures to hang on the branches.

Anna's oldest daughter reminded her of her husband, not only because of her straight blond hair and ruddy complexion covered with freckles, but because of her devotion to God and courage in adversity, virtues Anna once had before...

The door flew open, and the burst of frigid air chilled the room and blew out one of the candles.

John stepped inside with a recent Lenape convert who had been baptized under the name Paul. Anna was glad the man had converted. Brother Paul was six feet tall and built like a tree.

Her husband was almost as tall and as broad across the shoulders, with a pleasant look that seemed to want to break into a smile at the slightest provocation. John's strength helped her feel safe, as if being wrapped in a warm blanket. Even though she'd lived among Lenape most of her life, Brother Paul made her uneasy.

Belinda and Lisel ran to their father and gave him a tight embrace. Katrina tugged on his trouser leg until he picked her up and ran a hand through her brown ringlets. Katrina was the only one of their children who favored Anna.

"Papa," Belinda said. "I'm writing Scriptures to hang on the tree, and I helped Mama with the buns for the feast. We're almost ready."

John hugged his oldest girl. "You're such a blessing to your mama." He said the words in English, which was odd. They spoke Lenape when natives were around, especially ones who hadn't learned English.

John would normally remind the girls to speak Lenape when they had a guest.

"I helped, too." Lisel allowed her lower lip to almost reach her chin.

"No sulking." John patted Lisel's head. "There's enough work for everyone."

"I help Mama," Katrina said.

"Of course, you do." John set Katrina on the dirt floor.

"Children." Anna grabbed hold of Katrina's hand. "Give your father an opportunity to settle. Why don't you work on the Putz?"

Lisel clapped her hands together, and the girls gathered near the blazing fire where pinecones, cloth, and papers lay in a wicker basket. The children would make figures out of them depicting the Nativity, the wise men, and the Exodus from Egypt. John had already whittled a small manger. Katrina, as the youngest, would place the pinecone baby Jesus in it on Christmas Eve after the Lovefeast.

Anna tucked a stray curl into her *Habba*, turned to Paul, and spoke Lenape to welcome him. "*Nulelìntàm èli paan.* May I serve you anything – coffee, water?"

Brother Paul shook his head. He wore a grey shirt and trousers, a buckskin coat similar to her husband's, and had shaved his Mohawk. But when he crossed his arms and leaned against the doorpost, he looked as intimidating as when he wore black and red paint around his eyes and dressed like a warrior.

"We'll need ashcakes." John now spoke in Lenape. His Adam's apple bulged as he grabbed the musket hanging on the wall over the fireplace. "And a couple canteens of water."

Anna wrapped the cornmeal ashcakes in cloth and poured water from the pitcher into the wooden canteens. "I've made some stew. Do you and Brother Paul have time to sup before your journey?"

"No, we must make haste." John glanced out the window. "It's already dark. We need to arrive at Gnadenhutten before it gets too late."

She motioned John to the corner of the cabin and whispered so the girls wouldn't be alarmed. "Something's wrong."

"A delegation from a nearby Lenape tribe arrived at Gnadenhutten. They have requested to meet with leaders from both of our villages." John touched her arm. "Don't be troubled. They mean no harm. They only want to know more about what we're preaching."

Anna's stomach knotted. "Is there any danger?"

"You fret too much." A smile played with the edges of John's mouth, but his brow furrowed. "They only want to converse, nothing more."

"How many will accompany you?"

"Brother Paul and Brother Luke."

Her shoulders relaxed. Brother Luke had been a trusted native helper to the Moravians since his youth. They'd known him for years in Pennsylvania. But Paul only showed up at the village a few months ago.

"Why must you go?" Anna wrapped her arms around John. "You

have responsibilities to your family. Let somebody without a wife and children take your place."

John enveloped her in his arms for a moment longer than normal when company was around. Then he pulled back to tilt her chin toward him. The lighthearted facade had been replaced by an intense gaze. "We came here to advance the Kingdom of God. Shall I pull back now?"

Anna wiped away the stray tear rolling down her cheek. "May the Lamb that was slain receive the reward of His suffering." She said the words in Lenape to reassure him, but they didn't make her feel any better.

"Amen." Brother Paul stepped over to them and put a hand on John's shoulder. "Brother, we must go now."

John nodded.

Anna swallowed back the lump in her throat and spoke in English. It seemed too intimate a moment with her husband to let Paul understand her words. "Will you be home in time for the Lovefeast tomorrow night?"

John's brow furrowed. "I don't know."

"You can't miss the celebration of the birth of our Savior."

"I'll try to be back in time." John's jaw twitched. "I promise to be home for Christmas."

Anna wanted to argue with him, tell him not to go, but it wouldn't do any good. She forced her breathing to slow to a normal pace. "Then I'll make it the best we ever had."

"That won't be hard," John said. "Any Christmas with you and the girls is good."

"Brother John." Paul nodded toward the door. "They're waiting."

"I'll meet you outside."

The door made a thumping sound as Paul closed it on the way out.

"Children." Anna placed her hands on Lisel and Katrina. "Papa's going on a journey. Come say good-bye."

The girls ran to their father and hugged him.

"When will you be back?" Belinda asked.

"Maybe tomorrow in time for the Lovefeast." John wiped his hand across his neck. "If not, I'll see you Christmas Day."

John took Anna into his arms once again and kissed her. The heat of the moment swept through her as she leaned into the kiss with parted lips. He rested his mouth against her neck, then pulled away. After strapping on his supplies and musket, he opened the door.

The blast of winter filled the cabin and sent a chill through her. She scampered to the fireplace, grabbed her ladle, and dished stew onto tin plates. "Children, come to the table to sup." The door shut with a dull thud behind her.

John was gone.

Chapter Two

The church bell resonated throughout the village announcing only five minutes until morning meeting would begin. It was later than Anna thought. Arising early this morning was harder than usual. She hadn't slept well without John by her side. The ropes on the bed sagged without his weight, but she didn't want to use the wedge to tighten them when he might be home tonight.

After rushing to dress the children in cloaks and boots, she stepped onto the stone walk outside the front door and breathed in the crisp winter air before heading to the dirt road. Her girls lined up beside her, with Belinda holding Katrina's hand. Anna tried to hold Lisel's, but the child wanted to walk on her own. Anna reluctantly let her.

Snow fell, and dark clouds forewarned that it would cover the ground before the day was done. They passed the cabin two doors down when Lisel got distracted by large snowflakes and tried to catch them on her tongue.

Anna placed a hand on Lisel's shoulder. "Hurry. We'll be late."

Lisel's lower lip quivered, and Anna gave her a firm squeeze. This new habit of pouting needed to stop. Lisel shrugged and ran ahead, but not out of Anna's sight. She had warned the girls how dangerous it was to wander off where they couldn't be seen. For once, Lisel listened.

Anna glanced at Lisel's boots that had been too big last winter, but barely fit this year. She should have bought new ones for the girls when the traders were at the village a couple of months ago. They probably wouldn't be back until winter snows thawed. The old boots would have to do. If they got too small, Anna would cut out the toes and add some cowhide to them. If that didn't work, she'd make some deerskin shoes.

That would make Lisel happy since she had recently fussed that she wanted to wear moccasins like some of her Lenape friends at school did.

The walk was short since their home was only five cabins away from the new church. It had only been built three months ago and was such a blessing. They didn't have to meet in the crowded schoolhouse anymore. The roads of the village formed in a T shape with the church in the middle and the school across the path.

Pastor Zeisberger, the leader of the village, lived next door to the church. Other cabins lined the roads. A few of them had a second floor or two rooms. Some even had wooden floorboards, but most were simple one-room log cabins with dirt floors like theirs, not nearly large enough for their growing family. John promised to build them a larger cabin like the one they had in Bethlehem as soon as he had a chance.

At least the land was fertile. During the summer, crops would be planted in the fields bordering the village. Behind the church was the field where corn, beans, and squash, known as the three sisters, were planted together. Each family had their own plot to raise potatoes, turnips, cabbage, and a small herb patch. The village had already been enclosed with wattle fences to keep out rodents and wild animals.

But it still didn't feel like Bethlehem. It didn't feel like home.

The round cabins on the far end of the T were built by the newly converted Lenape. They weren't really round like the wigwams many Lenape lived in. They were called that because the natives didn't have the tools to shape the round logs. Beyond them was God's Acre, the village cemetery. They'd only been there a year and a half, and already Phoebe's child and Rebecca's husband had been buried there.

Anna remembered the graves they'd left in Bethlehem. She inhaled deeply through her nose and released it through her mouth to keep the anxiety at bay. Worry was a sin she repented of often.

The bell tolled again. Meeting would begin soon.

Hurrying their pace, they passed Brother Luke's cabin, and a knot curled up inside Anna's stomach. John was headstrong and took risks, but she tried to hold onto the thought that Brother Luke would keep the peace.

Paul was a different matter.

The son of a chief, he arrived in the village a few months ago, wearing a beaded headdress with a few eagle feathers sticking up. The war paint on his face in the shape of a mask around his eyes dripped down his cheeks. He wore earrings and had a tattoo of a bear on his arm. He told John it was because he fought like Yakwahe, a mythical bear, in battle.

Anna kept the girls close by when warriors visited the village. But when Paul showed up, she wouldn't even let them out of the cabin.

Pastor Zeisberger, Pastor Jungman, and John talked to Paul for hours, explaining the salvation of the Lord. In the end, Paul had converted and was baptized.

Within a week, with John's help, he had built a round cabin, not much bigger than a wigwam, near the end of the T.

John had made it his mission to disciple the young brave and invited him to supper at least two or three evenings a week so they could study the Bible together, and he could teach Paul to read his native language.

On those evenings, Anna cleaned up and tucked the children into bed.

The girls loved Paul. Lisel would constantly pester him to tell her stories about his tribe. He would tell the girls his yarns only if Lisel would recite the Bible story she learned recently. But his adventures were too violent for young girls to hear even if they did have heroism and romance in them. Lisel was already too enamored with the Lenape ways.

Even though John had grown close to Paul and remarked often at how quickly the young brave absorbed Scripture, Anna wasn't sure about him. His conversion seemed too fast to be genuine. She tried to caution John about trusting his new convert at face value and suggested maybe they should meet in Paul's cabin, away from the girls.

John dismissed her fear, saying she allowed her troubled thoughts to consume her.

Maybe she did. But she had reason to be concerned.

Anna entered the church, and the tension throughout her body floated away. Something about stepping into the house of God alleviated her fears. The Spirit of God lived inside all His children, but she felt His presence here. Lately, it was the only time she did.

Paintings of Jesus' life filled the right wall above the fireplace, and paintings of the Exodus from Egypt, David facing Goliath, and Daniel in the lion's den were on the wall to the left, scenes reminding her that the saints of old also faced trials. How were they able to trust in God without being plagued with worry?

On the raised platform in the front, Pastors Zeisberger and Jungman, and Brother Davis sat in chairs behind the sturdy wooden table that held a brass candle holder and a large Bible. Sometimes John would sit in one of the three chairs. She missed seeing him there.

The candles on the walls and hanging from the ceiling weren't lit. They had meeting almost every morning but only lit candles when they had special nighttime services like the Christmas Eve Lovefeast taking place this evening.

In the middle pews, widows chattered away in the widow's choir, but one young Lenape girl, Rebecca, sat quietly. A beauty with narrow brown eyes, high cheekbones, and smooth bronze skin, she looked out of place among the older women.

Two of the widows, both white women, were at least twice Rebecca's age. Nobody knew the age of the third widow. Sister Mary was a Lenape who joined the Moravians when her children were young. The sagging skin covering her face, and the age spots and tired lines around her eyes and mouth showed that was many years ago.

Rebecca had left a nearby Lenape tribe, a year ago, when she married a native who had been with the Moravians since his youth. It was the first marriage to take place in the village.

A month later, she stood over her husband's grave. The elders urged her not to grieve over her husband since he had gone to be with his Lord. They urged her to move into the widows' cabin so they could take care of her.

Anna wasn't sure that was what was best. Rebecca was only nineteen years old and was required to lodge with women who had already lived their lives. How was she supposed to ignore her heartache and not grieve?

Losing a husband had to be hard. Anna couldn't imagine what it would be like to experience the pain of loss without John by her side to comfort and protect her.

Phoebe interrupted Anna's thoughts. "Are you well?" The Lenape woman spoke in English even though the Lenape language was spoken in church. She wanted to learn the language of the Moravians.

"Why wouldn't I be?" Anna answered her in English, and then turned to Belinda and spoke in Lenape. "Take your sisters to the children's choir and make sure they stay with you."

Belinda nodded and grabbed Katrina's hand.

Lisel crossed her arms. "Can't I sit with my friend, Deborah?"

"You'll sit with Belinda." Anna delivered her mama glower. "Last time you sat with Deborah, you talked during service."

Lisel's lower lip drooped.

"Go!"

Lisel abandoned her pout and followed Belinda and Katrina to the children's section in the back.

Anna and Phoebe took their seats on wooden benches on the left side in the married women's choir. Anna took Phoebe's hand. "Now tell me, why wouldn't I be well?"

"I heard Brother John and some others went to Gnadenhutten to meet with some Lenape warriors who showed up there."

"Yes, that is so."

"The tribal chief is with them." Phoebe looked at the floor. "Brother Paul's father."

Anna drew her hand to her mouth. "John didn't tell me." Heat flushed her face.

Brother Paul's father had disowned him when he became a Christian. "Why didn't he tell me?"

"This is a good thing." Phoebe swiped her tongue across her lips. "Brother Paul has a chance to tell his tribe about Christ."

Anna pressed her lips together and glanced at the painting of Jesus suffering on the cross. John should have told her. It wasn't the first time he had tried to shield her. They'd quarreled about it often. She told him how much harder it was not to worry when he hid the danger.

What if Brother Paul's father meant them harm? They could be abducted or killed.

Her stomach churned, and she placed her hand over it.

The bell rang once more, and service began.

As they sang the morning hymn, Anna tried to focus on the words, but her mind kept wandering to how John had deceived her about the peril he faced, danger brought to them by his new convert. What if something happened to him?

He had lied to her. Again.

After the hymn, Pastor Zeisberger stood to lead them in prayer. He said something about remembering the missionaries in Gnadenhutten and praying for the visiting Lenape tribe to convert, but Anna couldn't concentrate enough to form words to petition the Almighty.

Nausea rose within her, and she ran out the side door and toward the field to throw up. She wiped her mouth with her sleeve. If something happened to John, what would she do? She couldn't manage on her own with three children and one on the way.

They never should have come to Schoenbrunn Village.

Chapter Three

John sat at the sturdy wooden table with Brother Luke and Brother Paul drinking his coffee near the fireplace. The guest cabin in Gnadenhutten was larger than most, with a wood floor, two rooms on the lower level, and a loft where guests slept. When Sister Esther, their hostess, was there, she slept in the smaller room on the main floor that was just large enough for a straw mattress.

Esther, a widow in charge of hospitality in both villages, was in Schoenbrunn today to celebrate the Christmas Eve Lovefeast. She had another guest home there, but this cabin was always available.

Outside, behind the cabin, a large fire pit had been built, and a hog had been roasting on a spit since before dawn. A feast of roast pig, cornbread, cabbage, and boiled potatoes would be served to the Lenape tribal leaders when they arrived later today, as a gesture of good will. The aroma filled the cabin, making John's mouth water.

They had ashcakes for supper last night and hadn't had breakfast this morning. Esther wasn't there to cook and none of the men were gifted in womanly arts.

John's stomach growled, making him wish he'd taken time to sup before he'd left for Gnadenhutten. Anna was one of the best cooks in Schoenbrunn.

If only yesterday's meeting hadn't lasted so long, he could have made it home in time for supper. But everyone on the council had an opinion on how this meeting should be handled. In the end, they decided to allow Brother Paul to decide. John and Brother Luke would offer support where needed.

John moved his head in a circle to get the kinks out of his neck. Sleeping upstairs away from the fire, on a straw tick mattress with his two friends, didn't allow him a restful night. There weren't enough warm blankets, and he'd tossed and turned until the rooster crowed. He missed

ANNA'S CHRISTMAS PROMISE, Tamera Lynn Kraft

Anna sleeping by his side.

If his wife knew he didn't tell her everything, she would be angry, but he didn't want her to fret. Ever since they'd lost their son, Noah, she'd changed.

When they were courting, they would talk often about how God would use them in mighty ways if they yielded to His will. But now, fear and worry overwhelmed her more than her faith sustained her.

He didn't know how to help. When he hid the danger, she became indignant, as if he'd betrayed her trust, but he still found himself deceiving her to shield her from knowing the worst of the threat they faced. He had no choice. The truth would only make her anxious.

It was hard to lose a child. Even though it had been two years ago, it bothered him, too. More than he would admit.

Noah, their oldest, loved adventure and claimed that one day he would explore the wilderness beyond the Mississippi River and bring the Gospel to the natives there.

He'd been out with his Lenape friends, but they weren't to blame. They'd done everything they could.

Joseph, Noah's best friend, had told John what happened. They'd found a cave opening on a wooded hill near their village and climbed in. It was too dark to go much past the opening, but Noah had the idea of lighting a torch.

With torch in hand, he led Joseph and three other friends through a cavern to an opening where a stream fed the cave. Noah stepped closer, and the floor fell away. Joseph and the others used a rope to climb down the hole. When they reached the bottom, about ten feet deep, Noah was senseless. They couldn't wake him. They pulled him out, and after making a travois out of tree branches, carried him home.

Anna was so distraught it scared John. He'd never seen her like that before. He tried to reassure her that everything would be all right. He was so desperate to calm her that he promised Noah would recover even though he knew it was beyond his control. He prayed God would fulfill the oath he foolishly uttered, begged God to save his son. But two days later, it was the first of many promises he'd broken.

Noah never woke.

The Moravians called it "going home" and encouraged the congregation not to grieve. John was glad his son was in Heaven, but he couldn't manage not to be sad the boy wasn't still with him. Noah would have been twelve last month.

What made it even harder, Anna's parents had gone home two months earlier after succumbing to influenza. She didn't have their strength to help her through it.

She'd insisted she would give John another son, that somehow the

90

next child would make up for losing Noah. When she didn't get pregnant, she'd retreated into herself. She eventually came out of it, but the joy and faith that were once such vital parts of her were gone.

Before Noah died, Anna would never have refused to go to Ohio. She would have insisted on it. Sometimes John wondered if they should have stayed in Bethlehem, at least until she recovered from the loss.

Anna's grief didn't leave. Instead, it turned into fear that harm would come to John, or to another one of their children. She'd become overprotective and, since coming to Schoenbrunn, never left the girls alone. She always walked the children to school and church, and never let them play outside without her there to keep an eye out.

John swallowed another gulp of coffee. At this point, he wasn't sure she'd ever completely recover.

In a few hours, Brother Paul's father and some tribal elders would walk to the village, and the meeting would begin. Hopefully, it would be soon so John could get home in time for the Lovefeast. That would ease Anna's fears.

He glanced at his friends. Paul hadn't spoken two words since their three-hour trek to Gnadenhutten the night before. Always a man of few words, he seemed more stoic than usual.

"Brother Paul, help us know how to prepare to greet them," John said. "You're the one they requested to see."

"I should meet them outside the village." Paul stood and poked at the fire. "There's no reason to put you in danger."

Brother Luke leaned back in his chair and crossed his arms. "If you decide to do that, we'll go with you, so you might as well stay here."

A muscle in Paul's jaw twitched. "My father is not interested in converting to Christianity. He'll bring me back to the tribe, or he'll see me dead. No reason for you to follow me to my grave."

"Brother Luke is right." John took a gulp of coffee. "You're part of our family, now. We're staying with you. If it means we go home to be with our Lord, then God's will be done."

They were brave words, and John meant them. But he couldn't help but think of how Anna and the girls would fare if something happened to him.

Chapter Four

After dropping Belinda and Lisel off at school, Anna held tightly to Katrina's hand as she marched to the widow's cabin. She didn't know why she hadn't thought to ask for Rebecca's help before.

"Mama, I can't walk fast. My legs are too short."

She leaned down and kissed Katrina's cheek. "I'm sorry, child. Mama forgets, sometimes. But we're here, so you won't have to walk any further." She knocked on the door of one of the larger two-story cabins.

Sister Mary opened the door. "Sister Anna, it's so nice of you to visit. We don't get company too often. And you brought your little one with you." She pinched Katrina's cheek.

"Ow, that hurt."

"Katrina." Anna squeezed her daughter's shoulder.

"The child is right," Sister Mary said. "I do squeeze too hard." She leaned down to Katrina. "Would you like some sweet cornbread and milk?" Katrina nodded.

"Well then, come in." Sister Mary stood aside.

Anna and Katrina entered the cabin, but Rebecca didn't raise her eyes to greet Anna as she spun yarn at the spinning wheel in the corner.

The other widows made up for it with a flurry of activity that almost made Anna forget why she'd come. They all moved at once, preparing the table for their guests. Sister Berta poured milk, and Sister JoAnn sliced the cornbread, as Sister Mary got out tin plates and some butter they must have churned recently.

The spacious cabin had plenty of room for the large oak table and benches. The blazing fireplace warmed the home, already filled with plenty of kindness and hospitality. Sister Mary motioned Anna and Katrina to sit, but Rebecca didn't join them while they ate cornbread together.

Anna finished her milk and stood. "Ladies, would you mind watching Katrina while I talk to Sister Rebecca alone?"

"Not at all, my dear," Sister Mary said. "Why don't you two young ladies go in the other room for some privacy?"

Rebecca followed Anna quietly as if she were afraid her footsteps would unsettle the cabin and bring it to rubble if they were to be heard. The other room was where the widows slept. Two rope beds were on the wall near the window, and on the wall by the door rested a trunk and a small table where a pitcher of water and a wash basin sat. This room alone was as big as Anna's whole cabin. The elders made it a priority to take good care of the widows.

Anna sat on one of the beds and motioned Rebecca to join her. Rebecca eased beside her.

"I wanted to ask you something," Anna said.

Rebecca gazed at her with dark, round eyes, but said nothing.

"I've been assigned to provide the refreshments for the Christmas Lovefeast. I've heard you make the best coffee in the village. Could you make the coffee for the Lovefeast and help serve?"

Rebecca looked at her feet. "I don't know."

"I know you miss your husband."

"I do." Rebecca glanced up. "I miss him more than you can imagine."

"This might help. It would give you something to do."

"I miss Samuel." Rebecca bit her lip. "But I also miss home."

"I don't understand." Anna furrowed her brow. "You mean the cabin you and Brother Samuel lived in?"

"No. When I converted to Christianity and married, I moved away from my home, from my family, from the wigwam I grew up in, from the ways of the Lenape. I missed them, but I had Samuel. Then he died, and everything changed." She wiped her face. "I don't know why I'm here, living with women I hardly know, in a place that seems so strange in so many ways. I try, but it isn't home."

"If you feel that way, why don't you return to your family?"

"I can't. If I did, my father would marry me off to a Lenape warrior. I couldn't live as a Christian. My new husband wouldn't permit it."

"I'm so sorry." Anna placed her hand on Rebecca's.

"Sister Mary and the others try to help." She wiped a stray tear from her cheek. "And God is with me. He'll see me through this dark time."

"It would help to do something, to focus your thoughts on serving others instead of dwelling on your grief."

Rebecca's mouth turned up slightly. It wasn't exactly a grin, but it was closer to one than Anna had seen on her face since Samuel had died. "I'd love to serve the coffee."

Maybe if Rebecca could start to come out of this melancholy, there was hope for Anna to overcome the anxiety that plagued her.

Chapter Five

John stood among the men from the village who had gathered, waiting to share the feast with the visiting tribe. The women and children stayed in their cabins as a precaution.

His stomach fluttered as a dozen Lenape warriors, a medicine man, and Paul's father, chief of his tribe, marched into the village.

Chief Swantaney came in full attire. On his head was a beaded headdress with many eagle feathers pointed straight up. He wore a deerskin breechcloth, leggings and a fur mantle on his chest. Large rings hung from his ears, and a string of animal bones dangled around his neck.

John let out a silent prayer that the red and black paint around the chief's eyes was ceremonial and not a declaration of war.

Standing next to the chief, the Lenape medicine man wore a leather bag around his neck, a wampum belt around his waist, and a satchel over his shoulder. The warriors, with various designs of red and black paint on their faces, stood behind the chief.

A couple of men with bulging muscles carried cedar logs in their arms. When they stopped, they dumped the logs in a pile and rubbed their arms as if they'd carried them during the entire two-hour trek from their village.

None of the Moravians had guns. John had left his musket in the cabin. Weapons would have violated their determination to show the Lenape the love of Christ, but the delegates from the Lenape tribe had no such motivation. They carried tomahawks, knives, bows, and arrows.

A young Lenape warrior beat a cadence on his drum. It mixed with John's beating heart and intensified the trepidation he felt.

Chief Swantaney held up his hand. The drum stopped.

Brother Luke greeted the visitors as the head of the Moravian delegation. "Nulelìntâm èli paan. We are honored to have you visit our village."

The chief nodded but said nothing.

"We have prepared a roast pig. Please join us in a meal."

The Lenape waited and watched as the chief pinched his lips together. "We will eat."

John let out the breath he was holding. If the Lenape had refused the meal, it would have shown they had no desire to come to a peaceable conclusion with the Moravians. Eating with them was a good sign.

As the braves sat on the ground and waited to be served, John helped the Moravian elders serve food first to the chief, then to the medicine man, and then to the warriors.

Paul stood back from the delegation, leaned against a tree with his arms crossed, and watched with quiet fortitude, refusing any food offered to him. Few emotions ever showed on Paul's face, but John was fond of the man and could usually see through him.

The Lenape convert had been a warrior from his youth, and that didn't change when he became a Christian. He just decided to fight in a different war, a spiritual one.

John knew that Paul was determined to stand strong in the face of this challenge, but it was hard to go against one's father no matter what age he was.

They had conversations together during their Bible studies where Paul had asked how he could honor his father without denying his Lord.

John didn't have an answer, but he did have confidence that Paul would allow God to guide him. Even though Paul had only been a Christian a few months, John had never met a man who had surrendered his life more thoroughly to his Lord. That was why, when Paul was baptized, John recommended his new name. The change was as drastic as when the Apostle Paul had been confronted on the road to Damascus.

The feast was over, and the food was cleared away.

Luke stood and addressed Chief Swantaney and the Lenape warriors. "We are honored to have you visit our village. We understand you wish to discuss some things with us. We would also like to share good news with you. As our guests, we honor you and insist that you speak first."

"We will smoke the *hapakan* with the sacred *kshate* tobacco before we talk," the chief announced.

"Father, no," Paul said. "I no longer participate in the Fire of Peace, nor do I worship the Great Spirit *Kishelamakank*. I have a new God."

"Silence, Yaweha," the chief bellowed.

Paul, whose Lenape name was Yaweha, stepped back.

John pulled on his collar.

"Wait," Brother Luke said. "We will smoke the pipe with you as a gesture of goodwill, but we will only pray to our God." He placed a hand on Paul's arm but didn't look away from the chief. "Smoking the pipe does not mean we worship your gods but that we do seek peace between the Lenape and the Moravians."

Chief Swantaney turned to the strong warriors who had carried the logs. "Prepare the fire of peace."

The warriors built a fire pit using the cedar logs they'd carried into the village. It didn't take long before the fire blazed and warmed everyone standing around it. The medicine man pulled a long-stemmed pipe out of his satchel, lined it with sweet grass, and packed it with the tobacco from his pouch.

The chief pointed to the fire where he motioned them to sit in a circle.

John took a seat on one side of Paul, and Luke sat on the other. The other Moravians and natives filled in the circle. The cold ground under them made it hard to find a comfortable position.

Swantaney plopped down opposite Paul. The medicine man next to him lit the pipe and handed it to the chief. It was passed to each Lenape warrior, who took a puff, and then to each Moravian. When the pipe reached Paul, he glared at it.

John held his breath. Paul was not known for his patient compliance, but this was not the time to offend the chief by refusing to take part. He'd already dishonored them enough by not partaking in the meal with them.

One Lenape warrior placed his hand on his knife. Nobody spoke as everyone stared at Paul, and for a moment, it seemed that even breathing had stopped.

Paul's jaw clenched as he took a puff and handed the pipe to John.

John smoked the pipe and let the smoke escape his nose and mouth as he squelched the urge to cough. Moravians didn't believe in polluting their bodies with tobacco, but they did partake of the peace pipe when the

Lenape leaders insisted. Not to do so insulted the Lenape before a word of the Gospel was spoken.

After the peace pipe was laid aside, Chief Swantaney stood. "As you know, we, the Lenni Lenape, serve *Kishelamakank*, the Great Spirit. He is our god and has sent us nature spirits to guide us." The chief moved his arms and spoke in a clear, loud voice. He was a good orator. "My only son has offended the Great Spirit and embraces the religion of the white man. Is that not so?"

"Yes, Father," Paul said. "But I have not rejected you, or our people. I am Lenni Lenape."

"Not true." Swantaney pointed at his son. "The great prophet Neolin warned *Kishelamakank* would not be pleased if we turn from the Lenape traditions to the ways of the white man. Son, you have done that, as have all the Lenape who have turned away from their heritage to join the Moravian tribe. Your soul is in danger, and I will allow this no longer."

A murmur traveled through both delegations.

The noise stopped when Paul stood and faced his father. "I am the son of a chief. That hasn't changed. But you know how troubled I was after disease killed many from our tribe, my wife, my son—your grandson."

Chief Swantaney crossed his arms. "All the more reason to pray to the Great Spirit."

Paul wiped his hand over his face. "I did pray to the Great Spirit, and I watched the medicine man do everything he could to stop the plague, but they still died, along with many strong warriors." His jaw set, he turned slowly, looking at each brave. "I needed to know the truth. If the Great Spirit allowed this to happen for a reason, I would accept it as his will, but I needed to be sure. I decided to go on a spirit quest until I had an answer." He turned to his father. "I left with your blessing and was gone for many moons on this quest." He locked eyes with the medicine man. "I vowed to not return until I had a revelation from the One True Master of Life, the only God."

"No." Swantaney stood. "If your revelation was true, you would not have rejected *Kishelamakank* and our people."

"Father, you did not see my vision. It was from the one true God. He spoke from a bush that burned, but was not consumed, as He did to the prophet, Moses, written about in God's book. He told me to go to the Moravian tribe; that they would tell me how His Son died to save me, and that they would teach me His ways."

"You will return to the tribe and embrace the traditions."

"No, Father." Paul crossed his arms and glared at the fire. "I will not reject my Lord now that He has shown me the truth."

"Think carefully." Swantaney gazed into his son's eyes. "If you do not return with us within a moon, we will make war with the Moravian tribe."

A gasp escaped John's lips.

Chapter Six

Anna tried to ignore the dread welling up inside of her as she started home with Katrina. She was glad she went to visit the widows' cabin and asked Rebecca to be one of the Dieners, but it reminded her how quickly everything could be taken away, how easily she could lose her husband, or another child.

Before she left, she'd convinced Rebecca to sup with them on Sunday. Somehow, Anna hoped she could help by befriending the young widow.

Katrina held up her hands to be carried.

"You're a big girl. You must walk."

"Mama, carry me."

Normally Anna would have insisted. Being strict, but kind, was the best way to help her daughters mature into godly women, but she didn't have the energy or the heart to argue. "Just this once." She picked up Katrina and carried her home.

When they stepped into the cabin, Anna sat in the rocker and hugged her youngest daughter tight, too tight, afraid to let her go.

"Mama, you're squishing me."

Anna set Katrina down. "My pardon." She wiped her eyes.

"Mama, are you sad?"

"I'm all right, little one," Anna said, hoping Katrina wouldn't see through the lie. "I miss your papa."

"Me, too," Katrina said.

Work would keep the anxious thoughts away, and Anna needed to get busy if she would be ready for Christmas. She needed to bake more sweet buns and had planned to make a squash pie for dessert, John's favorite. When she'd spent a whole week boiling maple syrup to form sugar crystals for the sweet buns, she made sure she had enough for the pie and to sweeten the cornbread.

The main dish would be a problem. John had no time to hunt a pheasant or wild turkey for Christmas dinner, so she would need to serve maple-cured ham or kill one of the chickens. They'd had their fill of ham, but she only had a couple of chickens, and she hated losing one of her egg-layers. Ham would have to do.

Before she started, she needed to bring more water up from the creek. While grabbing the water pails off the shelf, she heard a rustling sound behind her.

She turned in time to see Katrina climbing halfway up the tottering

Christmas tree. She pulled her daughter back right before the wood frame, boughs, and candles crashed to the ground.

Katrina sobbed.

Anna pulled her youngest daughter into her arms. "Shhh, hush now." She trembled as Katrina wailed. Her chest felt as if the wooden frame had fallen on it.

Katrina could have been killed.

~~~~~

"Chief Swantaney." John stood and faced him. "Brother Paul, Yaweha, is your son, even if he chooses to live away from his people. Will you not listen to his words before you decide to war against his friends?"

The chief crossed his arms and said nothing. None of the other men, native or Moravian, seemed to want to be the first to break the silence.

Paul stared at the fire, his jaw clenched.

John cleared his throat. "Chief Swantaney." Paul grabbed his arm, but he pulled it away. "I too have lost a son, but my son died. You still have yours, even if he doesn't share your beliefs."

"My son might as well be buried, as my grandson was." Chief Swantaney hunched his shoulders. "Who will take my place when I join my ancestors in death? I have no son or grandson to become chief and lead our tribe."

Luke cleared his throat. "I am Lenape, and I have lived with the Moravians for many years. They are friends to the Lenape. They mean no harm to you. Your son has made the decision to stay with us."

"Because you deceived him, with your talk of a Son of God. The Great Spirit has no sons."

"No, Father," Paul said. "I was not deceived. I chose to become a Christian and give my allegiance to God. Will you not hear me?"

Chief Swantaney sat at the fire and nodded. "I will listen."

The other braves sat around him, and Paul moved to the center. He set forth the Gospel message and how he came to know the truth.

John gazed at the men. Some jutted out their chins. But Chief Swantaney gave no indication what his response would be. He prayed God would give Paul wisdom as he spoke.

A few braves leaned forward. One man nodded.

Paul ended with a passionate plea for the braves and his father to come to know Christ.

Some of the braves looked visibly shaken. The one who nodded his head stood. He looked like he might say something but glanced toward the chief and swallowed any words he was tempted to utter.

Paul's father stood. "I will consider what my son has said. Tomorrow, we will meet again. I will let you know my decision, then." He marched out of the village with the braves following him. The man who stood looked toward Paul, even took a step in his direction, paused, and then ran off to join the others.

John swallowed the lump in his throat. Tomorrow was Christmas Day. He wouldn't be home in time.

Chapter Seven

As Anna led her children on the path to the church, she kept her gaze focused outside of town. An inch of snow had covered the ground, but it wasn't as bad as they were expecting. The snowstorm fizzled into light flurries.

They reached the church, and she took one last look before they entered. No sign of the men. She bit her lower lip. John had said he might not be back in time.

The lit candles gave the room a warm glow. A blazing fire in the fireplace added to the mood.

Anna ushered the girls to the children's choir and set the baskets of sweet buns on the wooden table in front. Rebecca had already arrived with the pot of coffee she'd made, and Phoebe had provided a pitcher of juice for the children.

She joined Phoebe and Rebecca on the bench in the front in the married women's choir facing the congregation. Even though Rebecca's place was in the widow's choir, since she volunteered to make the coffee and be a Diener, nobody minded this breach of tradition. Anna was glad Rebecca decided to help. It seemed to lighten her mood to know she could be of service.

The meeting opened with Pastor Zeisberger reading the Scripture in the book of Matthew about Jesus's birth. He went on to say how Jesus's birth was a promise that God would always be with the people of this world. That was why He was called Emanuel.

All Anna could think of was John's promise to be home for Christmas. She glanced toward the door. No sign of her husband.

Pastor Zeisberger prayed over the meal, and Anna joined the Dieners in serving the sweet buns and pouring the coffee and juice. When all were served, she returned to the bench to enjoy the meal with Phoebe and Rebecca.

As she took a bite of bun, she squelched the nausea rising in her stomach. The morning sickness didn't normally affect her this late at night, but worry would sometimes cause it to flare up. She tried not to fret, but all she could think about was the child growing inside of her. If something happened to John, he'd never know she was expecting. She could finally give him another son, although they could never replace the son they'd lost. Maybe she should have told him before he left. She might have if he'd told her the truth about the danger he faced.

Anna chided herself for pondering all the bad things that could occur. Nothing would happen. John promised he'd be back for Christmas. She glanced again toward the back where the door stayed firmly shut.

After sharing the meal together, they were instructed to pray for one another.

Anna set her tin cup on the floor. "Why don't you go first, Phoebe? How would you like us to pray?"

"I'm with child." Phoebe's eyes watered, but she brushed the tears away. This was the third time since they came to Schoenbrunn Village that Phoebe was expecting. She'd only carried one child until it was ready to be birthed, the stillborn boy buried in God's Acre.

"That's wonderful news," Anna said. They prayed for Phoebe's child to be born healthy and full-term.

Rebecca spoke next. "I lack faith. I need to trust God's grace to get me through this lonely time and to provide me with a Christian husband. I miss Samuel, and I miss my home. Sometimes at night, I can't stop crying."

Anna swallowed as she remembered grieving for Noah. If she hadn't had John when Noah died…she cleared her throat and prayed for Rebecca.

Phoebe placed her hand on Anna's arm. "How would you like us to pray?"

She glanced at the door even though she promised herself she wouldn't keep looking for John. "I am well."

Phoebe raised an eyebrow.

"Really," Anna said. "I need no prayers. My husband and children are healthy, and we had a good crop this year. God is good."

"God is good, Sister Anna," Phoebe said. "But one of His greatest gifts is a community of believers who pray for one another. So give us your request."

Heat rushed to Anna's face. She couldn't say it, couldn't allow herself to think that things might go wrong in Gnadenhutten. "I told you, I am well."

Rebecca wrapped her arm around Anna. "Do you think we are so easily deceived? Your eyes are puffy from crying, and your face is as red as mine. We are sisters in Christ. Let us be there for you, as you have helped us in time of need."

Anna blinked to keep her tears from being shed. She'd planned to comfort Rebecca. Instead, Rebecca was helping her through this. "Pray for my husband's safety." She swallowed. "And for God to move among Brother Paul's tribe."

"Lord," Phoebe prayed, "keep Brother John and those with him safe until they return and make their mission fruitful with many converts."

A tear rolled out of Anna's right eye. She wiped it away.

"And keep Sister Anna in Your peace as she goes through this dark night," Rebecca prayed. "Let her know she has sisters in Christ to rely upon and that You promised to always be with her, that You are God with us."

The lump in Anna's throat threatened to choke her. Promises had a way of being broken. This last one had to be different. She couldn't lose John. She glanced toward the closed door.

He'd make it. He'd keep his promise this time.

Brother Davis passed pure beeswax candles with red ribbons tied around them to everyone in the congregation, including the children.

Pastor Jungman lit the candles with a flintlock tinder lighter.

A choir of children, including Belinda and Lisel, came forward to lead the singing of *Morning Star, O Cheering Light*.

This was always Anna's favorite part of the Christmas Eve Lovefeast, but somehow the words in the last verse struck her like never before. "Morning Star, my soul's true light, tarry not, dispel my night."

She willed the door to open as she prayed for Jesus to tarry not in dispelling her night. The only way that could happen would be for her husband to come home—safe—and fulfill his promise to her.

More hymns were sung, Scriptures were passed out to the children, and the doors in the back of the church opened, not to let John in, but because the Christmas Eve Lovefeast had come to an end.

Anna hugged Phoebe and Rebecca and headed toward the children's choir. Before she made her way to the back, Pastor Jungman and his wife, Sister Margaret, approached her.

Pastor Jungman taught the girls at the village school and always had a kind word when she went to fetch them. "With Brother John gone, I thought you might be in need of meat for your Christmas supper. I shot a pheasant and a wild turkey today."

"It's too much for our family," Sister Margaret said. "You'd be doing us a favor by taking the pheasant off our hands."

Anna blushed. Were they helping her because Pastor knew the danger John was in? Did they already consider her a widow? "Thank you. It would be a godsend."

So, this was what she had to look forward to, the men of the village taking care of her as they did Rebecca and the other widows. But if something happened to John, Anna had young children. She wouldn't live in the widows' cabin.

She would be alone.

"I'll bring it by tonight," Pastor Jungman said.

"If there's anything else we can do to help," Sister Margaret said, "you send Belinda to fetch us." She placed her hand on Anna's. "Don't worry. The men will be home in the morning. Gnadenhutten is only a three-hour walk. God is good. All will be well."

"All will be well." Anna tried to keep the catch out of her voice but failed.

The Jungmans pretended they didn't notice and excused themselves. Anna collected the children and walked home. She peered into the night but couldn't see any images in the distance that looked like men returning to the village.

Lisel skipped ahead and was swallowed up in the fog.

Anna's heart raced as she picked up Katrina and ran to catch up. When she reached Lisel, she set Katrina down and swatted Lisel's bottom. "I warned you not to run ahead. Do you want a savage to grab you, and take you away?"

Lisel's bottom lip quivered, and tears fell from her eyes.

Anna swallowed the lump in her throat. She'd never spanked the girls before. They'd always disciplined in other ways. "Lisel."

Lisel sobbed.

"I'm sorry." Anna hugged her daughter. "I love you. I don't want anything to happen to you. Do you understand?"

Lisel wiped her face and nodded.

"Good. Now let's get home so we can prepare for Christmas."

"I'm sorry, Mama."

"I forgive you." Anna wiped Lisel's tears away with her sleeve.

Lisel grabbed hold of her hand, and they headed to the cabin. After entering, she paused to latch the door. Without John home, she felt safer with the entrance locked.

The children rushed to the tree to hang their candles and Scriptures. Belinda set her candle on the highest beam. After Anna lit them, the girls stood and admired them. Lisel's eyes widened at the sight.

A knock sounded, and Anna ran to the door. John had kept his promise. She unlatched it and threw it open.

Pastor Jungman stood there holding a pheasant in the air.

Anna placed a hand over her stomach and tried to tamp down the disappointment.

"I wanted to bring it over tonight so you'd have plenty of time to prepare it tomorrow. I know how Brother John likes his fowl well done."

"Thank you kindly, Pastor Jungman." She grabbed the pheasant and set it on the table. It was heavy enough to land with a thud.

"Pastor Jungman." Lisel grabbed his hand and pulled him into the cabin. "See our tree. Isn't it wonderful?"

Pastor Jungman patted Lisel on the head. "You have a very fine tree.

Your papa will be pleased when he returns."

Anna tucked a stray curl into her *Habba*. "Would you like to stay for coffee or sweet buns?"

"Thank you, no. My wife and children are waiting for me to light the candles on our tree." He turned to go.

Anna stirred up the courage to ask. "Have you heard word from Gnadenhutten?"

Brother Jungman turned. He had compassion in his eyes, or was it pity? "No word, yet. But take heart. I'm sure it took longer than they expected. That's why they're not home. Brother John and the others will make an early start in the morning. You'll see. They'll be home by midday, just in time for Christmas supper." Brother Jungman opened the door and paused. "Sister Margaret and I will pray for your husband's safe return." He closed the door behind him.

It made the same thud as when John left.

"Can I put Baby Jesus in the manger?" Katrina asked.

Anna nodded. She hated John not being home for this. Katrina carefully placed the Baby Jesus pinecone in the manger.

"Mama," Belinda said, "can we keep the candles lit until we slumber?"

"As long as you go to sleep right away."

"We will," Lisel said. "Will Papa be home early?"

Anna turned away. "I don't know." She let out a breath and faced her children. "Perchance he'll be here when you wake up. Now, to bed, all of you."

The children prepared for bed and crawled onto their straw tick. Anna kissed them each goodnight. She draped a cloth around herself, dipped the pheasant in a pot of boiling water to loosen the feathers, and settled in the rocker with the bird in her lap. While plucking feathers, she watched the girls sleep under the flicker of candlelight. When the pheasant had been stripped and the feathers had been gathered in a sack to be cleaned later, Anna placed the bird in cold salt water to draw out the rest of the blood.

Katrina let out a soft snore, and Anna blew out the candles, but she couldn't sleep, not yet. She stepped outside and watched the road.

The moon shone brightly against the blanket of snow covering the ground. It was a clear night. She could see the Big Dipper and the North Star. If John was on his way home, he'd be facing north. He would see it, too. The wind whipped around Anna, causing her to shiver. She needed to go inside to bed.

Tomorrow was Christmas.

John promised to be home.

Chapter Eight

John spun to the left, batted the pillow, twisted to the right. Luke snored beside him. It sounded like the snorting of the pig he'd butchered so his family could have meat this winter. The grunting of Luke's snores and waiting for Paul to come to bed made it impossible for John to sleep. At least, those were the excuses he told himself.

He sat on the side of the bed and looked out the small window at the foot of the loft. The North Star shone brightly. That was the direction he should have been heading this evening, north toward Schoenbrunn Village, toward Anna and the children, but instead, he was stuck here for one more evening while Chief Swantaney decided what to do.

Another broken promise.

Thirteen years ago, he and Anna had watched the North Star on another Christmas Eve.

After another Lovefeast in Bethlehem, Pennsylvania, Brother Radul, Anna's father, invited John to come to their home to share a meal with them. That wasn't the real purpose for the visit. John had asked him for his daughter's hand in marriage. Brother Radul seemed pleased by the prospect.

John asked Anna to walk with him, and she said she would. They strolled along the banks of the Lehigh River and stopped near a white oak tree. It hadn't snowed since Thanksgiving, and the tree was barren, but its orange leaves crunched under their feet as they walked.

The clear sky displayed too many stars to count.

John pointed to the north. "There's the Big Dipper, and that's the North Star."

A brisk wind gusted, and Anna pulled her cloak in tight. John wrapped an arm around her.

She leaned her head onto his shoulder. "The stars are beautiful tonight."

"I was lost in the forest once." John gazed at the North Star. "It was on a hunting trip, and I'd traveled too far away from the village. I was able to find my way home following that star."

"It reminds me of God's Word," Anna said. "At times, we may lose our way, but just like the North Star, God's Word will guide us home."

John pulled back. Anna's dark, round eyes gazed at him in the moonlight, and the brown curls trying to poke their way out of her *Habba* gave him pause at the wonder of this night, this perfect moment. "I have something to say." He swallowed hard. The words wouldn't come.

"Brother John, I would hope by now you know you can converse with me about anything."

"Yes." John wiped his face with his handkerchief. "That's why I want to ask you…" He took her hands in his, and a tingle traveled up his arm. "Anna, will you marry me?"

"I have a fond affection for you, John Brunner. That I can't deny." She drew her hand away. "But I need a promise from you before I commit to pledging my troth."

John's heart beat faster. "I don't understand."

"Promise me that our lives will be spent advancing the Kingdom of God and sharing the Gospel with the Lenape, no matter what the cost. Do that, or no matter how deep my affection for you, our nuptials will never take place."

John cleared his throat. "Have I ever given you cause to believe I would want otherwise?"

Anna gave a half smile. "I've never known a man who serves our Lord with more fervor than you." She lowered her eyes. "Except maybe my father. I've often hoped you would speak of marriage with me. But I made a vow to our Lord that I would only marry a man who would pledge thus."

John placed a hand on his chest. "I promise that our lives will be spent serving the Lord and spreading the Gospel to the Lenape."

"Then my answer is yes. I shall marry you."

~~~~~

John had broken so many promises to Anna since then. He gave his word Noah wouldn't die, and that they'd be safe if they moved to Schoenbrunn Village. Not arriving home in time for Christmas would be one more shattered pledge. But he didn't break his first vow to her, and he never would.

He climbed down the ladder to the main room. If he wasn't going to sleep, he might as well provide companionship to Paul and stay close to the fireplace where it was warm. It was so cold in that loft that sleeping there wasn't much better than pitching a tent outside.

Paul sat with his legs crossed on the floor near the fireplace, staring at the Bible open in his lap.

John hesitated to interrupt him if he was spending time with God and started back up the ladder.

"You're not disturbing me," Paul said without looking up from the book. "I desire your fellowship…and your guidance."

John sat on the floor next to Paul and spread his hands in front of the fire to warm them.

"I've been reading about my namesake, the Apostle Paul." Paul looked up and closed his Bible. "He didn't let anything stop him from spreading the Good News of Jesus Christ."

"That's true," John said, not sure where the conversation was headed.

"I've done some wrong in my life. When I was a warrior, I raided villages, stole livestock and horses, killed people. Not just from tribes we were at war with." His Adam's apple bulged. "I've murdered Christians."

"I know." They'd talked about this before. Although most Lenape tribes were peaceful, Paul's tribe often plundered other tribes and villages. John had often assured Paul he was forgiven.

"Paul did the same thing. He persecuted the church. He even says he was the worst of sinners."

John didn't say anything.

"Yet he didn't let anything dissuade him from sharing the Gospel. He was beaten, imprisoned, shipwrecked, chained. Nothing stopped him."

"That's true."

Paul's jaw twitched. "He willingly was arrested and sent to Rome as a prisoner to fulfill his goal to convert the Romans."

"I'm not sure what you're trying to say," John said.

"Did you see the faces of some of the braves yesterday? After I spoke to them?"

"They seemed touched by your words."

Paul stood and poked the fire. "I would do anything to deliver to Christ the reward of His suffering by sharing the Gospel with the young braves of my tribe, to convert my own people."

John's breath caught. "What are you thinking?" He stood. "You can't go back there."

Paul leaned one arm against the fireplace. "I haven't decided what I'm going to do."

John grabbed Paul's arm. "You can't do it. Your father would never let you practice your Christian faith. And what happens if your tribe raids another village? You would be required to don war paint and take part."

Paul pulled his arm away and shrugged. "I would never do that. I've given my allegiance to God. I won't go back to the old ways."

"Then you're putting your life in danger."

Paul's chin jutted. "So did the Apostle Paul."

"Without the Moravians' fellowship, you would have to choose between going back to your sinful ways or death." John wiped his hand across the back of his neck. "All of the ways of your people will be calling you to the life you once lived. You won't have brothers in the faith to go to for advice or admonishment. You'll be on your own."

"Weren't you listening, tonight?"

"I don't know what you mean."

"The verse they quoted at the Lovefeast. You know I have a good memory. I can quote it if you'd like."

"I know the verse."

Paul grinned. "I'm still going to quote it. Matthew 1:23 says, 'Behold, a virgin shall be with child, and shall bring forth a son, and they shall call his name Emmanuel, which being interpreted is, God with us.'"

John let out a sigh. "God with us."

"So wherever I go, I won't be alone. That isn't the only verse where Christ promised He will always be with me. There are many more. If you like, I could quote them."

"I thought your ability to instantly memorize the written and spoken word was a good thing, but now you're using it against me."

"Don't you think God gifted me with that ability for a reason? Perchance He knew I would need to learn the written language of the Lenape in a short time so I could bring God's Word to my own tribe."

"Being able to read the Bible and memorize Scripture doesn't qualify you for this." John locked his gaze on Paul, hoping to show him how earnest he was. "You're new in the faith, and you'll be subjecting yourself to the same sins that were a big part of your life before. Even if God is with you, your Christian brothers and sisters won't be. You won't have anyone there to pray for you."

"You'll pray for me."

"But there won't be any more experienced brothers to help you when you get into trouble. I'm against this."

Paul spread his feet into a wide stance and squared his shoulders. "I had hoped you would take this to the elders with me. I plan to talk to them before we meet with my father."

"I'll go with you. But if they ask my judgment, I'll tell them what I told you."

"Even if you don't agree," Paul said, "you've been a good friend."

"I'm honored to be your friend."

"So tell me, friend, why are you awake at this hour? You're not just concerned about me."

John pressed his lips together. "We might not be home for Christmas."

"I know you would like to be home with your family, but under the circumstances, Sister Anna will understand."

Guilt lodged in his throat. "I haven't exactly been truthful with her."

"You lied to her?"

"Not exactly. I told her we were coming here to share the Gospel with a delegation of Lenape. That part's true." Heat flushed John's face. He had lied no matter how much he tried to justify it.

Paul stared at the fire. "You didn't tell her that my father was part of that delegation?"

"No." John lowered his eyes.

"You deceived her."

He swallowed back the lump in his throat. "Yes."

107

"Isn't that lying?"

At that moment, John felt more like a chastened boy than the man who had mentored many Lenape. "It's worse than that. I promised her I would be home for Christmas."

Paul delivered a scorching glare. "Why would you disdain your wife like that?"

"It's not disdain." John cleared his throat. "I told you about my son, Noah. Since he died, Anna's been different. She worries about everything and is frightened easily. I wanted to make things easier for her."

"By lying to her?"

He stared at his hands. "I was trying to help her."

"No, you just didn't want to have to help her with her fears. You hid the danger to avoid the problem."

John felt like he'd been hit in the gut. Was he lying only to make things easier for himself?

Paul sat down beside him. "Brother John, you've been a good mentor to me. I know I haven't been a Christian for long, but if I struggled with worry and doubt, what would you do?"

"That's different. You're not my wife."

"Still. What would you do?"

"I would pray for you, and I would admonish you to read Scripture and to trust God to help you through it."

"Sound counsel. Maybe that's what you should do for your wife. I would do anything to go back and be able to lead my wife to trust Christ." Paul headed to the ladder. "I'm going to bed."

John watched him climb into the loft and out of sight. He poked the fire, poured himself a cup of coffee that had been brewing on the cinders for too long, and wrapped his hands around the cup to warm them.

He'd disappointed Anna, and tomorrow, when he showed up late, it would be one more broken promise.

God, forgive me. Give me guidance.

When he returned home, he would do everything he could to help restore his wife's faith in God. He would stop making empty promises to keep her fears at bay. He could see now he was only destroying her trust in him.

With God's help, this would be the last time he failed his wife.

Chapter Nine

Anna rose while it was still dark. She stretched, stoked the fire, dressed, and placed the pheasant on the spit over the fireplace to cook. She was grateful for a few moments to herself before the children woke.

Her husband wasn't home yet. He hadn't arrived in the middle of the night like she'd hoped, but now she realized how foolish it had been to expect that. If the meetings with Brother Paul's father lasted late, it was more likely for the men to start out at dawn than to try to traipse the forest at night. It was a three-hour trek in good weather. With the snow, it might take more.

He would surely be home by noonday. They could read the Scriptures hanging on the tree before Christmas Supper. The only things he would miss were the morning preparations and breakfast, maybe the noon meal.

They could still have a wonderful Christmas together.

She promised herself it would be the best Christmas ever. It would be hard to have a better one than when John proposed marriage, but when she told him about the child growing inside her, that would make it almost perfect.

This time she would give him another son.

That first Christmas beside the Lehigh River was so special. Anna wished she had the courage and faith she did then, when she wanted to spend her life with a man who would risk everything to serve God. It had been the promise John had kept, but she hadn't been as faithful.

The rooster crowed as the dawn peeked through the window.

Lisel jumped out of bed first. "It's Christmas. It's Christmas." She shook Belinda and Katrina.

Neither of them seemed vexed for being awakened so brusquely.

Katrina wiped her eyes.

"Can we play with the Putz first, Mama?" Lisel asked. "Can we?"

Anna took a deep breath in through her nose and let it out through her mouth. She wouldn't let on that she was worried. John would be home by noon, and the girls would never know the danger he faced — or that this Christmas was different than any other.

She tied on her apron. "Morning chores and breakfast, first. And all of you get dressed this instant."

The girls finished their chores faster than they normally did. Even Lisel didn't dawdle. By the time Anna finished cooking bacon and eggs, the girls had set the table.

"Mama," Belinda said as they sat on the benches, "where's Papa? He said he'd be home by Christmas."

"He promised." Lisel's lower lip drooped.

"He'll be here," Anna said, working to exude a confidence she didn't feel. "It takes time, and he probably waited until this morning to start. I'm sure he'll be home soon."

That seemed to satisfy the girls. They held hands, and Anna offered the blessing. Before she could say amen, Belinda interrupted. "Lord, protect Papa and bring him home safe."

"And help Mama to stop worrying," Lisel prayed.

"Amen."

Anna cleared her throat. "Amen."

~~~~~

It was almost noon before Swantaney and his tribal leaders showed up. John tried to figure out what the chief's answer would be by the look on his face, but it did no good. The man was as stoic as his son.

Paul was easier to decipher, especially after the conversation last night, and the meeting with the elders early this morning. Luke agreed with Paul, and despite John's reluctance, the council believed Paul was hearing from God, and that if the chief required him to return to the tribe, they would support whatever he chose to do, provided he followed guidelines they laid out and kept in contact with the Moravian council in Schoenbrunn.

Paul's squared shoulders and jutted chin showed he'd made his decision.

If there was a way to change this, John would do it, but sometimes, he couldn't protect the people he cared about. Sometimes he had to leave them in God's hands. All he could do was pray and hope the chief didn't force the issue.

Brother Luke greeted Chief Swantaney.

"I have a decree to make." Swantaney strode to Paul.

The warriors around him gripped their spears with a firmness that had been lacking yesterday. Not a good sign.

Not at all.

The chief glared into his eyes. "Yaweha, you will return home where you belong, and you will forget about this white man's religion. You are Lenape, the son of a chief. It's time you act like it."

"Father." Paul's posture straightened, until it looked as if he'd added a couple of inches to his height. "I, too, have made a decision."

The chief crossed his arms. "Go ahead."

"I will return to the tribe."

A low murmur rushed through the crowd.

"Silence." Chief Swantaney lifted his hand.

The noise stopped.

"It is good, my son. You have made the right choice."

Paul's jaw twitched. "You have only heard part of it."

Chief Swantaney backed up two steps. Sweat beaded his forehead. "Tell me. Now!"

"I meant what I said."

John glanced at the warriors behind the chief, the ones gripping their spears.

"I shall return, and I shall become the next chief." Paul cleared his throat. "But no matter where I am, whether in the Moravian village, or in the Lenape tribe, I serve only one God, the God of the Christians."

The chief's Adam's apple bulged. Two warriors took a couple of steps closer and stood on either side of the chief, gripping their spears with both hands.

John shifted his weight as the muscles in his chest tightened. If they made a move, he'd defend his friend no matter what the cost. For now, all he could do was watch.

"Father, I will not fight you or your men." Paul shifted his position into a wide stance and held his hands out with his palms open. "If you wish to have me killed, I will make it easy for your braves. I will not resist."

Heat traveled up John's back. For a cold day, he felt unusually warm.

"But if you allow me to return to the tribe, I will share my new faith with the other braves. I will convert as many as I can, and I will bring my Bible with me, God's Word written in the Lenape tongue that the Moravians have taught me to read. Those are my conditions."

Nobody said anything.

Paul crossed his arms as if nothing more needed to be said.

Chief Swantaney's face turned red. "I am the chief and your father. You dare tell me your conditions!"

"And I am a grown man, the son of a chief, and a Lenape warrior." Paul stepped toward his father and placed a hand on his shoulder. "I will not denounce my God, but I'm still your son."

The other warriors readied their weapons.

The Moravian men moved back, respecting Paul's decision to offer no resistance.

John couldn't bring himself to do so and took a couple of steps forward until he stood beside Paul. He couldn't stand by and not do anything.

The braves' glances shifted from Chief Swantaney to Paul, and then back to the chief.

A chill filled the air as a gust of wind blew through. Snowflakes fell from the sky. Everybody waited.

Chief Swantaney spoke. "My son, you have given me your conditions. Here are mine."

Chapter Ten

The smell of pheasant filled the cabin as it roasted on the spit. Anna cut up potatoes, slipped with the knife, and sliced the tip of her finger.

Holding it tightly in her apron, she blinked back the moisture filling her eyes, and dumped the potatoes into the iron pot.

The girls hadn't asked about their father, but as the day went on, they grew more subdued. At the noon meal, they hadn't chattered on about the day. Even Lisel didn't want to play with the Putz anymore, and Katrina didn't fight sleep when Anna made her lie on the rope bed and take a nap. When Katrina finally woke, it was an hour until Christmas supper, and John still wasn't home.

Anna glanced out the window. Clouds darkened the sky and obscured the sun. The winter storm had finally arrived in full force, and white gusts filled the air and blanketed the ground. If John hadn't left before the storm started, he would be trapped in Gnadenhutten—if nothing had happened to him. Her stomach knotted, and an overwhelming dread fell on her as dark as the snow clouds outside. She couldn't see the light of God's love through it.

Please, Lord, restore my faith in You.

Now that all the preparations had been made, it was time to gather around the tree. Usually, John would read the Scriptures hanging on it. It was a treat to see what verses held special meaning to each of them and the girls that year. Except this time, all the Scriptures had been written by Belinda, or given to them by the church. Anna couldn't bring herself to write out any, and Lisel didn't ask her to write the verses she'd learned in school. She was too busy with the Putz.

"It's time to read the Scriptures," Anna announced. She needed to follow the traditions of her family or she would...she couldn't bring herself to think that this might be the last normal Christmas—or maybe, not so normal. She blinked and wiped her face on her apron as the children gathered around the tree.

"Papa normally reads them," Belinda said.

"Belinda, you're the oldest. Why don't you do it this year?" Anna couldn't keep the catch out of her voice.

"Mama." The whine in Lisel's voice was gone. She sounded calm, composed, maybe too calm. "When's Papa coming home?"

"I don't know." A sob came from deep inside Anna, and she couldn't hold it back. She slumped into the rocker by the fireplace.

Lisel and Katrina climbed into her lap. Lisel wrapped her arms around Anna as far as they could reach.

Tears filled Katrina's eyes. "Don't cry Mama." She patted Anna's arm. "Don't cry."

Belinda stood behind her and hugged her from the back.

"Come here." Anna pulled Belinda around and scooted Katrina over so Belinda could have room in the chair.

Belinda cautiously sat. "The chair will break."

Anna wrapped her arms around her girls. "I don't care. I want to hold you, all of you." They sat hugging each other and allowing tears to flow freely. Anna wiped her eyes. "That's enough. No more tears. I don't know when Papa will be home, but we're going to celebrate Christmas. Whatever happens, God will see us through."

"Mama." Belinda stood and walked to the tree. "Shall I read the verses, now?"

Anna blew her nose and pulled Lisel and Katrina closer. "Yes, Belinda. Go ahead."

Belinda pulled the paper off nearest to the top. "This one's my favorite Christmas verse." She read it out loud. "Matthew 1:23. Behold, a virgin shall be with child, and shall bring forth a son, and they shall call his name Emmanuel, which being interpreted is, God with us."

"Why is it your favorite, Belinda?"

"I know Jesus has always been God, but when He was born, He became God with us. His name even means God with us. And He'll be with us forever. This year I wrote out the verses where Jesus promised to be with us and to help us."

Lisel laid her head on Anna's shoulder. "Is Jesus with us even when Papa isn't?"

"Yes, child. And He's with your papa, too." A lump formed in Anna's throat. "Belinda, read another promise."

Belinda pulled off another verse and cleared her throat. "John 14:7 says, 'Peace I leave with you. My peace I give you.'"

Anna's oldest daughter pulled off more verses and read the promises Jesus made, and Anna listened as Belinda read His pledges, that nothing would separate them from the love of God, vows that He would always be with them. Verses Anna had forgotten.

She'd been too intent on the promises John had made. He kept the first promise, the one about serving God, no matter what. But the promises he'd made since, about Noah, about not being in danger, and about returning in time for Christmas, were ones he had no control over keeping. Those things were in God's hands. She'd relied on empty oaths, no matter how well-intentioned, instead of turning to Jesus, God with us, for the peace she needed.

Belinda ended with Hebrews 13:5. "Never will I leave you, never will I forsake you."

"Children, join hands with me and pray." Anna prayed like she hadn't since Noah died, asking God to forgive her for her doubt and to give her His peace. By the time she'd prayed for protection for John, warmth swept through her. No matter what happened, no matter how hard it was to go through, God would be with her.

"Girls, come to the table." She stood and placed the pheasant on a large platter. Picking up her butcher knife and fork, she paused.

The door burst open, and a gust of snow blew into the cabin.

Chapter Eleven

John marched through the door and dropped his bedroll and rifle on the bed.

Paul followed him in but stood next to the door.

When John had invited him to Christmas supper on the way home, Paul insisted he wouldn't stay unless Anna asked him to sup with them.

Anna had a knife and fork in hand, ready to cut into the bird.

John grinned at the sight of her trying to carve a pheasant. She wasn't very good with knives. "You're not going to eat Christmas supper without me, are you?"

"Papa!" The girls, in one accord, ran to him and encompassed him in hugs and kisses.

Anna dropped the fork and grabbed the side of the table. Her olive complexion had turned as white as the snow on the path outside.

"How about you, wife?" He tried to tease her, but he couldn't help but allow a smile to overtake the corners of his mouth. "Is this the kind of greeting I get? No kiss or hug."

"Oh, John." She sank onto the bench. "I thought you were..." Tears flowed out of her eyes, breaking his heart.

He ran to her side and took her into his arms. "I'm sorry I worried you." He kissed her. "I'm so sorry."

Anna wiped her eyes. "Supper's getting cold, and the pheasant still needs to be sliced." She handed the knife to John. "Brother Paul, will you stay and sup with us?"

"Thank you." Paul dropped his gear by the door and sat at the foot of the table. "I would be pleased to sup with you."

John picked the fork off the ground, wiped it on his trousers, and prepared to cut into the meat. "Pheasant? I didn't manage to bag anything before I left." He winked. "Don't tell me you went hunting and shot a pheasant?"

"No." Anna's mouth twisted. "Pastor Jungman was kind enough to provide for your family."

He couldn't tell if there was animosity in her statement. He imagined there would be plenty of making amends after the children went to bed.

After he'd sliced the bird, they all sat at the table, prayed, and dished out the food. Anna had outdone herself by fixing all of his favorites. The fowl melted in his mouth, and the sweet cornbread was wonderful. She must have boiled maple syrup for days to have enough for the sweet buns

114

and the cornbread.

Nobody said anything. Normally he would have to chide Lisel for speaking too much, but she focused on her food.

John swallowed. He understood the silent treatment. He deserved it. But this was Christmas day, and they had a guest.

"So Brother Paul." Anna gazed at John. "How does your father fare?"

A flush crept across John's cheeks as he pulled on his collar. "How did you know we were meeting with Chief Swantaney?"

Paul said nothing and focused on his food.

"Phoebe mentioned it." Anna took a bite of cornbread, never taking her gaze off John. She swallowed and drank a sip of coffee to wash it down. "She was concerned I might be worried about you. Seems everyone in the village knew, except me."

"Anna." John set down his fork. "I'm sorry I didn't tell you. I only wished to save you needless apprehension."

She tilted her head toward the children. "We'll talk of it later, husband." She turned to Paul. "Forgive me, Brother Paul, for bringing you into this. I really would like to know how you fared with your father."

Paul drank some coffee. "I'm grateful to you, Sister Brunner, for inviting me to Christmas dinner."

"You've been in our home often enough that I believe it would be appropriate for you to call me Sister Anna. Don't you?"

Paul nodded. "Sister Anna. Tomorrow I leave to return to my tribe."

Anna clasped her hand over her mouth.

"Don't be concerned," Paul said. "This is by God's design. My father has agreed to allow me to live as a Christian in the tribe and to share the Lenape Bible with the other braves. I will be a missionary to my people."

"Your father agreed to that?"

"Not at first. There was some discussion, but in the end, he agreed. His only requirements are that I marry a Lenape woman from my tribe, provide him with lots of grandchildren, and take his place as leader when it's time."

"That is good news," Anna said. "How will you find a Christian wife from among your people?"

"I'm trusting in God to take care of that." Paul drank some coffee. "I am ready to marry again."

Anna leaned forward. "Didn't Sister Rebecca come from your tribe?"

"The young widow?" Paul lowered his eyes and grinned. "Yes, she is from my tribe. I'd forgotten."

"It won't be easy not having any Christian brothers to strengthen you." She tilted her head as if she was really interested.

"That's the best part." John stared at her, trying to decide what had changed. She seemed different. "Since the tribe lives only a three-hour walk from here, the chief has agreed to allow Brother Paul and any braves who wish to join him to come to church on Sundays. They'll stay overnight at Brother Paul's cabin."

Anna gazed at John. He couldn't tell what she was thinking, or if she was still angry. "Will you meet with him after church for a Bible study?"

John cut a piece of meat off the bone and tried to sound casual. "If you are willing to have him and the Lenape he brings in our home." No answer. "Or we could meet in Brother Paul's cabin."

"I wouldn't hear of it." Anna dished out more pheasant. "Brother Paul, you and your friends are welcome here, anytime. I'll make Sunday dinner for you and whoever you bring."

John had a bite of meat in his mouth when she said it and choked on it. He placed a napkin over his mouth while he tried to stop coughing. What was she up to?

"I hope you don't mind that this Sunday I've invited a guest," Anna said. "Sister Rebecca. She's been lonely since her husband's death. She misses her home with the Lenape."

Paul's face flushed. "I would love to spend time with Sister Rebecca."

"Good, it's settled, then."

John drank a sip of coffee. He had a sense something had just transpired between Anna and Paul, but he couldn't figure out what. "Anna, we tried to get home before now. Chief Swantaney wanted time to think about Brother Paul living a Christian life among his tribe. Then on our way home, a snowstorm blew in, delaying us further."

"Mama cried," Lisel said.

Anna placed a finger in front of her mouth to silence their daughter. "Lisel, eat your pheasant."

John placed his hand on Anna's. "I'm so sorry I was late."

Lisel ate a bite of pheasant, but it didn't keep her quiet. "Belinda read verses from the tree to make her feel better."

John would have said something if he could have thought of anything to make the situation better. Now Anna would be more fearful than ever, and he wasn't sure she'd ever forgive him.

She stood and cleared the dishes. "I made squash pie for dessert."

"Squash pie? After all the sugar you used in the corn bread?"

Anna nodded.

"What a treat." He turned to Paul. "I married myself a fine woman."

"Yes, you did," Paul said. "You need to be a good husband to her."

Heat traveled up John's back. He hadn't been the husband she deserved, but that would change.

Anna dished out the pie and set the biggest piece in front of John. "Belinda and Lisel sang at the Christmas Eve Lovefeast."

"I'm sorry I missed it."

116

"Maybe they could sing for you and Brother Paul after dessert."

John was having a hard time keeping up with Anna's mood. Was she angry, upset, or just trying to make things nice for Christmas? With each comment she made, he was more unsure. "I'd like that very much."

"Good," Anna said.

John ate a bite of pie and let it melt in his mouth before swallowing it. Anna made the best squash pie he'd ever tasted. "Maybe after the girls sing, we could read the Scriptures on the tree."

"We've already done that, Papa," Belinda said. "Mama said I could read them since you weren't here."

"I see." John drank a sip of coffee. "I'm sorry I missed it."

They ate their pie, and the girls sang *Morning Star*. When they were done, John and Paul applauded. A lump formed in John's throat. He wished he'd been there to hear his girls sing it in church. They were growing up too fast. A few more years and men would be at their doorstep to court the girls.

"I need to go." Brother Paul patted his stomach. "Thank you for a wonderful Christmas supper, Sister Anna. I look forward to supping with you and Rebecca on Sunday."

"You're welcome." Anna lowered her eyes. "I'm sorry I haven't always treated you with hospitality. Please forgive me."

John's chin dropped.

"Thank you for that, as well." Paul draped his supplies over his shoulder. "You've more than made up for it today."

Anna scooted to the door and opened it. "I will pray for you to have great success among your people."

"Thank you. I covet your prayers."

John strode toward Paul and shook his hand. "I'll miss you."

"You've been a good friend, but there's no need for long faces. I'll see you Sunday." Paul closed the door behind him.

Lisel kept Katrina occupied by playing with the Putz while Belinda helped Anna with the dishes.

John drank a cup of coffee and tried to figure out what had happened with Anna and if it was a good thing or a bad one. Either way, he needed to make amends. He had wronged her by making promises he knew he couldn't keep and by lying to her.

On the walk home, after trying to justify it to himself and to Paul, he'd come to the truth that his deception was a lie and a sin. He'd do as she asked and wait for the children to go to sleep before he talked to her about it, but he would make things right.

Anna stacked the last clean dish on the shelf. "All right, children. Time for bed."

The children hurried into their nightgowns.

"Belinda," Anna said. "You and Lisel are old enough to walk to school by yourselves starting tomorrow."

John spewed coffee across the table.

"Thank you, Mama," Belinda said. "I promise we'll be careful."

"I know you will."

"Good night, Mama, Papa." Lisel kissed them and helped Belinda pull the tick out from under the rope bed. They all settled in under the wool blanket.

Another new development. John wiped his mouth on his sleeve.

Lisel didn't pout as she had every night for months, and the girls were soon asleep.

This was the moment John had been looking forward to and dreading at the same time.

Chapter Twelve

Anna sat in her rocker, gazing at her husband.

John stood by the fire but wouldn't look at her.

She wondered which subject she should discuss with him first.

"Anna." He knelt before her. "I am so sorry for lying to you. I was wrong for not telling you we were meeting with Paul's father."

That surprised her. Normally when he deceived her like this, he would try to justify it by saying it was to keep her from worrying. "This isn't the first time. How can I trust you if you don't tell me the truth?"

He lowered his chin but kept his eyes focused on her. "There's no way I can answer that. I have lied to you many times and made promises I couldn't keep. I know that. All I can do is be truthful from this point on and hope that someday I can earn back your trust."

"Oh, John." She wiped a tear falling onto her cheek. "I do understand why you did it. You were trying to protect me. But don't you see, you can't take the place of God in my life. You can't promise that things will always work out. Nobody can."

He nodded but remained silent.

She placed her hand on his cheek. "I love you, and I do forgive you."

John swept his arms around her and kissed her.

She pulled back. "But it will take time before I trust you again. Trust is built on you telling me the truth, no matter how hard it might be, or how upset I might get. And no more promises you can't keep."

He covered her hand in his. "I understand."

"The only promises I can trust are the ones God has made. He promised to be with me always and to never leave me or forsake me. I'm not saying I won't doubt again, or that fear won't grip my heart, but I need

118

you, my husband, to remind me of who Christ is and the promise He made when He was born. A Christmas promise. God with us. Can you do that?"

"I don't know." John's Adam's apple bulged. "But I'll do my best with God's help."

"That's all I ask." Anna leaned over and kissed her husband passionately. "I have a surprise for you. I'm with child."

John beamed, his expression bright with hope.

"If it's a boy, I want to name him after our Noah. If she's a girl, I'm thinking of Faith."

"Both fine names," John said. "You have made this the best Christmas ever."

"A Christmas filled with promise." Anna grabbed John's hand and led him to bed. She was glad to have him home in their little cabin in the Ohio wilderness.

For it truly had become home.

The End

Dedication

I dedicate this book to my loving husband, Rick Kraft, who has supported me through my writing journey. He is my biggest fan.

CHRISTMAS IN CADBURN TOWNSHIP
Michelle L. Levigne

A Book & Mug Mysteries tie-in

Chapter One

With only an inch of snow on the sidewalk, Saundra Bailey seriously considered giving up walking to work at the Cadburn Library. Here it was the first week of December, and the walk down Overview from her apartment building to the municipal complex holding the schools, city hall, fire department, and library seemed to be a whole city block longer every morning. Besides, while she didn't mind walking in the dim dawn light, walking in growing darkness at the end of the day left much to be desired. She still had flashbacks to her first week living in the township, when Cigar Man had tried to run her down.

Despite that, she did enjoy her walks. Cadburn had looked like a holiday postcard even before the snow started falling. Twinkling lights were everywhere, some of them multi-colored and the rest either white or golden. Pine garlands and pinecone wreaths and thick, velvety red ribbons graced the light poles and street signposts and benches. When she stopped by Book & Mug for their current decadent coffee special, the aromas made the approaching holiday feel closer: cinnamon, apple, and plum. Kai's staff all wore floppy elf hats and every few days more bits of Christmas décor joined the extravaganza of pinecones and garlands.

Despite the holiday glitz, she felt more mopey with every day that passed. She had sniffled a few times last night, listening to Kai and Olivia, the head barista, discussing the long list of rehearsal schedules for community activities to ensure that everyone on the coffee shop's staff could participate in their favorite activities. Kai took such good care of his staff. He didn't seem to mind taking on the huge headache of juggling everyone's schedules so they wouldn't miss out. There were church choir rehearsals, community choir rehearsals, caroling parties, cookie decorating parties, and ice-skating hours on the temporary rink erected in the park. A team of people were preparing to erect the Santa Claus village next to the library where children could stop after school and make ornaments and talk to Santa in his workshop.

Despite four story hours today with children fighting to sit on her lap or next to her during story times, Saundra increasingly felt alone. Abandoned. All the children, teachers, and her co-workers talked about plans for Christmas. Presents for all the people in their lives, presents they hoped to get, plans for Christmas Eve and Christmas Day. It was ridiculous to feel left out, with Christmas still weeks away.

"You're not alone, you dope," she muttered, and smiled as fresh snow dusted her face.

Should she worry that Aunt Cleo hadn't contacted her yet, letting her know when she would arrive in Cleveland for Christmas? With Saundra so new in her home and job, she couldn't take off and fly to wherever Cleo was working as she usually did every Christmas. It made no sense to feel depressed just because Cleo hadn't called her. After all, this was only the first week of December.

Besides, how could she feel alone when she had so many new friends? Starting with the cousins at Book & Mug, and then Pastor Roy and Patty at Cadburn Bible Chapel, and spreading out through the township from there.

Saundra couldn't wait for Aunt Cleo to show up. She would get to be hostess, at long last, and pamper her aunt for a change, instead of being the one who was taken care of.

Even better, she wouldn't have to endure a command performance at Grandfather Mulcahy's house. Everyone dressed in black, sat in the shadowy grand parlor, and murmured among themselves. Rarely to her. Except for the yearly interrogation about her job situation, her dating life, and the usual complaints about her father being a vast disappointment. Since they rarely looked directly at her even then, Saundra wondered if anyone would even notice she had left town.

"Christmas resolution," she told the snowflakes drifting away from her on a change in the wind. "I'm not going to wear black until at least halfway through January."

She stopped multiple times on her way home that night to tap notes into her phone with ideas for treats and activities when Aunt Cleo showed up. Each time, she had to take off her glove, because she couldn't get the phone screen to react to the touch of the yarn covering her fingertip.

Full dark had fallen, leaving her to walk through a multi-colored wonderland, by the time she reached her apartment building. To her delight, when she stepped into the old-fashioned brass cage elevator, she discovered someone had decorated the inside with green tinsel garlands from the central light to the four corners. She eyed the crumpled bit of greenery and white berries half-buried by the tinsel in the center, as the elevator rose to her floor. Her phone rang as the elevator clattered to a stop. She bit at the first two fingers of her glove to tug it off while she pulled her phone out of her purse with the other hand, and hurried to step out of the elevator before it closed on her. Cleo.

"Hey, I was just thinking of you." Saundra hurried down the short hall to her apartment door.

"That sounds ominous." Cleo laughed.

"Oh, no, all good! I've been getting all sorts of ideas for when you come for Christmas. I mean, there's so much to do in the Cleveland area, I could keep you busy until Valentine's." She laughed and nearly dropped her keys.

The silence from her aunt didn't strike her until she was inside her apartment and turned the deadbolt on the door.

"Cleo?"

"I'm so sorry, dear." Her aunt sighed. "I've been dithering over this decision for nearly a week now. Maybe I should have called you sooner."

"You're not going to make it, are you?"

"It all depends on ... well, there are a few leads I've been sidling up to. Depending on the reaction from the people I'm testing right now, that will influence if I'm home with you for Christmas. Don't hate me too much, darling. What I'm working on is so absolutely vital ... it's sort of a family legacy when you think about it." A breathy chuckle escaped her. "I've lost you again, haven't I? Because I haven't felt safe to tell you about the legacy. Until now."

"Cleo?" Saundra stepped into the kitchen and opened the door to the little balcony greenhouse. Moist, warm air smelling of green growth and soil spilled into the kitchen. Comforting her. She needed to assure herself that nothing had changed while she was away all day. Which made absolutely no sense. None of the Mulcahys knew where she had gone, or likely even cared. Why would she fear that her nasty cousins had managed to break into her new home, ransacking it as they had done since she was three years old?

Still, there had been the oddest feeling at times today that someone was watching her ... She would have blamed Nick West, who took an almost fiendish delight in sneaking up on her, since buying a condo in Cadburn Township, but she knew he was out of town on another of his research trips. So what had triggered that feeling that something was off?

She shook her head to stop those thoughts, as her aunt started talking again.

"Now that you're safely away from ... well, the less said about those schemers, the better." Cleo chuckled. "Do you remember how you used to love to hold the heart locket? Trying to see all the bits of gold dust and streaks of color woven through it?"

"Yes, what about it?" Saundra braced for the instructions she had been waiting to receive, ever since discovering that Eden Cole had a Venetian glass heart locket almost exactly like the one she guarded for her aunt. Sometimes, she regretted telling Cleo and Nick what she had seen. She feared confronting her about the locket would risk the growing friendship with Eden and her cousins, Troy and Kai. Maybe especially Kai.

"I think in honor of your new freedom and safety, you should wear the heart for special occasions. There should be plenty coming up. Roy loves talking about all the little community celebrations and activities."

"Cleo … even if you're ready to tell me all the family secrets and what's behind the locket, this isn't a conversation to have over the phone." Saundra muffled a groan. She was starting to sound like a bad spy novel.

"You're right." Her aunt echoed that sigh, ending on a rippling chuckle. "I promise to tell you everything when we're together. Face to face. Go ahead and wear the heart. Let people ask questions. Just … never let it leave your possession when you're out in public. All right?"

"Of course. You can trust me."

"I know. How I got so lucky, to have you to hand the legacy on to, I don't know."

"Okay, you're starting to sound all mysterious." Saundra laughed. Cleo did love her puzzles and secrets. If playing along and not asking too many questions about all her research trips and secrets made the elderly woman happy, Saundra was glad to do it. Even when her parents had been alive, she had felt closer to Cleo than anyone else.

"Sorry, dear. Occupational hazard. Now, tell me about this young man Roy says you've been stepping out with."

"Stepping out?" Saundra shrugged out of her coat, then closed the greenhouse door and settled at her kitchen table. "I have no idea who he's talking about. I've been far too busy getting involved in the community and learning my job to 'step out' with anyone, as you say."

"You can be a talented little liar when you want to be, but never with me. Especially when Nick adds his two cents."

"Nick has too much fun playing at being my big brother. The interfering, trick-playing kind, not the one you turn to for advice." Saundra sighed and contemplated using her key for Nick's condominium to play some sort of trick on him. Change something, maybe fill it with candles in a particularly poofy, feminine scent he didn't like. Some sort of scent bomb that would build up for however long he was out of town this time.

"When we have very little in the way of family, we do tend to go a little overboard with what we do have, don't we?" her aunt murmured. She chuckled. "Big brother and little sister goes both ways, dear. I'll leave it up to you how to teach Nick a lesson he deserves. Now, as for your very bad evasion, I'm talking about that very nice, hard-working young man from the coffee shop. Roy is sure you two are clicking quite nicely."

"Pastor Roy is a dear and has quite a romantic streak in him. I can't wait to see what he does when Valentine's Day comes around."

"Oooh, she's looking ahead to Valentine's Day. Must be serious."

"Cleo!" A moment later, Saundra laughed, and her aunt with her. She wasn't surprised to feel extra warmth in her cheeks when the merriment faded. "I don't know why you're asking since I've talked about Kai and his cousins often enough. If there is anything ... well ... I'm taking it very slowly."

"Sweetheart, just because those vicious cousins of yours —"

"No, this has nothing to do with Edmund setting me up with that slimebag lech to settle his debts." Saundra sighed and thought yet another prayer of thanks for Nick West who always showed up when she needed him. Even in embarrassing situations. "Kai and Eden and Troy are all my friends."

"Yes, so Nick has told me. And I'm grateful they've taken you under their wings."

"Nick needs to have his tattletale mouth slapped. Especially since most of it is his imagination."

"Really? Nick, letting his imagination run away with him?" Her aunt chuckled. "I am a little concerned, dear, since both he and Roy say the cousins aren't part of the Kingdom. I want you to be happy. And I trust you not to go too deep into a relationship that can't extend into eternity. While I don't advocate missionary dating —"

"Stop. Just stop there."

"That's just it. I trust you to stop before you get hurt. Now, you're going to send me a picture of him, aren't you? So when I do come to town, I'll know him?"

"Cleo ..." She sighed, with just a touch of laughter in the vocal signal of surrender.

Chapter Two

Saundra waited several days before wearing the heart locket. Breaking the habit of secrecy and protection was harder than she could have imagined. Yet when she thought it over, wearing the glass heart helped her feel closer to her aunt.

Her first time wearing it was at the community children's choir concert, in the park on Sunday afternoon. The lights and colors and the dusting of snow in the air and the children's excitement helped her get over that first little blurp of nervousness. She enjoyed the children's voices raised in song, especially the ones who called out when they saw her sitting in the second row. There was something spectacular about the afternoon concert, the delightful contrast of bright sunshine with sparkling snow swirling around. Maybe part of that came from the sparkle and weight of the glass heart, resting in the thick cowl neck of her green sweater. The sweater was thick and warm enough to let her wear a vest jacket and gloves and be comfortable. Everything was perfect.

Nick stepped out of the shadows between two refreshment booths, as the children leaped down from the risers set up in front of the gazebo and ran to find their parents in the crowd of listeners. He shuffled over to the side at the same time she tried to sidestep him. For a few seconds, she couldn't move, with people moving past her on both sides.

What was he doing back in town? Not that he had to clear his schedule with her, but still, some warning would have been nice. She hated the feeling of being spied on. Granted, that came from her Mulcahy cousins always sneaking around and prying into her life—and trying to prove she had the heart locket. Nick wasn't the one she had to worry about breaking in and stealing the locket. The exact opposite, actually. Still, she resented how he always seemed to step from the shadows when she least expected him.

"Isn't it a little early for Valentine's Day?" His mouth smiled, but there was some darker sparkle in his eyes that made her shiver, as if the gobs of snow sliding off the shelter roof had gone straight down her neck.

She reached up and pressed two gloved fingers against the heart. "The perfect colors for Christmas, so why not? Why does love have to be limited to February?"

"Why indeed?" One eyebrow went up high enough to make Spock jealous. "You should take better care of treasures like that. Never know who's going to try to snatch it." He raised a hand.

Saundra muffled a yelp and jumped back two steps, while pressing both hands over the heart.

"Gotta be faster than that, to stop a really determined thief."

"You taught me enough self-defense tricks, I can probably have a thief singing soprano before he realizes what happened."

"You hope." The amusement left his eyes. "Cleo—"

"She encouraged me to wear it." Saundra bit back the justification that if Eden or her friend, Charli saw the heart, that might prompt them to bring out their own Venetian glass hearts, to compare.

"She did, huh?" He nodded. "Doesn't it just renew your faith in mankind in general, when Cleo changes the rules without any explanation?" Before she could respond, or even decide if he was being snide or mysterious or just silly, he winked at her and turned and sauntered away.

126

~~~~~

"Troy?" Eden's voice tightened enough to distract Kai from trying to find Saundra in the churning crowd moving through the park. He turned to look at her, then past her to Troy.

His cousin looked like someone had whacked him between the eyes with a snow shovel. He slowly shook his head and stared toward the now-empty choir shelter.

"Oh ..." Eden stepped up next to him and she got that look for a moment. A few muttered words slipped between her lips. Kai didn't catch them, with all the people chattering and laughing and calling greetings around them, but he could guess. Eden only slipped into the nameless foreign language the three of them barely remembered when she was stunned enough to forget herself. The words that sounded like they were partly French, partly Latin, conveyed so much roiled emotion they worked better than curses. Especially when nobody else in the world but the three of them could speak the language.

Kai stepped up next to his cousins, so they were all in a row, and he could look exactly where they were staring. He saw Saundra. Was something wrong with her? As usual, she was bent over, talking with a handful of children. Her expression was bright with laughter and her affection for them. Kai got a funny twisting sensation in his chest, watching her. The children had good reason to adore her. Then she raised a hand to her neck and something glittered, gold and red. She held it in her glove, moving it out for one of the children to get a better look.

"Oh ... heck." He couldn't find the words to express what he felt because he wasn't sure what he felt. "That isn't ... Is it?"

"That's what we need to find out," Eden said.

"She doesn't look like us." Troy hooked his arm through Eden's and moved her aside as several people came hurrying past, talking about hot chocolate and roasted chestnuts at the refreshment booths. "Not another cousin."

Kai got his feet stepped on, but ignored it, his gaze locked on the Venetian glass heart in Saundra's hand. She was only fifteen feet away from him, but he couldn't get a deep enough breath to call her through the happy sounds of the crowds.

"So that part of our theory could be wrong. It's not a family heirloom," Eden said.

"Maybe it's a lookalike." Kai moved out of the flow of traffic with them.

"That's what you need to find out," Troy said.

He watched Saundra tuck the heart back into the folds of her sweater and stand up straight, smiling at the children chattering with her. He almost said, "Why me?" but he knew.

127

Then Saundra's gaze met his. She grinned and gave him a little finger wave, then bent down to one of the children again.

"I can't just go up to her and ask if it's a locket, and what color the stripe is on the back, and if she's figured out how to open it, and what she found inside," he said.

"Sounds like a plan to me," Eden said.

"She'll think I'm crazy. Especially if it's just a lookalike."

"Do we hope it's a lookalike?" Troy gestured with a jerk of his chin at Saundra, who was exchanging words with the parents of the children. "Start out slow, just get a closer look at it."

"This is really something that needs to be discussed in private. Especially if the heart is a real one." Eden squeezed Kai's arm. "Whatever is growing between you two ought to help."

He nodded, holding back the question: What if confronting her about the Venetian glass heart locket ruined everything between him and Saundra? He watched her while they walked away. He hadn't felt this helpless since he was maybe eight and the social workers tried to put him in a foster family separate from Eden and Troy.

Focus on the heart, he told himself, as Saundra wove through the dispersing crowd to meet up with him. *If we're lucky, now there are five hearts in the world, and another piece of the puzzle could have just dropped in our laps.*

"Hey, there you are," she said.

"Here I am." *Oh, real smooth.* "What'd you think?" He gestured at the crowds dispersing among the refreshment booths and little gift shops set up around the park. "Are you having fun?"

"Oh absolutely."

"Good. That's the important thing." His mind went completely blank, so he turned and gestured in the general direction of the refreshments. "Want to get something?"

"If I remember, you said something about Mr. Green having an incredible hot spiced cider recipe he won't share with anyone."

"Oh, yeah." They fell into step. He wished for a moment that Saundra, who seemed so good at reading the minds of the tongue-tied and scatter-brained children during story time, could read his mind now.

Or maybe he didn't want her to. Not with that glass heart sparkling within his reach and him afraid to look close enough to visually compare with the three he knew better than the back of his hand, locked away in Eden's apartment.

They reached the double-sized tent dispensing Mr. Green's famous cider. He couldn't ask her about the heart in front of all these people. They didn't get away from the tent for at least a good fifteen minutes. People chatted with them about the music, the Christmas-themed activities for

128

children at the library, the holiday menu additions at the coffee shop. Kai was glad people talked to Saundra like she had lived here for years. Yet he itched to get her away from all these interruptions, so he could ask her about the heart. If he could look at it. All it would take was five minutes to hold it in his hand, to see what color the stripe was across the back, run his fingernail along the indentation that revealed it was a locket, with the hinge cleverly tucked inside the heart, and find the tiny pinhole to insert a long stick pin to trigger the hidden lock.

A gust of sleety wind blowing horizontally through the doorway of the tent gave him the excuse he wanted.

"Had enough of Northeast Ohio winter?"

"Does it show?" She laughed.

"How about I get you indoors? Maybe drive you home?"

"That'd be nice."

It would have been nice, and he imagined sitting in the back corner booth with Eden and Troy and having their help as they asked Saundra about the necklace, but nothing went as he envisioned. He glanced over at Saundra as they left the park. No heart.

"Something wrong?" she asked.

Kai realized he was staring, and about to walk into a fire hydrant. "Your ..." He raised his hand to his throat. "I thought I saw something there."

"Oh, yeah." She patted the neckline of her sweater. "Safely tucked away. The cord it hangs on is old and kept slipping during the singing. I had a vision of the knot coming untied and it falling and breaking. So I tucked it away where it'll be safe."

"Good. It looked pretty. Whatever it is."

Oh, yeah, real smooth.

"It's an antique glass heart my aunt gave me. Well, not gave me, gave me. More like taking care of it, and she gave me permission to wear it. For special occasions only." She chuckled. "Sounds a little melodramatic, doesn't it?"

"Sounds like a great story."

He filed that bit of information away to share with Eden and Troy. So did that reduce the chances of the heart being like their three, and the one Saundra's friend, Charli, wore that one time in the coffee shop? Before he could frame the next question, a handful of mutual friends caught up with them. They were all on their way to the Book & Mug to warm up, and chattered about the music, about a sledding party they hoped to have tomorrow and even a few pestering questions about the specials. Someone was always trying to change the menu and schedule for the specials. Still, it was nice to know that some people had their favorites and wanted to drink them more than twice a week.

The chattering, laughing, and pretend complaints took them to the coffee shop. Kai went through the front door with them and Saundra.

He prepared his words, to get Saundra away from everyone, to the back corner booth where Eden and Troy waited. While Leo was assembling all their drink orders, Millie came out of the back room to report the dishwasher was acting up again. Kai knew better than to put the problem aside for morning. For one thing, he refused to let dirty dishes pile up. There were health code regulations to consider. With his luck, an inspector would show up just as the morning crew was opening the doors. Better to handle the problem now. He apologized to Saundra and gestured toward her, hoping his cousins would get the hint, as he walked past their booth.

An hour later, he came out, his sleeves and back wet, his hands cut from digging a fork out of the rotator mechanism for the fifth time this month. Why always a fork? Why never a spoon, considering how many spoons they used? Eden's apologetic expression told him everything before he even looked to the front booth where Saundra had been sitting with their friends. They were all gone.

Kai left Leo to close up the coffee shop for the night and went upstairs with his cousins. He reported what he had learned from Saundra. Eden settled at her computer and got to work, following the inspiration that made her such a brilliant investigator. Kai headed upstairs and changed out of his repairs-soiled clothes. He felt a little better, returning in flannel shirt and sweats, barefoot.

Troy leaned over the back of Eden's desk chair, studying the screen with her.

"Something interesting?" Kai stopped at the long conference table that sat in the open side of the office, like a partial barrier between that half of the floor and the door to Eden's apartment.

"Just checking something we found earlier, checking out Saundra's connections, when we found out she was a Mulcahy." Troy stepped back and settled on the edge of the hip-high bookshelves that lined the wall and fit neatly under the windows on that side of the building.

Eden tapped her mouse and the screen closed down. "Interesting little legal action she faced from the rest of the family when her mother died. Lots of nasty accusations recorded in all those legal filings, and a lot of dirty laundry aired in the newspapers during the fight. Seems the Mulcahys didn't approve of Saundra's mother marrying her father, and they were looking for something they claimed she stole from them during the marriage. Funny thing is, they would never say what exactly it was. What stuck in my head is that they tried to include Cleo Bailey in the legal proceedings, claiming she had custody of the item. They refused to describe the item and could never provide any proof Saundra's aunt had it, much less that her mother had the item."

"The heart?" Kai wasn't sure what that suddenly hollow feeling was in his chest. "How long ago was this? Like maybe they knew about the seeds hidden in the hearts before they latched onto Troy and me?"

"We need to first make sure Saundra's heart is like ours." Troy knuckled his eyes. "And find out just how much she knows about the hearts."

"If that was what the Mulcahys were trying to get hold of in the first place," Eden said. "You have to feel sorry for her, having relatives like that. You have to wonder how much she knows, how deep into the secret she is, and more important, what her Aunt Cleo knows. She did say her aunt was taking care of the heart and gave her permission to wear it. Like it was finally safe, she was finally far enough away from the Mulcahys to wear it in public."

"So, how do we find out if we're right, or something else is going on?" Troy said.

"Bait." Eden reached into the neck of her sweater and brought her glass heart out. Kai flinched, seeing it. She wrinkled up her nose at him. "I remember when I used to wear this all the time, like a good luck charm. I have to wonder how many clues we might have missed, because I was so afraid of the wrong people seeing it." She rubbed it with her thumb a few times before letting it slide back into hiding. "If Saundra is part of protecting a heart, she'll be curious when she sees mine."

"And if some of those wrong people happen to be hanging around?" Troy said.

She crossed her eyes at him. "I don't know about you two, but I am sick and tired of going on nothing but theories and foggy memories. Someone wanted us lost, when we were separated from our parents and tossed into the System. Maybe if we take some risks, irritate enough people, we'll find out who, if not why."

Chapter Three

Monday morning, Saundra wore a plain white turtleneck, to show off all the colors and glitter in the Venetian glass to their best advantage. The story time children, especially the little ones who saw magic in everything, would love it.

She was right and regretted her decision by the time lunch rolled around. The littlest children followed true to form. When they saw something sparkly, they wanted to hold it. Even put it in their mouths. After the fifth child reached for the heart, she tucked it inside her shirt for the rest of the day. There was something comforting about the feeling of the glass resting against her skin.

Saundra wore the heart on Tuesday. She had a meeting about library holiday activities before starting work, with refreshments provided. She couldn't justify swinging by Book and Mug on her way to work to get coffee. She laughed at herself for feeling so disappointed, and even a little worried. What if Kai didn't notice she wasn't stopping in?

More important, how could she get a reaction from Eden, seeing Saundra wearing a Venetian glass heart so much like her own? Seeing the heart would open up a line of discussion Saundra had been waiting for all her life, not just since moving to Cadburn Township. What could she find out about the hearts before Cleo came to town and finally had that talk with Eden?

Wednesday morning, the sleety-slushy weather meant she needed to drive. Her heart beat a little faster as she approached Book & Mug. She spotted two parking spaces, separated by three cars, right in front. An unusual occurrence at this time of the morning.

Saundra caught her breath, panic choking her. She sped up instead of slowing to maneuver into the second parking space. She was halfway to the next intersection before her conscious mind recognized what she had seen.

The twins, Edmund and Bridget Mulcahy, stood in front of the inset display window of the bookstore side of the coffee shop. Edmund faced the street, while Bridget leaned against the window, looking inside. They had always mocked her for her love of books, so she doubted they were window shopping for books.

No, common sense insisted, it was just her imagination working overtime. She just saw a couple who looked enough like her cousins to frighten her. Why would Edmund and Bridget be in Cadburn? Looking in the window of a bookstore? Impossible. Totally out of character.

"Get a grip," she scolded herself.

By the time she got to the library, she obeyed what her survival instincts insisted. Even if this was a case of mistaken identity, she couldn't take any chances with the glass heart. Nick had told her repeatedly that she should always listen to her gut, even if it contradicted what the people around her were saying. Her instincts said not to wear the glass heart out in public any longer.

She took the time to tuck the heart inside her shirt before she got out of the car at the library. When she went home that night, she put the heart back in its box sitting next to her jewelry tray. She wrote to Cleo, even knowing her aunt might not have access to the Internet right now. She felt somehow as if she had failed Cleo. What if she hadn't seen those people, whether they were her cousins or not?

"Thank You, Lord," she whispered. "I'd rather have false alarms than no alarms at all."

What if she had ignored that moment of panic, parked, and went into Book & Mug, and against all common sense, her nasty cousins had somehow followed her to Cadburn Township and saw the heart?

~~~~~

"Never rains but it pours," Troy announced, slamming open the door from the stairwell into the storeroom, and then stomping into the office while Kai was taking his lunch break upstairs. "Guess who's slithering around town?"

Kai turned in his seat at the conference table and saw the thundercloud darkening Troy's face. He dropped his fork into his ramen noodles bowl. "What happened now?"

"The twins are here."

"What twins?" Eden's tone indicated she was only halfway listening, studying her screen, shoulders hunched, and frowning.

"Mulcahy," Troy enunciated.

The scent of his lunch turned sour, and Kai pushed the box away a few inches. His sense of, *We should have known this day would come,* pulsed in his head for a moment, before switching to, *They're here to hurt Saundra.*

"That can't be good," Eden said, finally turning around from her computer. The three cousins exchanged glances as Troy came up to the table and braced his arms on it.

"The question is if they know we're here," Troy gestured between himself and Kai, "or if they're here for Saundra."

"The question is if we warn her, or we ..." She sighed, closed her eyes and rubbed her temples. "I know I'm going to sound horrible and heartless, because I trust her, and I don't want to test her anymore, but ... for our own peace of mind, maybe we should let this be a test?"

"I'm with Kai. She's as much a victim as we might have been." He tugged out a chair and sank into it, giving Kai a look that he could only label "guilty." "Do we let her be bait in a trap? If they're here for us, then we're protecting her by not revealing we know her. If they're here for her, we're protecting her and us, by not letting those two know that we're friends."

"If they realize we do know her, they could try to use her to get to us," Kai offered. He slid the lid on the ramen noodles box. Dump it, or save it for later when he might feel hungry again?

"Bigger priority," Eden said. "Making sure they don't get into the greenhouse."

"Don't suppose you've figured out how to install real lasers out of Star Wars or whatever and facial recognition in the security system?" Kai said.

Some of the tightness in his chest eased when Troy and Eden grinned at his half-joking comment. Then Troy's face wrinkled again with a new, clearly troubling thought.

"Saundra's greenhouse. If they get to it ..." He shrugged. "They might finally leave us alone."

"We don't know if Saundra has plants from the same seeds, so how could her cousins?" Eden sighed. "Well, look on the bright side. If they're here on your trail, they didn't get what they wanted from that scientist who sold us out."

"They'll just keep coming back until they get what they want."

"They don't have a reputation for playing by the rules. Nobody at Mulcahy-Dresden does. All they need are a few leaves, some notes, enough evidence to hand over to their crooked lawyers to try to prove that they developed the plants and we stole the prototypes from them."

Kai raised one hand and waved it, as if he needed to get their attention. "And what if they're here for Saundra, and they don't know we're here?"

That silenced his cousins.

"I'm all for dropping boiling oil on them when they come to the door," he continued, "but your home improvement insanity removed all the windows with hinges. Nothing opens."

Eden gave him a withering look that held for all of five seconds before she slouched in her chair and weariness took over her expression. "Lay low. Try not to be spotted and recognized. Sorry, but I'm not going to be seen in public with either of you until the red alert is over."

"Makes sense." Troy nodded. "And if they come here and actually have the gall to ask for us, never be available."

"Kai, Bridget first made contact at the coffee shop where you were working," Eden said slowly, as if thinking aloud. "Maybe it'd be good to turn everything over to Olivia and stay out of sight until they leave town. Reduce your visibility, on the off chance they come in here just to get coffee. I mean," she gestured at the glass block windows at the front of the office, with white smears collecting in the corners as evidence to the bitter winter weather, "even spies need to get warmed up and take a break."

"Fine, but what about Saundra?" Kai said.

"If you think about it," Troy said, "we can't warn her, because then we have to explain how we know her cousins, and all the research Eden did on her and ... could get ugly."

"Let's just wait and see what they do, all right?" Eden said. "We all lay low, we stay away from Saundra, we keep watch, and hope this is just family politics and has nothing to do with the seeds."

"And be ready to race to the rescue, if they do attack," Troy said.

Kai had to agree, but he felt like a coward and a liar.

~~~~~

That afternoon, Saundra had just settled back at her desk after finishing the afternoon story time when a commotion at the front desk made her turn. Vinnie, the newest intern pointed at her. A police officer she didn't recognize turned to look at her. From clear across the library, she saw him frown.

Had something happened to Aunt Cleo? Was this how she would learn all that globe-trotting and investigating had turned dangerous? Maybe even deadly? A notification delivered by someone who didn't even know her?

No. She refused to believe it. If Cleo had been hurt or even killed, Saundra believed she would know before anyone had to tell her. Something else had happened. The only way to find out was to go meet the officer instead of making him come to her.

"I'm Saundra Bailey. You're looking for me?"

"Are you sure?" His frown flickered into confusion, almost a smile. Then he shook his head. "I'm sorry, I've got a woman outside who can't seem to keep her story straight. The man with her doesn't help matters. They insist your name is Mulcahy, not Bailey, and they insist you're their cousin."

"What do they want? What happened?" Saundra followed him to the front door, wrapping her arms around herself in anticipation of the icy breeze swirling snowflakes around outside like a snow globe scene.

"They were raising a ruckus at your apartment building, trying to get inside. Claimed you had to be sick or dying or something, because they couldn't get you to open the door. Wanted the superintendent to open the door." He snorted, giving her a momentary grin. "Got into it with the old cuss something good. He kept saying you weren't sick, saw you leave for work this morning. They wouldn't listen. Wanted me to arrest him and break your door down. Then they got into it with him that your name was Mulcahy, not Bailey like he had in his files."

They stepped outside, and there were Bridget and Edmund pacing in front of the deputy's car. Another officer leaned against a big, dark luxury car with rental stickers. He was probably the reason they didn't follow the first man into the library.

Bridget let out a little shriek and came running to throw her arms around Saundra, while Edmund held back. She was at her twittery, teary worst, exclaiming about the heartless lawmen who refused to listen to the instincts of family and break down the door. What if her darling cousin Sandy had been lying there on the floor, dying of a fever or something worse?

"Saundra, not Sandy," Saundra muttered.

They would have wasted time coming to the library to check on her. And besides, what kind of protection could they give the town when they couldn't keep her name straight? She had grown up with Sandy, of course she knew what her name was. Why did they keep arguing with her when her darling cousin Sandy's life was probably at stake?

"Saundra. For the billionth time," Saundra muttered, "my name is Saundra, not Sandy."

For just a second, Bridget's mask of twittery, silly concern cracked, showing the shrew underneath. Then she was back to scolding the officers and doing a retro Valley Girl routine. Honestly, what kind of lawmen argued with her family over her name?

"But I wasn't sick and dying on the floor, and my last name *is* Bailey," Saundra said, when Bridget finally ran down. Edmund reached over her shoulder to shove a clean handkerchief nearly into her face.

He gave Saundra a smile that was nine-tenths reptilian, like the crocodile gave Captain Hook, and smugly smirky. Why did she think Nick smirked? His expression was friendly and open and warm compared to cocky, God's-gift-to-women Edmund Mulcahy's expression.

"But—but that's ridiculous!" Bridget wiped at her face and gulped, then wiped again.

"Why are you here?" Saundra asked, trying to keep her tone calm. Letting the twins know they had rattled her or irritated her would just encourage them to keep going with this totally uncharacteristic pretense of caring. They wanted something. They needed Saundra to get it.

"What a silly question. We're family. Why shouldn't we check up on you? What's wrong with dropping by and checking in, asking how your life is going? So tell us, favorite cousin." Bridget was always dangerous when she slid a little Southern sweet tea into her voice. "What have you been doing with yourself?"

So many answers. So many of them barely adequate to even begin to fling back all the nastiness those two had inflicted on her all her life. Saundra swallowed and licked her lips, and swore she tasted bitterness.

"You know, the same old thing." She shrugged. "Working. Doing community things."

"That's the Sandy we know," Edmund said. "Always busy. Bet you love it here." He gestured back toward the center of town. "Great big Hallmark card, you know. This whole place. Nice. Suits you."

Who were these people and what had they done with her cousins? Edmund never said anything that nice. He had made a study of all the things she valued, the things she enjoyed, just so he could mock them at every opportunity. His tone of voice was warm. She didn't trust it for a moment.

If Kai were here, she would have turned to him and asked him to look for pods in the back seat of the car, because chances were good her cousins had been body-snatched.

"Are you sure everything's all right, Miss Bailey?" The deputy winked at Saundra from behind Edmund and Bridget. "You know these people?"

"Yes, I do." She barely refrained from adding, *unfortunately.* "Thank you."

"I can't believe —" Bridget let out a delicate sound that couldn't quite be termed a snort, then waited until the officer got in his car. The second man stepped up, handed Edmund a set of keys, then got in the patrol car and they drove away. "Why are you holding to that silly little game?"

"What silly game?" Saundra thought she knew what Bridget referred to, but it was fun to aggravate her. How many times in her life had she been able to get away with that?

"Your name," Edmund said. "All along, we thought you went through that silly process to punish us for — well, for not standing up with you against the old farts." He stomped over to the rental car, opened all the doors, and proceeded to thoroughly examine it while Bridget and Saundra talked.

Uppermost in her mind was relief that she didn't have to leave work and drive those two back to her apartment to get their car.

"No. I took my mother's maiden name in all seriousness. No game at all."

"But ... why?" Bridget said, after sputtering for a few seconds, visibly discarding different words. She turned to Edmund, but he was too busy searching the car. Just what did he think the officers had done to it? "You're a Mulcahy."

"I've never been a true Mulcahy, and everyone let me know it from the day I could understand all the undercurrents in the family."

"Oh, but that's just silly. And that was the old farts' idea, not ours. We're all grown up now, and we really should be friends. Take it back, please?" She fluttered her eyelashes.

"Why are you here?" Saundra knew better than to get into one of those, "But you know you really want to do it our way," arguments. The longer she tried to reason with her cousins, the more ammunition she gave them to use against her. She caught herself before reaching up to check that the glass heart was safely tucked away out of sight inside her sweater.

"Making amends, if you want to get down to it." Edmund shrugged. "Been a lot of things happening. Weird things. To make your eyes open. Make your hair go white."

"We split from the old guard. Got our eyes opened and we realized what a big ugly mess Grandpops and the uncles and our own father made." Bridget held out a slim hand in a glossy red glove. "We figure, you're the only really decent Mulcahy in the whole world, so we just ..." Another shrug. "About the only decent advice Grandpops ever gave us was to never give up on family. You're family."

"So we want to get tight, you know?" he offered, when Bridget just stood there, and Saundra just stood there, and she looked at them and they looked at her long enough to be awkward.

"That's nice, but ..." Saundra couldn't come up with any words. Period. Nothing caustic. Nothing heavy with sarcasm and doubt. Which should have been her first reaction. Nothing encouraging, either. She didn't want to encourage them. Bridget and Edmund regularly tried to pull the "we're sooooo sorry, can't we be friends?" trick on her when they were children. She learned from the first time, and ever after, Saundra had to be bullied and shamed into accepting their overtures of friendship. She never believed them, so she had never been hurt when the two of them went on the offensive within days of their latest reconciliation forced on them by their grandparents.

Common sense said not to trust them.

Then again, they had never gone so far as to say they had broken from the rest of the family. Bridget had never referred to the elder generation as the "old farts." She was in too much fear of them. Or maybe it was just fear of irritating someone badly enough they cut her off from all that Mulcahy power and money.

"Why?" she asked, when the three of them had stood there, looking at each other, long enough for the last of the warmth to seep out of her sweater. She needed to get rid of them and get inside before she caught a cold.

"We want to be friends," Bridget said. "We're the next generation. We need to work together to rule when our time comes." She gestured at the car. "Get your coat, and let's get going. There's just gobs of things we can do. We've got so much fun to make up for now that we're friends."

"Bridget, I can't. I'm working." Saundra gestured at the library building behind her. She knew better than to respond with the words pressing on her lips: *We're not friends, we will never be friends. Who are you really and what did you do with the real Bridget?*

"Oh, pooh! What do you need to worry about a job for? You're a Mulcahy. You should be setting down roots and preparing for the day we're going to be in charge. Until then, have some fun!"

"I like my job. And you really should have called ahead. I would have told you I'm not going to go running around town when I have obligations and responsibilities."

"Who taught you such big grown-up, boring words?" Bridget giggled.

Edmund slammed the trunk shut, then three of the four car doors. That seemed to startle his sister.

"No," Saundra said when Bridget demanded her phone number, so she could call ahead next time. If she had her way, there would never be a "next time." She braced herself to say she was cold, she had to get back to work, anything to avoid the argument that would break out any second now.

Of course, now that her cousins knew where she lived, how long would it take for them to find someone willing to break rules, for enough money, and help them invade her privacy once again? Just what had driven them to come looking for her, and how long had it taken them to find out where she had moved?

"You're such a goody-goody. You'll come around, sweetie!" Then she stunned Saundra by hugging her, briefly, before turning and mincing across the sidewalk to the car. Edmund looked bored, but not irritated. That was probably a good thing.

Saundra waved as they pulled out of the parking lot and wrapped her arms around herself. She was colder inside than outside. What did those two want? How long would they keep up this game before they had a temper tantrum and stomped away and left her in peace again?

Chapter Four

The next afternoon, Saundra took advantage of the clearer weather to run up to The Office on her lunch break for some stationery supplies, to finally get started on her Christmas cards. She returned to find Bridget and Edmund waiting, perched on her desk. They looked slightly ridiculous in their uber-sophisticated clothes, heavy on black and silk and leather, framed by all the toys she got to work with as the children's librarian.

Twila hissed at Saundra as she passed the front desk and gestured at the Mulcahys. As if Saundra couldn't see them for herself? She didn't say anything, and Saundra supposed she would get an earful once her cousins left.

Bridget bubbled over with plans for them to have a fun evening. Saundra could barely keep up with all the options. Of course, even though her cousin kept saying it was up to her, she knew from experience they would end up doing what pleased them, not her. Not that she would give in. Still, some of it sounded like fun. Some military exercise demonstration on Lake Erie. An exhibition at a private gallery downtown. Dinner at a fancy restaurant. A private museum tour. A private concert for the East Side elite. Saundra couldn't imagine doing all those things in one evening. She was about to say so when Bridget held out her hand and asked for the keys to Saundra's apartment, so they could wait for her to come home after work, instead of, as she put it, "bumming around the sticks." That sounded like the old Bridget.

Saundra wouldn't hand over her keys if it was the end of the world and her apartment was the last safe place to hide.

Kai stepped into the library. He took about five steps toward her, then stopped. From twenty feet away, she saw his mouth flatten, and his expression went pale and grim.

Saundra's desk phone buzzed. Loud. Someone—she had a good idea who—had turned the volume up after she had turned it down again.

"You have a visitor," Twila said through the intercom. "Does Mrs. Tinderbeck know about all the personal time you're using up?"

"Thank you, Twila." Saundra turned and glared at the woman from across the library. That seemed to knock everything back into motion. Kai finished crossing to her area but stayed away a good eight feet. "Hi. Something I can help you with?"

"Ahh ..." He shrugged and made a point of not looking at either of her other two visitors. "Just wanted to know if you were free for pizza tonight. We ended up with a pizza baker as a joke and well ... if you're up for risking your stomach and your life ..." Another shrug.

"Thanks, but my cousins are here from out of town, and I might be tied up." She gestured at Bridget, then Edmund. A cold thread moved through her, insisting something was very wrong here.

Kai clearly avoided looking at them. He wasn't the kind of guy to ignore strangers.

Then something else struck her. Kai could have called. Why make the effort to walk over here from the coffee shop?

"Oh, okay." He nodded to them. Still not looking at them. "Some other time." One corner of his mouth quirked up. "If we don't die of indigestion." A shrug. "Well, back to the salt mines. You'd think in this weather nobody would want to put up buildings, but these new clients are lunatics. Later." He nodded to her and turned and left.

Salt mines? Since when did he refer to the Mug as a salt mine? He loved the place. And what was with talking like he was doing construction?

A queasy chill ran through her, at the sudden certainty Kai knew her cousins and was throwing up a smoke screen. Why?

"That was weird," she murmured, and looked to see what Twila was doing.

Just like she thought: on the phone, her shoulders hunched and one hand cupped around the receiver. It was far too late for Twila to hide the fact she was a constant tattletale. With Roger Cadburn in jail and his stooge, Carruthers fired from the police department, just who was she spying for now?

"You have no idea," Bridget said with a gusting sigh. "Please, oh, please, Sandy, tell us you're not falling for that slimebag's come-on lines?"

"Come-on lines?" She muffled a chuckle. "Why would you think that about Kai?"

"Because we know him," Edmund said. "They're rivals of the family. They're out to destroy the company. Stay away from that guy. His girlfriend is a private investigator. At least, she claims to be. I'm more inclined to call her an industrial spy."

"She stole something big, something so hush-hush important, nobody at the top would tell us what it was," Bridget said, softening her voice. "She stole it from the main offices of Mulcahy-Dresden. Got Edmund in huge trouble." She fluttered her eyelashes and twisted her lips to look pouty for a moment. "Poor guy, nearly broke his heart before he realized she was just there for what she could get. Came on to him like— like a—like a zombie. Just tried to suck him dry."

"You mean a vampire?" Saundra muffled a chuckle. They couldn't honestly be talking about Eden, could they? For one thing, she was Kai's cousin, not girlfriend. And to imagine Eden playing up to a man to get inside information and steal something? Ridiculous!

"Whatever." Bridget fluttered her hands, waving away the correction. "The point is, she played him. Made him think she was in love. It was just awful."

Edmund had sidled over behind Bridget while she talked, and now he shook his head and mouthed "No," several times. Saundra swallowed hard to muffle another chuckle. She wasn't going to ask what part of the story was real and what was exaggeration. She needed to find a way to avoid going out with her cousins even more desperately now than just ten minutes ago.

"What is he doing here? Why is he glomming onto you?" She squeaked and sat up straighter on the edge of Saundra's desk. "Oh, I know, you're so good at research. I mean, you're a librarian. He must be using you to get free research and digging into classified records and things. That must be it."

"No, Kai is a friend from … well, from the Chamber of Commerce. We're working on some things together for the Christmas festival," Saundra said.

"Chamber of Commerce?" Edmund's face wrinkled up like he couldn't believe what he was saying.

"He owns a business here in town."

"No. It has to be a front. I bet they're all in on some big scheme together." Bridget slid off the side of the desk and gestured at the door. "Oh, Sandy, we have to get you out of here. It's not safe for you. They know you're a Mulcahy. They followed you here to town. They're after you to get to us, to destroy the family business."

"I don't think so. Kai and — well, Kai has been here for five years. He was here long before I got here."

"You're sure?" Edmund caught hold of Bridget as if he had to hold her back. Saundra's words seemed to reassure him, but Bridget couldn't be reassured. She insisted on leaving immediately, getting entirely out of Cadburn. She wanted to take Saundra with them, completely out of town, don't worry about her things, the family would replace everything.

Mrs. Tinderbeck came to Saundra's rescue. She walked over with that calm, steady, no-nonsense stare, her left eyebrow cocked up just slightly. Bridget's bubbling, fake panic died away. She even flushed a little. Saundra knew that wasn't embarrassment, because she couldn't imagine either of her cousins feeling embarrassed about anything. Frustrated, yes. Foolish, yes. Flustered and unable to think clearly, most definitely yes.

"I'm sorry, but this is a library, if you haven't noticed. I'm sure you believe this emergency of yours is important, but I must insist on you letting Saundra complete her duties without any more distractions. If you're feeling distressed, perhaps I should call an EMT or send for an ambulance to take you to the hospital?"

"No, thank you, Mrs. T," Saundra hurried to say. "They were just leaving."

"I overheard you talking about plans for this evening. Did you forget your committee meetings for the Christmas festival? You can't miss any of them, Saundra. This is very important for our public relations effort."

"Of course. Thank you. I'm sorry. I completely forgot." She fought not to grin, or worse, laugh. Mrs. Tinderbeck was the head of the committee for the Christmas festival, and they had met last night. She would hug her boss as soon as her cousins were out of there.

Under Mrs. Tinderbeck's calm, disapproving gaze, Bridget and Edmund made their farewells and hurried out of the library. Saundra immediately got on her phone and called the superintendent of her building, asking him to be on the lookout for them to come back and try to get into her apartment. She said a quick prayer that her cousins would slink away to pout and drink themselves some encouragement. If she was lucky, they would decide whatever they were looking for wasn't worth the trouble. Then she hurried to Mrs. Tinderbeck's office to explain what that newest mess was all about.

~~~~~

By the time Kai got back to the Mug, the Mulcahys had left the library. Relief fought with guilt as he listened to the recording Eden had made, thanks to the tiny wireless microphones installed in the library, courtesy of Nick West. While the man's know-it-all attitude and his relationship with Saundra still irked him, he had to admit that knowing they could check on her made up for his interference in their lives over the last few months. Granted, Kai felt some irritation that Eden hadn't revealed the existence of those microphones until Saundra's superintendent, Owen Miller, called to tell them that the two "fancy-dressed snots" who tried to get into her apartment the other day were back, and this time headed for the library. Eden sent him over to the library deliberately to get a reaction from the Mulcahy twins.

He could almost laugh at the ridiculous story Bridget told, until he realized that the twins knew about Eden, despite the care he and Troy had taken to keep them from finding out about her existence. What else did they know or just suspect about him and his cousins?

The conversation between Saundra and Mrs. Tinderbeck was reassuring. He had to head back downstairs to the coffee shop since he did have a business to run. Eden promised him when Troy got back, they would plan the next step to protect Saundra. Maybe it was time to have that talk with her, find out what she knew about the Venetian glass heart lockets, and share what they knew and guessed.

~~~~~

Thursday on her lunch break, Saundra stayed at the library because the weather was still miserable. She checked her email on her phone during the fifteen minutes when Twila wasn't in the lunchroom. Among all the spam emails, advertising services she didn't need for bank accounts and exercise equipment she didn't own, she found an email from Cleo.

> *You'll have answers soon enough. Some leads and possibilities are finally coming together, and if the allies I anticipate are real, and not illusions like so many others have been over the years, then I can finally entrust some wonderful secrets to you. You're absolutely right. You have the right to know.*
>
> *For now, though, be doubly careful. I share your doubt that this new friendship from your cousins is anything but a ruse. Put the heart away, back where it can't be found. I asked Nick to be on the alert for their next nasty move.*
>
> *Hold on and be patient just a little longer, darling.*

There was a time, Saundra reflected, when her aunt's taste for mystery and adventure had been exciting. She had been delighted to be included in little puzzles and sleuthing games. Today, though, somehow it all made her feel tired. And a little afraid. Just what was Cleo involved in, and who was she involved with?

When she got home, she went straight to her bedroom, before she took off her coat, and picked up the box to put the heart back in the strongbox in the secret compartment in the window seat.

The box felt too light. There was no sliding sound and shifting of weight as the glass heart moved across the bottom of the box. Saundra swallowed hard and opened the box.

Empty.

She thought long and hard and prayed just as hard, and nearly called Pastor Roy and Patty to ask for their help. If Nick had been watching her cousins, there was no way they could have gotten into her apartment to take the heart. The most likely scenario was that they had gotten in that first day her superintendent caught them, and they pretended to be trying to get in, rather than admitting they had been caught leaving the building.

How did they know that after all this time, she had the heart? They wouldn't have wasted all that time and effort on a guess or hunch. Yet if they had the heart, why were they hanging around town, and trying to make nice with her? What more did they want?

Who could she turn to for help? She didn't want to tell Cleo what had happened until she had absolutely no hope at all.

Chapter Five

Friday morning, Saundra parked a block away from Book & Mug and hoped the extra hour she had given herself before she had to be at work would be enough. Eden could work faster than the police. Maybe she could influence the authorities to put out a warrant for Bridget and Edmund. They hadn't come back yet to pester her to come play, so most likely they were already safely back home with the heart, basking in the praise of their relatives.

As if thinking of her had been a cue, Eden came walking down the sidewalk toward Saundra, while she was still in her car, gathering her thoughts. Saundra watched her, trying to plan how she would approach Kai's cousin. Maybe she should make it an official visit to Finders, Inc.? Would she be taken more seriously if she called ahead before she walked into the coffee shop and asked to go upstairs? That sounded like a good idea. Call, leave a message, and be waiting in the coffee shop when Eden came back from whatever errands she was running. Saundra pulled out her phone.

A streak of sunlight illuminated a sparkle of gold and red at Eden's throat, just as she came even with the nose of Saundra's car. Something went cold and still inside her chest as the familiar sparkle and shape and colors mesmerized her. She raised the phone and snapped three pictures before Eden walked past her and reached for the door of Green's Grocery.

The images caught on the cell phone were too small to do her any good. When she made the pictures bigger, they turned the red and gold sparkles into blobs.

Saundra didn't need the proof of the pictures. She knew what she had seen.

Eden was wearing that Venetian glass heart she had glimpsed back in September.

Saundra took several deep breaths, and closed her eyes, and prayed one of those hurting, simple prayers of *Please, God, help?* First, she needed to verify Eden had another glass heart locket, not just a lookalike. She got out of her car and walked down to Green's Grocery.

The sun was bright, sparkling on all the Christmas decorations on the old-fashioned light poles. Tinsel and pine garlands and oversized metallic blue and red and gold ornaments, and twinkle lights everywhere. Visible in the big front window of the grocery, Eden tugged down the long red plaid scarf covering her mane of sable curls. She talked to old Mr. Green in his white apron, white shirt and black pants. He was busy filling tilted bins with potatoes and onions, green apples and oranges.

The glass heart vanished, likely hidden under the scarf, and Saundra relaxed a little. Now would be the perfect time for Bridget or Edmund or both to show up and cause a ruckus and try to get at the heart. Those two thought too quickly, coming up with a dozen lies in as many seconds.

Saundra waited until Eden came out with her two cotton bags of groceries. She called greetings to various people as she headed back to Book & Mug. Saundra followed, but slowed her steps, so she wouldn't seem to be following her. She flinched every time friends called out to her. Maybe this wasn't such a good plan after all. Maybe she should have gone straight to Kai and asked for his help? The friendship growing between them was in jeopardy if this all went horribly wrong.

As if thinking of him conjured him, Kai appeared in the doorway of Book & Mug, meeting Eden as she reached the door. He took the two grocery bags and she turned around to leave.

"Don't you dare!" Kai called, as Eden headed down the street in the other direction. "Don't even think of bringing some foreign coffee into my place."

Eden just laughed, turning to walk backward a few steps. She passed Saundra, who stood by the light pole and pretended to check her purse. Then she was past.

Kai's gaze swept over Saundra as he turned to go back into the coffee shop. His face lit up and something seemed to crack open in her chest.

"Your favorite on special today," Kai called. "Cinnamon cappuccino."

"Umm, maybe after I ..." Saundra gestured down the street.

"I like a lady with her priorities in order. Exercise, freeze yourself getting errands done, then come in and drink something hot and loaded with sugar." He winked, and she had to laugh, despite the ache threatening to choke her.

"Sounds good." She took a few steps back, her heart racing with the panicky realization that Eden had probably vanished. So much for her first attempt at tailing someone.

"Later, pretty lady."

By the time Saundra had followed Eden across two intersections, heading east toward the park, her hands were chilled, and she had to jam them in her pockets. The day had been mild enough to leave her gloves in the car. What had she been thinking, first tailing Eden, and now going without gloves? It was December in Northeast Ohio, for heaven's sake.

Eden stopped at a window display of glass ornaments with tiny lights inside. The store, Illumination, was new and had opened on Black Friday. Saundra ducked into Iris and Aperture, a store featuring prints and art supplies, specializing in photography. The deep-set display windows in the old-fashioned building let her keep an eye on Eden even when she stepped into Illumination.

A man smelling of English Leather lime stepped up to the bin of photos next to her. She didn't think they made that scent anymore. Her father wore it. The man flipped through the matted photos with a careless speed that had her glancing at him to make sure he really was looking at the prints. For just a second, she thought she was looking at Troy. The same high cheekbones, sable curls, hazel eyes. But no, not Troy. About four inches shorter, with wider shoulders. Dressed in his usual leather bomber-style jacket, Nick West had a camera hanging from a thick, indigo strap around his neck.

"New at this, aren't you?" He gave her a slow smile when she tipped her head up to meet his gaze. "Tailing someone." He gestured with a jerk of chin at the back of Eden's pea coat, barely visible now in the other store's front window.

"Me? Why would I?"

"You really need to work on lying more convincingly." He picked up the camera and clicked it on, then turned it to show her the screen. Saundra tried to step around him and he blocked her. She had to look.

There was the glass heart, framed in the collar of Eden's pea coat.

"Yes, you do." He gave her a smile that would have been charming at any other time.

"Look—"

"I like this one the best." He clicked through the catalog of shots, and Saundra couldn't turn her gaze away.

In clicks of just a second or two at a time, she saw the locket. Against her green cowlneck sweater. In her hand, against her high-necked gray dress, which she had worn to the library on Tuesday. Nick had a picture of her studying the heart when she checked it during the day.

"Just how long ago did Cleo ask you to check on me? Maybe since she told me to wear the heart? Is that *why* she told me?" Saundra's stomach twisted, at the thought that her aunt had been using her as bait. Didn't they trust her to carry through her part in luring Eden out into the open to discuss the heart?

"Come on. The suspense is killing me." He looped his arm through hers and pulled her along with him.

"Hey!" She didn't resist until they were three steps out of the shop and turning to go into Illumination.

Eden wasn't there.

He muttered something and turned, looking up and down the street.

"Do you mind?" She tugged her arm free when his turns threatened to yank her off her feet. "Maybe your technique needs some work, too."

He let out a growly sort of sigh. "Might as well combine our resources."

"What might those be?"

He grinned. "Feisty today, aren't you? Marian the librarian might not suit you after all."

"Gee, I never heard that one before." She wanted to laugh, and she wanted to punch him. It made her head hurt more.

He moved out ahead of her. She supposed she had the choice of running along after him or being left behind.

Nick led the way at a brisk pace. At the next intersection, he looked to the right and gestured for her to look left. He had put away the camera, probably tucked into an inner pocket of his jacket. How come men's jackets had those convenient inner pockets, but she could never find a woman's jacket with at least one? It wasn't fair, even considering that women could get away with purses.

No sign of Eden. How had she vanished so easily, so quickly? Granted, they had been distracted. Nick raked one long-fingered hand through his hair.

"She's good. Kind of makes me proud, when you really think about it." He huffed and looked both directions. "Well, head down to the shop or double back? "

"Why?" Eden emerged from a shadowy doorway right behind them.

Saundra had the satisfaction of seeing Nick flinch.

"Just what are the two of you up to, shadowing me?" Eden crossed her arms over her chest and spread her feet, visibly ready to stand there a good long time.

"What have *you* been up to, to *need* to be alert enough to notice someone is shadowing you?" Nick started to cross his arms, then his smirk went crooked and he clasped his hands behind his back instead.

"Every time you show up, there's usually some kind of trouble." Eden flicked her gaze to Saundra, then back to him. "Granted, you help solve it instead of start it, but we've learned to be paranoid. Troy has started calling you 'the spook,' by the way."

"Well ..." Nick bared his teeth, and Saundra wondered if he was at a loss for words. For probably the first time since she had known him. He usually had a witty remark, or as Aunt Cleo would say, a half-witty remark, for every occasion. "I guess I'm losing my touch. Or maybe it just runs in the family."

When Eden didn't respond to what certainly struck Saundra as an opening, fishing for a reaction, his amusement faded a few degrees.

"We need to talk."

"We need to talk about your heart locket," Saundra said.

"Why?" Eden tipped her head to the right and raised her gloved hand to her scarf-swathed throat.

"Maybe the more important question is why Saundra's not wearing hers," Nick said.

Saundra felt like a load of slush had slid off a storefront canopy and right down her collar. Knowing Nick, he probably knew her cousins had gotten in and stolen the heart.

Knowing Nick ... maybe he already had a plan for getting it back? But if he did, why was he wasting time harassing her and stalking Eden?

"No, the more important question is why she hasn't approached me, since I've been wearing my heart to lure her in." A bright smile wiped away Eden's guarded expression.

"We need to talk," Nick repeated.

"Yes, we do." She turned and gestured toward the gold twinkle lights wrapped around the arched trellis in front of the door to Book & Mug. "Let's get comfortable."

"If you wanted to talk to me, you could have just said something," Saundra said. "Instead of ... instead of playing tricks and being all mysterious."

"It was a test. Come on. We'll be more comfortable inside." She turned and walked away and didn't bother checking to see if either of them followed her.

When they entered the Book & Mug, Kai was on the phone and writing on a pad of paper. He cocked an eyebrow at them and turned his head to watch as Nick and Saundra follow Eden to the back corner booth, all the while saying, "Uh huh," and "Large?" and "Right, the usual." Eden gestured for them to sit, then stepped away, down the back hallway.

Nick half-bowed and gestured for Saundra to slide into the bench seat ahead of him. She didn't think until she was already seated that now she wouldn't be able to get up and leave without asking him to move. Or sliding under the table. Maybe she could get up on the seat and climb over to the booth behind her.

Eden came back without her coat, the chain visible but the heart tucked inside her sweater. She stepped behind the counter and snagged a serving tray. Saundra watched Eden work around Kai, who manipulated the different coffee spigots and steamed milk nozzles and pump bottles of flavored syrups, filling two carryout trays of cups. They didn't seem to be talking to each other, but Saundra caught a couple of glances they exchanged, nods and shrugs. Silent communication from long practice. Eden returned to the booth with three mugs on a round tray. All cinnamon cappuccinos with cinnamon candy canes and whipped cream piled high enough to threaten to spill over the side.

"You're good," Nick said as Eden slid their mugs to them and sat down. "How long did it take to figure out I was doing recon?"

"Troy saw you when he was following up on a report that the Mulcahy twins were trying to get into Saundra's apartment. You were focused on them."

"They didn't, did they?" Saundra said.

"Oh, ye of little faith," Nick muttered.

She muffled a gasp of exasperation and contemplated the proper angle to jab him in the side with her elbow.

"We debated if you were just careless and didn't see Troy, or arrogant and didn't react, maybe figuring he wasn't a threat. We decided you were testing us."

"So you left me dangling in the wind, is that it?" He saluted her with the mug as he raised it to his lips. His gaze locked with Eden's as he took a long, slow sip.

"We figured you were up to something since you didn't contact Saundra. Why would we think that?" Eden swirled her candy cane through the whipped cream. "She didn't gripe about you. She does that every time you show up. Didn't you know?"

"Now I do." He gave Saundra a sideways glance through narrowed eyes. Then he leaned back in the booth and chuckled. She wanted to give him a shove hard enough to have him sprawling on the floor.

"So … we were trying for a reaction from Saundra when she saw me wearing this. Get things out in the open, start people talking." Eden rested two fingers over the bulge of the locket under the neckline of her sweater. "What does the heart mean to you? Why do you have it?"

"My aunt is guarding it," Saundra said.

At the same time, Nick said, "It's a family heirloom."

"Which is it?" Eden's tone went cool.

"Both." Nick shrugged, never moving from his slouched position. "My grandmother entrusted that heart to me when I was … probably younger than you three when you hit the foster care system. Cleo is an old family friend. Her family inherited mine as a duty, like you see in those

PBS Masterpiece dramas, where the servants inherit their positions from their parents. With the kind of life I lead ..." He shrugged. "Cleo is a better guardian than me."

"Runs in the family," Saundra whispered. She caught her breath when Eden went so utterly still she thought her friend had even stopped breathing. "Are you ... cousins to Eden and Kai and Troy?"

Nick shrugged. "Time will tell, won't it?"

Eden muttered something that sounded familiar yet wasn't English. Saundra understood the intent, if not the words. She had heard Cleo and Nick speaking a similar language.

"Miss Cole, I am shocked. Such language coming from a lady of your breeding," Nick said. How did he manage to speak so clearly when his face was stretched in that smirking, evil grin Saundra always wanted to slap off his face?

"Why do I have the feeling you know a whole heck of a lot more about my so-called breeding than I do?" Eden lowered her voice so no one outside the booth could have understood.

"Sorry ... I really am sorry." The amusement fled his face. He sat up and put his elbows on the table. "I don't know much of anything. No solid, hard facts. Just a lot of stories and speculation. We were all kept in the dark to protect us. And those." He gestured at the lump under Eden's fingers.

"What is in your heart?"

"Nothing."

Eden studied him, then glanced at Saundra, eyes narrowing to slits. "Okay, you want to get nitpicky? What *was* in your heart?" She shook her head when Nick just tipped his head to the left, as if in confusion or question. "Seeds for those interesting plants Saundra is growing for her aunt?"

"Uh huh. Saw them, did you?"

"Would you two stop it?" Saundra barely refrained from slamming her fist down on the table. "We should be working together."

"Why?" Eden said. Not in a nasty way. Just curious.

The words caught in Saundra's throat. She couldn't look Eden or Nick in the eyes for a few seconds. How could she confess the heart had been stolen? She needed to work up to it.

"Bridget and Edmund —"

"We know about them. Kind of shocked us to find out you were a Mulcahy."

"I'm not," Saundra growled. "I never was. They made it very clear, my whole life. I wasn't good enough for them."

"The only thing her father ever did that earned the family's praise was marrying her mother. Everything went sour when they discovered she didn't have a glass heart. The Mulcahys have suspected for years that the Baileys have custody of one. They want the seeds some of the hearts are guarding," Nick said. "I'm guessing since you asked, and since you have that fascinating greenhouse on your roof, your heart had seeds too?" He leaned even closer, softening his voice more. "And let's make another guess. You were the trusting little souls who went to the wrong botanist for help in identifying those seeds, and he tried to sell you out to Mulcahy-Dresden, and that put the clan on your trail?"

"How do you know that?" Eden said.

"That's my chosen task. Keeping an eye on the clan, ensuring they don't make any headway. The Mulcahys used to be family retainers, just like the Baileys. Only they decided turncoat paid better. They've got a long tradition of selling to the highest bidder and then running off with whatever goodies they can grab, so someone else takes the fall when the latest crime lord finds out the treasure vault has been emptied out."

Eden studied him for a few moments. One corner of her mouth quirked up. "I thought you said you didn't know much."

"Like I said, mostly stories, few hard facts. Very little proof."

"What do you know, then?"

"What color is the stripe down the back?" Nick said.

Saundra barely stopped herself from asking the obvious question: *Do the hearts have different colors on the back?*

"Every heart locket looks the same on the front." He picked up his mug, cradling it in both hands and gazing down into the creamy depths. "Unless they're put next to each other, lined up, you can't find the minor differences. You'd think they were all made from the same mold, but they're not. They were hand-made, to order, at the same time, decades ago. With specks of gold and silver and gem dust to make them individual and unique. And each locket has a different color on the back. They were made to help identify the people they were given to and their descendants." He glanced sideways at Saundra. "What color is mine?" He grinned. "I assume you've studied it often enough to know it on sight?

She wanted to give him that shove right off the bench. "Green. Dark enough to look black," she admitted, meeting Eden's gaze.

Nick cocked an eyebrow at Eden. She slowly reached into the collar of her sweater and pulled out the heart. She turned it over, cupping it in both hands, shielding it when she held it out so only Saundra could see it. The stripe down the back was raspberry. A little squiggle of what looked like gold leaf crossed the raspberry line in the middle.

Nick rested his hand over Eden's, pressing them flat and apart, so he could see the heart. He went very still for three heartbeats. Then he nodded, his mouth stretching in a flat smile.

"Interesting. I had heard about the crowns, but never thought I'd see one."

"Why don't I believe you?" Eden fluttered her eyelashes at him.

"How long ago did you get that locket from your mother?"

"None of your business."

"It might be. If I'm right about you. Which I'm sure I am." He exhaled loudly and turned sideways in the booth to face Saundra full-on. "Why aren't you wearing the heart?"

"Well, duh," she said, making a sour face to hide the guilty fear dropping ice into her belly. "As soon as my cousins showed up, I knew better than to take that chance."

"Yeah, smart." He cocked an eyebrow at her, as if he expected her to say something more. When she didn't respond, he turned back to Eden. "I'm going to hazard a guess that trying to follow up on the clues, figure out where you came from, that got you started in the sleuthing business."

"Maybe. You know, this has gone on way too far without including the guys." Eden slid out of the booth. "And more secure surroundings. Without any handy listening bugs you might have planted thinking you're protecting people."

Nick flinched. He didn't look at her, but Saundra suddenly knew.

"You did it again, didn't you?" She punched his arm, then turned to Eden, aching with a sense of betrayal. "He's bugged different places where I worked, when my cousins were getting their slimy fingers in and making things hard for me. Did he plant bugs at the library? And you knew?"

"We gave him the benefit of the doubt that it was to protect you." Eden shrugged. "Sorry. You know now."

"Get out of my way you big—" Saundra shoved on Nick's arm and spat some of the nastiest-sounding words in that foreign language she could remember. She had no idea if she was even pronouncing them correctly, or what they meant, but from the widening of Eden's eyes and the momentary shock in Nick's, she was close enough for them both to understand.

Nick got out of the booth and stepped back to let her slide out.

Her phone chimed, the generic marimba going up and down the scale. Saundra checked her watch even though she knew by the alarm what time it was.

"I have to go to work. Don't let this big bully run over any of you." She took a breath. "And you'll at least tell me what you all talked about, since he's too busy playing James Bond to talk to us little people?" Saundra barely waited for Eden to nod. She turned and stomped out of the coffee shop, muttering, "Family retainers."

Chapter Six

Kai texted her less than an hour later, with breaks of ten and fifteen minutes between each message, likely taking care of customers. They were full of emojis that made her laugh, in between complaining that life was so unfair, if there was even a remote chance Nick West could be a distant relative. Because he couldn't possibly be distant enough. He promised to send her a copy of the audio recording Eden had made of the whole meeting between the four of them, comparing what they knew. Nick even admitted Cleo knew far more than he did. She was something like the archivist for the search to find all the scattered members of their clan. Other hearts were supposed to hold bits of paper, lists of names and places and dates, and even pieces of a map. What the map led to, he had no idea. According to Nick, there were twenty-six hearts, with the colored stripe indicating which of the original five siblings the holders of the hearts descended from. That meant the three cousins were cousins, but in several branches of the family line since each of their hearts was a different color.

Saundra nearly dropped her phone when she read that. Kai and Troy had Venetian glass heart lockets too? Then she laughed aloud at his next text.

The spook is ticked that Eden has one of the crowns. It means she's descended from the clan patriarch. Could almost read his mind. He wants to be the boss. Before he breaks into your friend Charli's place to see if her heart is the real thing, do you know what color is on the back of hers? Have you gotten close enough to see that?

Sorry, she texted back a minute later, after waiting for Twila to skulk back to the checkout desk. Fortunately, she was on a break between story sessions, but Twila acted as if there was no such thing as privacy as long as she was within the library's walls. *I've never had a chance to examine it. I was planning on confronting her one of these days, wearing my heart. Well, actually, Nick's heart. I never knew it was his. I thought it was Cleo's.*

Kind of explains some things. Guy doesn't have a heart.

Saundra muffled a snort.

Can you ask her? Maybe invite her over to meet with us? Gotta team up against Cousin Nick before he gets too bossy, y'know?

Oh, I know all too well. Saundra sighed and thought a moment before confessing. *Charli's grandmother took it with her on a trip to Europe. As a good* luck charm. Definitely bring her into the defensive circle, but you can't look at the heart until probably February. It's a long, long trip. World tour kind of thing.

Wow, must be nice to be retired.

They texted back and forth a few more times, but she had kindergarten story time coming up and he had a business to run. He asked her to come to lunch, but she had a meeting with the middle school PTA to set up a library booth at the Christmas concert.

Kai responded with a sad face emoji. Then he went silent. There were a dozen things that demanded his attention as owner of the shop.

Then Bridget called, cooing in her Southern sweet tea voice, which meant something was up. Well, two could play that game, couldn't they? Especially since she was sure her cousins had gotten into her apartment, despite Owen Miller keeping watch. The security cameras around the greenhouse on her balcony had caught nothing, but chances were good her cousins would try again to get to the plants. Once they got the heart open and discovered all the seeds were gone, they would be back. Despite her seething irritation with Nick right now, she would call him and let him know what was up, what she suspected, so he could keep watch.

Bridget asked Saundra to come to dinner with her. Testing, Saundra agreed and asked where she was staying, and offered to pick her and Edmund up. Bridget gave the hotel name and address a little too easily, but she didn't say if Edmund was or wasn't joining them. Definitely, something was up.

By the time Saundra hung up, she already had a different plan to deal with her cousins.

Kai called during her afternoon break. Fortunately, Twila was busy on the phone, so she couldn't skulk over and try to listen in.

"Sorry, I already have plans for dinner," she said, as soon as he finished asking her to come after work. "In fact, I'm going to need Eden's help. Could you have her call me?"

"Nope." He chuckled. "She's right here. Hold on."

"Hey, what's up?" Eden said just a few seconds later.

"How good are you at picking locks? Break in while someone's out."

"Oh, please, tell me we're going to short-sheet the *ma'hoot's* bed?"

Saundra sputtered laughter. That was one of those foreign words Aunt Cleo used quite often, meaning several different derogatory things, depending on the intensity of the situation. Saundra didn't have to ask, Eden had to be referring to Nick.

"Better. My cousin, Bridget. The thing is ..." She closed her eyes and said a quick prayer for courage and the right words. "I can't tell Nick, but I'm pretty sure she and Edmund got into my apartment and stole the heart. Help me get it back?"

"Oh, you better believe it. After what they did to us, the cons they tried to pull ... yeah. Gimme the time and place. You're getting her out of a hotel? Both of them?"

"I'm pretty sure it'll be just Bridget and me, and Edmund will try to get into my place to have a go at the greenhouse. I've got alarms and cameras, and I'm going to file a report with the police, maybe I can get Allen Kenward to keep watch."

"The guys would pay to be part of this." Eden chuckled. "Gimme the details. We're gonna get them back good, and get your heart back, and Cousin Nick need never know."

"Thanks. You're saving me years of sniping."

"Is he that bad?"

"Actually ..." Saundra sighed. "No, Nick isn't the kind to say I-told-you-so, but if he can tease me about something, he will. Most of the time, I kind of like having an irritating older brother. He does look out for me, and he's really the only family I have, other than Cleo, but ... It's complicated."

"Tell me about it. No, remind me to tell you what it was like, growing up in the system, constantly having to convince a new batch of social workers and foster parents every few months that yes, we're cousins, we have to stay together."

"Sounds as bad as growing up with the Mulcahys."

"Oh, honey, sorry, but you've got us beat when it comes to misery and unfairness!"

~~~~~

Saundra's suspicions deepened when Bridget asked if they could go to dinner at Frenchie's, the English-style pub in Cadburn. That would add up to a lot of time spent driving back and forth, to the hotel downtown, and then back to Cadburn, and then downtown again when she took Bridget back to the hotel. She wasn't surprised at all that Edmund wasn't joining them. Bridget said he wanted to catch a hockey game. Saundra had to wait until they reached the restaurant to check the Cleveland Monsters schedule. Fortunately, Bridget went into the restroom as soon as they arrived at the restaurant, leaving Saundra alone long enough to get on her phone. The Monsters were playing a home match tonight. That didn't prove anything. The twins were experienced liars and knew how to back up their stories.

Before she could text Eden to update her, she texted Saundra.

Spook caught him. Troy says halfway up a ladder to your balcony. Cops helped.

Saundra muffled laughter, responded with a half-dozen grinning emojis, and put her phone away before Bridget came out of the restroom.

Bridget was still exclaiming over the calamari and fried green bean appetizers when her phone rang. She grimaced and ignored her phone. It stopped, then a minute later rang again. Stopped. A minute later, rang again.

"Salesmen," she muttered, and held up a hand for their waitress, Bernadette. "Honey, I really need something strong and big and sweet. What do you recommend?"

Saundra nearly spluttered her mouthful of green beans. What was Bridget up to, to play the sweet little thing card so strongly? Then her own phone chimed.

She reached for her phone sitting inside her purse on the chair next to her.

The text from Eden had one word: *Zilch.*

"Jerks," Bridget said, and flipped her phone into silent mode without looking at the screen. "Who's harassing you?"

"Not harassing. I'm on several committees for Christmas plays and parties and things, as a representative of the library. Always someone needing permission to change something." She shrugged and slid the phone back into her purse. The last thing she needed was Bridget reaching across the table to grab her phone and read the chain of texts. She wouldn't know who they were from, since Saundra merely had Eden's number identified with a capital E in her address book. Still, Bridget wasn't stupid by any measure, and she might put the string of messages together into a picture that could turn the evening very ugly in mere seconds.

"Oh, Sandy, you're such a go-getter! You really do need to have some pity on me and Edmund. Come back and get involved in the family business. We can't run things all by ourselves when everybody finally kicks off. I mean, yes, we have so many incredible ideas, and it's just going to turn things around big-time when we can finally do what we want without those old-fashioned dweebs getting in our faces, but ..." Bridget sighed. Then sighed louder and nearly snatched the tall glass off Bernadette's tray when she came to the table. "Oh, that is just what I need." She giggled, an uncharacteristically sweet sound. "Keep them coming, honey."

Bridget was trying too hard. What was she up to?

The second glass arrived, and still no food. Their dinners were taking far too long. Frenchies' prided themselves on serving high-quality food, fast and hot. Not that she was really hungry, after splitting the calamari and fried green beans. Something was going on. What?

Her phone pinged.

Eden: *Dinner has been delayed. Like some fireworks instead?*

Saundra stared at the text screen a heartbeat too long. Bridget giggled, but her tone was sharp as she asked who was bothering her now and couldn't those idiots leave her to eat her dinner in peace?

"Oh, hi," Eden called from the doorway into the dining room. She unwound her thick red plaid scarf as she crossed over to their table. "Didn't think I'd see you here tonight." Then she tugged open her pea coat, revealing the glass heart, glittering in all its antique glory.

Bridget choked on her next mouthful of drink. She barely got the glass down to the table before she dropped it. Her eyes got big, then narrowed in the greedy avarice and vicious cunning Saundra knew too well from childhood.

"Sandy! Look at that!"

"For the last time," Saundra snapped, "my name is Saundra. Not Sandy. When are you going to get it right?"

Bridget choked as she rose from her seat, pointing at Eden's chest. "But—but—Sandy, look what she's wearing! She stole it from you. That's some nerve! Call the cops. Somebody!" She waved her arms around as she stumbled around the table, reaching for Eden, who backed away from her with ease. "Stop her. Don't let her leave! That's a family heirloom! She stole it from my family."

Now Saundra understood Eden's plan. Bernadette had probably tripled the amount of alcohol in Bridget's drink, to slow her thinking. Not slow enough to keep her from accusing Eden of stealing Saundra's heart.

Zilch clearly meant Eden hadn't found anything while searching Bridget and Edmund's rooms at the hotel. So if they didn't have it ...

Maybe Eden was trying to drum up a reason to search Bridget? Was Edmund being searched at the police station right that moment?

Saundra's head hurt. She usually avoided alcohol, but she might just snag a gulp of what was left in Bridget's tall glass.

Officer Ted Shrieve stepped into the dining room, looking serious and official. He cocked a skeptical eyebrow at Bridget.

"Excuse me, ma'am, have you had too much to drink tonight?"

"Too much to—" Bridget let out a shriek and slammed her fist down onto the table, making several dishes jump. "I'm telling you, she's a thief!" She pointed a wobbling hand at Eden. "That heart belongs to my family."

"Really?" He turned to Eden. Then back to Bridget. "Just when did she take it? Because I've seen her wearing that pretty little heart before. My wife commented on it, liked it so much, I got her one from Etsy. Almost a duplicate."

Saundra muffled a snort and prayed Bridget didn't look at her, so she couldn't see her expression before she got it under control. Ted wasn't married. Clearly, he was part of Eden's plan.

She most definitely loved living in Cadburn Township, and all her new, wonderful, brilliant friends.

"If you say its yours, can you identify it?"

"Can I identify it? Look at it!" Bridget sputtered. She wobbled and had to brace herself on the table. Just how much alcohol had Bernadette put in her glass?

"What does the back look like?" Eden reached up and unfastened the clasp of the ornate blue and silver beaded chain and turned her back on Bridget before turning the heart over and showing it to Shrieve. "Describe the design on the back, if it's yours."

"Design?" Bridget gulped. She turned to Saundra. "Sandy, honey, help me out. You've seen the heart more times than me. Identify it, okay, so we can get it back? Officer, you have to believe me, our granny is just heartbroken over her heart being stolen." A bubble of giggles escaped her. "Heartbroken, heart stolen." Then she jerked herself upright again.

"I don't know what you're talking about," Saundra said, trying to widen her eyes and look innocent. "I've seen Eden wear that heart many times. As for heirlooms … I know when we were children, Grandmother accused my mother of stealing, but they got court orders to search our house and never found anything. I wish you had told me before it was a heart. I would have used my library search engines to look for anything like it."

Bridget stared at her for several seconds, going pale and then flushing so deep red Saundra thought maybe blood would trickle from the lip she gnawed on.

A steam engine shriek erupted from Bridget, and she flung herself at Saundra, hands twisted into claws. Fortunately, the table was between them. Even more fortunately, Officer Shrieve was fast, catching her around the waist and pulling her away. Bridget flailed her arms and legs in the air, shrieking and spilling profanity such that Grandmother Mulcahy would have made her eat an entire bar of soap, not just wash her mouth out with it.

Chapter Seven

"Now we'll never get the heart back." Saundra winced at the defeated tone of her voice.

The bright lights and colors filling the street and the competing strains of Christmas carols coming from businesses open late made an incongruous background as she, Kai, Eden, and Troy walked back to Book & Mug from the police station. She was actually surprised that many businesses still had their lights on. She thought they had been filling out reports for hours. She was exhausted and depressed, despite the glory of hearing Bridget and Edmund snarl and snipe at each other from opposite ends of the small jail cell area at the back of the Cadburn Township police station.

Naturally, her cousins had immediately gone into their standard mode of operations, a combination of "lie until everybody is dizzy" and "scorched earth." They hadn't prevailed and had no real defense other than Bridget being rip-roaring drunk. Officer Shrieve had his body camera turned on from the moment he walked into the dining room. He caught every word Bridget shrieked, including the threats she flung at him. Then she tried to seduce him and flung more threats when he talked about what a wonderful woman his non-existent wife was, and how much she loved the glass heart he found on Etsy. Just like Eden's, which she had admired for years.

Edmund's break-in attempt had been caught on the security cameras at the apartment building, as well as Kai, Troy, and Nick's cell phones. He claimed the ladder had been there, already propped against the balcony of Saundra's apartment, and he had heard her cry for help and climbed up because he was afraid for his darling cousin. The videos showed him breaking the lock on the garage at the back of the apartment building lot, hauling the ladder out, and fighting with it until he figured out the extensions. Another camera recorded him leaning it against the balcony, knocking flowerpots and decorations off several other balconies in the process.

Still, Saundra's good spirits kept taking a nose-dive every few moments when the truth bobbed up through her weariness.

"If the creeps don't have it, then who does?" Troy said, finally voicing what had probably been bothering all of them since Eden sent her *zilch* message.

"You know, if you had trusted me and told me," Nick said, stepping from a shadowy alley between two smaller shops, "I could have done something a lot sooner."

"Why didn't you? Aren't you spying on me all the time? How many cameras do you have in my apartment? Why didn't you catch the thief in the act?" Saundra stomped toward him. Her voice broke when Nick stepped back and nearly skidded across an icy patch in a low spot in the sidewalk.

"You don't trust me. That's the problem."

"Give her one good reason why she should?" Kai shot back. He stepped up and wrapped an arm around Saundra and guided her back to where Eden and Troy waited, with a good six feet of sidewalk between them and Nick. "She's referred to you as her big brother a few times, but honestly? Who needs family like that?"

"Big brother, huh?" Nick's expression smoothed out into that unreadable look that made her want to pound him sometimes. He nodded. "Fair enough." His glance slid over all of them. One corner of his mouth quirked up. Not quite a Nick West trademarked smirk, but close enough Saundra got over her fear that she had actually hurt his feelings. "I've got some strings to tie up of my own. Take care of my little sister for me, would you?"

Then he turned and walked away into the Christmas lights and shadows. Several storefront lights turned off as he passed them. Saundra wouldn't have been surprised if that was somehow planned by him, for effect. Nick loved a little bit of drama even though she knew he would deny it. That had to be the reason he lurked in the shadows and watched and waited until the perfect time to step in.

"We don't need to be asked," Troy said.

"We don't need permission," Kai said nearly at the same time.

Silence for a few seconds, then they laughed and the four started down the sidewalk again.

"What did Bernadette put in Bridget's drink?" Saundra asked, after discarding a half dozen other things she considered saying. "Alcohol doesn't usually affect her that quickly. Huh." She considered a new detail she had forgotten until that moment. "She's more a nasty drunk, not a sloppy, shrieky one."

"That's because it wasn't alcohol." Eden chuckled and hooked her thumb in Troy's direction. "The mad scientist there has found a couple interesting effects from parts of the plants he grew from the locket seeds."

"Not quite a truth drug, but it sure loosens the tongue and knocks down all those fun little inhibitions that keep people from spilling every thought in their head," Troy said.

"You. Are. Geniuses." Saundra sighed, chuckling, as half the tension of the night drained out of her, as if every footstep left it in puddles on the sidewalk behind her. "Adopt me? Please?"

"Sounds good to me." Kai let out a groaning sigh as they reached the doors of Book & Mug. "Got a new recipe idea that might be perfect for celebrating. Go on upstairs. I'll have Trent close up."

Eden invited them into her apartment, instead of sitting out in the office area around the big conference table. Troy excused himself while Eden was putting her coat away, and Saundra closed her eyes, soaking in the quiet, and sinking into the thick cushions of the futon couch. She might never get up and go to her own apartment if she sat too long.

"I've been thinking, maybe we need to have a bunch of decoys," Eden said, coming back into her living room. "Just in case other Mulcahys decide to challenge the story Ted and I came up with."

"That makes sense. I never really looked, but—" Saundra opened her eyes and stopped, mouth open, at the sight of three Venetian glass hearts sitting on a tray lined with midnight blue cloth.

Seen together, she could indeed make out differences in the placement of the sparkles and streaks of color among the red swirls of glass. They were unique, just like Nick had said. She caught her breath at the sudden ache, the sense of loss and failure. The heart Cleo had trusted her with should be there, sitting with the other three.

"So, do we bring Charli Hall in and find out what she knows, or wait until her grandmother comes back to town, and ask to see her heart?" Eden smirked, looking a little too much like Nick, as she handed the tray to Saundra.

"I'm too tired to think right now," Saundra admitted. "Is it okay if I ...?" She put the tray down on her lap.

"Go ahead. I'd really be interested in hearing what you know about the hearts. And I really need to talk to your Aunt Cleo now. I hope she knows a whole lot more than Nick does, and she's been keeping it away from him."

"I'll drink to that," Kai said, stepping through the door.

His newest drink concoction was more like a parfait, in tall, clear glass mugs, with layers of white chocolate whipped cream, frozen crème de menthe, frozen mocha whip, and crushed chocolate mint cookies. He laughed, a rough note in his voice, when he settled down next to Saundra and saw the hearts. He put his mug on the coffee table between the sofas and reached for one of the hearts, turning it over in his fingers a few times.

"Just occurred to me ..." He turned the heart over, showing Saundra and then Eden the backside, with a dark green stripe. "If he's right about the colors ... the spook is more my cousin than yours."

"Don't remind me," Eden moaned. Mischief sparkled in her eyes.

Saundra wished she had silly stories about Nick to entertain them with, so they could all laugh at him, but how could she laugh at the man who had been her hero through far too many miserable, Mulcahy-tainted incidents in her life? She was relieved when the cousins shared how they had fought for years to stay together and get the hearts out of the hands of interfering social workers. She laughed at tales of Eden's blossoming lockpicking and pickpocketing skills, and then ached for them as they related their early attempts to figure out who had deliberately lost them in the System and scrambled their records.

She had a great deal to think about when she finally got up to go home, through the buzzing of all that sugar in her blood that kept her wide awake despite the late hour.

The most important thing? The shy little kiss Kai stole, when she was settling into her car and the door was still open. He just bent down and brushed a kiss across her cheek, coming achingly close to the corner of her mouth. Then he stepped back, shoulders hunched, looking anywhere but at her. Saundra forgot how to breathe for several crucial seconds as he backed away, to the other side of the street and the side door of the Mug building.

"Kai!" She finally got her voice back.

He flinched and turned to look at her, and his grin looked like it might shatter.

"Mistletoe next time? I mean, it's Christmas."

His face lit up. She pulled the door closed and waved. He waved back. He was still standing there, watching her, as she pulled down Apple, heading for Overlook and the long straightaway to her apartment.

~~~~~

A tiny Christmas tree sat in front of Saundra's door, two steps inside her apartment. The aroma of pine filled her nose. An enormous, glittery red ribbon nearly hid the heart-shaped wooden box sitting under the tree. Saundra stayed in the doorway, staring at it, wondering how it had gotten into her apartment.

"Hello?" Her voice cracked, and the sugar buzz from Kai's Mint Chocolate Decadence drained away like air from a punctured balloon.

Nobody answered.

Seriously, why would someone break into her apartment and leave a Christmas tree to distract her before they attacked?

"I'm tired. Maybe I'm dreaming."

She detoured around the tree and headed for the kitchen for her biggest cooking knife, just in case. Then she peered into her bedroom, bathroom, and book room. She tugged aside the curtain of the front balcony. The snow covering it had no footprints, so no one hiding out there. She closed her door but didn't lock it, just in case she needed a quick exit. Then she picked up the box with one hand while holding the knife out with the other.

Underneath lay a note in Nick's distinctive, neat, square handwriting.

Early Christmas present for my favorite little sister. Cleo's coming in 5am Christmas day. Breakfast at my place.

Saundra looked around, although she knew if he had planted any cameras or microphones in her apartment, she would never find them after a week of searching. Certainly not now with her eyes getting fuzzy with weariness.

"Very funny, Nick. Did you enjoy seeing me losing my mind?"

Her phone had buzzed multiple times while they had been wrapping up Eden's sting operation at the police station, and she hadn't checked any of her messages yet. She didn't doubt there was an email, maybe even a text from her aunt in there. She tipped the box, wanting to throw it out the balcony door, choking on mixed laughter and a weary shriek. Yet again, how could she be furious with Nick when he had given her exactly what she wanted for Christmas?

Something heavy slid around inside the box. A solid *thunk* against the wood. Her heart stuttered a dozen beats as she sat on the arm of her sofa and dropped the knife on the cushion and pried up the lid.

Inside lay a Venetian glass heart, with a dark green stripe down the back.

Saundra laughed. Maybe later she would be angry. Later she would definitely find a way to pay him back for putting her through this. Mostly because yes, he was right, she should have gone to him the moment she realized the heart was missing. He probably had a good reason for taking it. He had probably taken it the moment he saw Bridget and Edmund slither into town.

For now, all that mattered was that she had the heart again, safe.

No, she realized a moment later, as she got up and went to her bedroom and put the heart on her nightstand.

What mattered was that the cousins trusted her with their secrets, and she was going to do everything within her training and vast librarian connections to find their answers. They had made her part of their family, and that was what family did for each other.

The End

Michelle started writing for fanzines in college, while earning a bunch of useless degrees in theater, English, film/communication, and writing. Her first professional publication came from winning first place in the Writers of the Future contest in 1990. She has over 100 published books and novellas in SF, fantasy, cozies, and romance. A tea snob, she freelance edits for a living and terrorizes writers and readers through two small presses she co-owns: Mt. Zion Ridge Press and Ye Olde Dragon Books. Be afraid … be very afraid.

www.Mlevigne.com
www.MtZionRidgePress.com
www.MichelleLevigne.blogspot.com
www.YeOldeDragonBooks.com
@MichelleLevigne

THANK YOU!

Thank you for reading this book from Mt. Zion Ridge Press.

If you enjoyed the experience, learned something, gained a new perspective, or made new friends through story, could you do us a favor and write a review on Goodreads or wherever you bought the book?

Thanks! We and our authors appreciate it.

We invite you to visit our website, MtZionRidgePress.com, and explore other titles in fiction and non-fiction. We always have something coming up that's new and off the beaten path.

And please check out our podcast, **Books on the Ridge,** where we chat with our authors and give them a chance to share what was in their hearts while they wrote their book, as well as fun anecdotes and glimpses into their lives and experiences and the writing process. And we always discuss a very important topic: *Tea!*

You can listen to the podcast on our website or find it at most of the usual places where podcasts are available online. Please subscribe so you don't miss a single episode!

Thanks for reading. We hope to see you again soon!

Printed in the USA
CPSIA information can be obtained
at www.ICGtesting.com
JSHW032241251123
52457JS00006B/131